MURDER SOLSTICE

Museum curator Finlay MacNeil had spent years trying to decipher the markings on the Hoolish Stones, the stone circle which for millennia had stood on the West Uist. He was suspicious of the cult-like group at Dunshiffin Castle, which was preparing to celebrate the summer solstice. It seemed that his fatal mistake was to challenge their beliefs on Scottish TV. Yet Inspector Torquil McKinnon had many other things on his mind. So when attractive Sergeant Lorna Golspie arrived on the island to investigate the way he ran his station, was it enough to distract him from the forthcoming Murder Solstice?

Books by Keith Moray
Published by The House of Ulverscroft:

THE GATHERING MURDERS
DEATHLY WIND

Keith Moray lives in Wakefield, West Yorkshire.

KEITH MORAY

MURDER SOLSTICE

Complete and Unabridged

ULVERSCROFT
Leicester

First published in Great Britain in 2008 by
Robert Hale Limited
London

First Large Print Edition
published 2009
by arrangement with
Robert Hale Limited
London

The moral right of the author has been asserted

British Library CIP Data

Moray, Keith.
    Murder solstice
    1. Museum curators- -Crimes against- -Fiction.
    2. Murder- -Investigation- -Scotland- -Hebrides- -Fiction.
    3. Police- -Scotland- -Hebrides- -Fiction.
    4. Cults- -Scotland- -Hebrides- -Fiction.
    5. Detective and mystery stories. 6. Large type books.
    I. Title
    823.9'2–dc22

    ISBN 978–1–84782–745–6

Published by
F. A. Thorpe (Publishing)
Anstey, Leicestershire

Set by Words & Graphics Ltd.
Anstey, Leicestershire
Printed and bound in Great Britain by
T. J. International Ltd., Padstow, Cornwall

To Kate, with fond memories of sugar
mice and early morning swims

Prologue

Winter Solstice

The single beam from the Lambretta scooter's headlight cut a meagre swathe through the afternoon mist and drizzle. To make matters worse the light was failing fast as the sun descended rapidly towards the horizon to start the longest, darkest night of the year. Already a watery full moon was making its progress across the sky.

'Bloody mad, I must be,' mumbled Calum Steele, the editor of the *West Uist Chronicle*, to himself. He raised a hand to wipe his visor and cursed again. 'Cold, wet and miserable I am, and just before Christmas too. The folk of West Uist don't know what we journalists have to go through to bring them the news of the outside world.'

He tried to snuggle his thick neck into his sodden yellow anorak as he negotiated the snaking Dunshiffin road. 'I certainly didn't expect to be coming up here again today,' he grumbled.

Winter solstices had come and gone all of his life without him paying them the slightest

1

bit of attention. Then The Daisy Institute, or as the locals called them, 'the flower people' had come and suddenly the solstices were big news. 'What do they think this is — a new Stonehenge?' he shouted to the elements, with a smug grin at his own joke.

Through the watery mist he could just make out the outline of Dunshiffin Castle, the recently acquired headquarters of The Daisy Institute. Several oblongs of light shone through the mist and he thought he could hear singing or chanting coming from within as he sped past.

'They have certainly had an impact on the island,' he said to himself. 'Them and their funny ways. I think I will have to write a series of — '

His attention was suddenly brought back to the task of controlling his scooter as he turned a bend and ran straight into a thick belt of opaque mist. He slowed down immediately, and then stared in horror as two headlights loomed out of the mist.

'Get over!' he cried in vain, as the vehicle hurtled towards him in the centre of the road. He swerved over to the side and almost lost his balance as he slewed precariously for a few seconds while a Jeep careered by at high speed with windscreen wipers working frantically. Calum stopped and looked round.

'And just what the hell are you playing at, Rab Noble?' he cried, as the tail-lights of the familiar Jeep rapidly disappeared into the mist. 'Are you drunk or what?'

But he knew that it was probably too early even for Rab Noble to be drunk, by a couple of hours at least. It was milking time, he guessed, which could account for his haste. He was obviously rushing from the farm to the milking parlour on the far side of the farm.

As Calum's initial ire cooled, he realized all too soberly that if he had not had his wits about him, the island could have just lost the star investigative reporter and editor-in-chief of the *West Uist Chronicle*. At that he permitted himself a smile of self-satisfaction before continuing his journey.

Rab Noble was at least fifteen years older than Calum, which he realized may have been part of the reason that Esther, Rab's wife, had rung him half an hour earlier with her stark message.

'Get here right away, Calum Steele, and I will give you the biggest story you have ever had. The sadistic bastard! I will blow the lid on him and his band of sickos.'

There had been no explanation, just the exhortation to be quick if he wanted his reward. And so, natural-born busybody and professional newsman that he was, he had responded immediately and turned out in the inhospitable squall. Calum had never been able to resist a story. More than that, he had never been able to stop lusting over Esther Noble, or Esther Harrison as he always thought of her. She had been in his class at school, along with his best friend Torquil McKinnon, now the local police inspector. Even then Calum had lusted over her, one of the best-looking girls on the island. As young adolescents they had groped each other on more than one occasion behind the bike sheds or in the bracken on the way home from school. She was bright too, which made it all the more surprising when she had left school at sixteen and married Rab Noble to become a farmer's wife, and a virtual recluse who rarely came into Kyleshiffin. Calum had barely seen her over the years, such was the way she had cut herself off from her roots, but as the man with his ear to every bit of gossip that was uttered on the island, he had heard that the marriage was stormy, presumably because as yet there had been no issue from the marriage. That and the fact that Rab Noble was a renowned drinker. And then there were the even darker rumours.

Calum turned off the road and headed up the track towards Hoolish Farm, catching a glimpse through the mist of the Hoolish Stones, the treble ring of megalithic stones a hundred yards or so out on the moor. They looked totally different from their appearance at sunrise when he had been up to watch the flower folk celebrate the solstice sunrise. He had written the article and was starting to put the *Chronicle* to bed when Esther had rung.

He heard the dogs howling before he turned the final bend and saw the lit-up windows of the dilapidated, sprawling farmhouse. He drew his scooter to a halt in the mud and dung-covered courtyard and switched off the engine.

There were three collies, all jumping and hurling themselves frenziedly about the wire-meshed kennel.

'Calm down, you doggies. Haud yer wheesht!' he cooed at them, to little avail. He thought that they looked fiercer than he remembered seeing them whenever he had come across Rab working with them on the farm near the castle. He tapped at the back door of the farmhouse, which was standing ajar.

'Esther? It's me — Calum.'

There was no answer, just the sound of a radio playing from inside the farmhouse. He pushed the door open and called again. Then he crossed the kitchen, avoiding bowls of dog food and entered the hall.

Esther Noble was hanging from the banister, her tongue purple and protruding from her mouth. A dog chain was cutting deeply into her neck and her face was livid, her eyes sightless and dead.

★　★　★

Half an hour later, Inspector Torquil McKinnon was patting the pasty-faced *Chronicle* editor's back while Dr Ralph McLelland, the local GP-cum-police surgeon, and another former school-mate, examined the body, assisted by Sergeant Morag Driscoll.

'And you say that Rab Noble almost ran you over?' he asked.

'Aye, Torquil. Like I told you, Esther phoned me to come up here straight away. She called him a sadistic bastard.'

'Well, we will see what he has to say soon enough. I sent Ewan McPhee to go and bring him back here. He will be milking the herd now, I am thinking.'

Calum was shivering slightly. He looked up at his friend. 'Suicide, do you think?'

Torquil shrugged his shoulders. 'Too early to say, Calum. And you know that, so be careful about what you write in the paper.'

'But I — '

Torquil's phone went off at that moment

and he raised a hand for quiet while he answered it. Calum watched him talking and could tell by his facial expression that all was not well.

'That was Ewan,' Torquil explained a moment later. The others stopped what they were doing to listen to him. 'He has just been sick, poor lad.' He took a deep breath himself, then, 'He found the cattle howling and moaning as he arrived. Rab Noble was there all right, but it was more like an abattoir than a milking parlour. He had shot three cows, and then blown his brains out with a shotgun.'

1

I

The Kyleshiffin market was always busy on a weekday summer morning, but during the heatwave of the previous fortnight the number of market stalls had seemed to double. Bric-à-brac, second-hand books, arts and craft stalls occupied the roadside positions, while local produce sellers naturally held to their traditional pitches along the crescent-shaped harbour wall. With the town packed with holidaymakers, as witnessed by a veritable flotilla of yachts and cruisers bobbing up and down in the harbour itself, and an influx of what the local people called New Age flower people, the market workers and the proprietors of the multi-coloured shops that formed Harbour Street itself were enjoying a thriving trade.

Perspiring slightly and looking forward to a refreshing cup of tea at the station, Sergeant Morag Driscoll weaved her way through the throng only to find her way blocked by an unbelievably good-looking, blond, blue-eyed young man in his early twenties wearing a summery white hoodie. His smile seemed natural, as if he was genuinely pleased to see her. He was standing in front of a stall bedecked with pictures of stone circles, well-known religious sites from around the world and posters of an older, but similarly smiling man dressed in a yellow hoodie. Morag thought that the hoodies were designed to give them a modern, slightly monkish appearance. On the table were stacks of books all bearing the same photograph of the older man on the front cover.

'Can I interest you in the experience of a lifetime, lovely lady?' he asked.

Morag Driscoll was a thirty-something single mother of three. She was attractive by any standards, although she herself believed that she had a weight problem. It worried her and she worked hard to keep as trim as possible, since her husband had died from a heart attack when she was twenty-six and she vowed that she would always be there for her children.

Over the years she had heard just about every chat-up line, but this one took her by surprise, coming as it did from one who was at least a decade younger than she and who had a monkish look about him.

'I am a police sergeant, young man,' she

replied, pointing to the three small stripes on the arm of her short-sleeved navy-blue shirt. Wearing jeans and trainers as she was, the shirt was the only indication that she was a police officer, the local force being well known for its liberal attitude towards uniforms. She took the leaflet he had thrust in her direction. 'Do you still want to give me a wonderful experience?'

Unruffled, the youth stood smiling at her. And, as he did so, she realized that his question was probably more to do with the spiritual than the carnal. She felt a slight tinge of guilt and put it down to the natural cynicism that went with the job of policing.

'My name is Peter, Sergeant. I am one of the acolytes with The Daisy Institute,' he explained, pointing to the simple logo of a daisy flower on the front of his hoodie. 'It will be the summer solstice in a few days. We will be holding an all-night vigil at the Hoolish Stones to celebrate the solstice sunrise. Why don't you come along? It might change your life.'

Morag dabbed her brow with the back of her hand. This young man could have turned her head had she been ten or fifteen years younger. 'I know about your celebration, Peter,' she replied, allowing herself the ghost of a smile. 'In fact, I might even be there,

11

officially. To make sure there is no trouble.'

'I will look forward to seeing you there then, Sergeant,' he replied. He reached over and tugged the sleeve of another white hoodie wearer. 'Henry, this lovely lady is a local police sergeant. I was telling her about the solstice celebration. We'll make her welcome if she comes, won't we?'

The hoodie wearer turned round and Morag found herself looking at another stunningly attractive young person with an enviable mass of auburn locks, a freckle-dappled face and glorious hazel eyes.

'Henry?' queried Morag, raising her eyebrows quizzically, for the face that had immediately fallen into a natural smile was most definitely female.

The girl laughed. 'Henrietta at birth, but Peter always calls me Henry.' She wrinkled her nose in mock disdain. 'He has a puerile sense of humour. But, of course, you will be welcome, Sergeant. Or you could come to one of our evening meetings. Scottish TV is doing a series on Logan Burns and The Daisy Institute every evening up at the Hoolish Stones. You might even find yourself on television.'

Morag glanced at the leaflet in her hand. It bore a photograph of Logan Burns, above a short text introducing The Daisy Institute, and explaining that it really stood for the DSY or The Divinity and Spirituality Institute. The reason for the daisy logo was thereby obvious. Morag suppressed the urge to tell them that she was sceptical of New Age religious leaders, gurus and cults, which was what Logan Burns and The Daisy Institute seemed to smack of. Instead, she smiled at them and shook her head.

'The trouble there is that like most police officers, I am a wee bit camera shy. But who knows.'

II

Ten minutes later as Morag pushed open the door of the Kyleshiffin Police Station, a converted pebble-dashed bungalow on Kirk Wynd, which ran parallel to Harbour Street, an evil odour assailed her sense of smell and she wrinkled her nose in disgust.

'Good Grief!' she exclaimed to PC Ewan McPhee, the large, freckled, red-haired wrestling and hammer-throwing champion of the Western Isles, and the junior officer of the West Uist division of the Hebridean Constabulary. 'What on earth is that awful stink? It is a thousand times worse than the fish market on a hot day like today. Is someone

13

boiling a sheep's head?'

Ewan grinned as she covered her nose and puffed out her cheeks as if she was about to throw up. 'Och, you will get used to it in a few minutes, Morag. It is the boss. He is seasoning his bag and cleaning his pipes.'

'His bagpipes! Does he have to do that here? Goodness me, what a stench.'

The door behind the counter opened and Inspector Torquil McKinnon, often known to his friends on the island as 'Piper', came out of his office, working a large sheepskin leather bag between his hands. Five large bungs protruded from points around it, stopping up the stocks of the three drones, blowpipe and chanter. The bag made a curious squelching noise as he pummelled it between his hands.

'Is that my favourite sergeant that I hear complaining about me seasoning my bag?' he asked with a grin.

Torquil McKinnon was a tall, twenty-nine-year-old man with coal-black hair, high cheekbones and a slightly hawk-like nose. To many of the West Uist womenfolk he was a desirable and eligible male, but to Morag he was more like an impish younger brother, even though he was her superior officer. And she often treated him as such. She stood facing him across the counter, her arms akimbo.

'Torquil McKinnon, I respect your professional ability as a police officer. I applauded
when you became the youngest inspector in
the islands and the West Highlands. I admire
your musical ability on the pipes. I was there,
remember, when you won the Silver Quaich.
But,' she said, slowly shaking her head, 'you
have a lot to learn about public relations.'

Torquil frowned, stopped pummelling his
bag and replied hesitantly, 'I am not with you,
Morag. *Public relations?*'

'We are supposed to be creating a warm,
friendly atmosphere for the public. We want
them to feel at home whenever they come
through that door. Instead of which you have
made the place smell like a charnel house. It
stinks in here, Torquil! It smells so bad that
no one will want to spend more than ten
seconds in this office. Just what odious
mixture are you using in that bag?'

Torquil had initially thought that she was
just teasing him, but now he realized that her
scowl and her slow advance towards the
counter flap meant that she was deadly
serious.

Ewan was feeling uncomfortable with the
way things were headed so he began edging
sideways towards the kitchen, the door of
which was lockable.

'It is a special formula prepared by Glen

15

Carscal's of Inverness,' Torquil replied tremulously. 'It doesn't smell too bad, does it? It is mainly beeswax, treacle and lanoline.'

'So no wonder it smells like you are boiling a sheep! Torquil McKinnon, you may be the inspector here, but I am the station sergeant and I do not appreciate you turning my station into a-a — '

Torquil had stepped back a pace at her continued advance. He was about to remonstrate when the entrance bell rang out and the door opened. A moment later five dogs on leads appeared, closely followed by an old lady dressed in an ill-fitting Panama hat and a cheesecloth frock. A prodigiously big shoulder bag swung hither and thither as she strove to control three chirpy collies and a zestful West Highland terrier, while a restrained and slightly disdainful German shepherd stood dutifully at her side.

'Ah, Sergeant Driscoll, Inspector McKinnon and Constable McPhee,' beamed Annie McConville, a lady of seventy-odd years who was known throughout the Western Isles both for her vague eccentricity and for the dog sanctuary that she ran single-handedly. 'I was wondering — ' She stopped abruptly and sniffed several times, her nostrils pinching with obvious distaste. 'Why, whatever is that disgusting smell?'

16

The three collies began barking in unison, followed a moment later by the Westie and the German shepherd.

'Wheesht, the lot of you,' cried Annie. 'Sheila and Zimba, you two ought to know better! I know it is an awful smell, but — '

'That is just what I was saying, Annie,' said Morag, darting a reproachful look at Torquil, who took it as his cue to beat a hasty retreat into his office.

'And what can I be doing for you?' Morag went on, tearing her gaze from the door that Torquil had left ajar.

'I was just going to ask PC McPhee if anyone had come in wanting to take any of these three beauties off my hands.'

Ewan had already made it to the kitchen door, behind which he vigorously shook his head and pressed his hands together as he looked beseechingly at his sergeant. Annie was well known for her loquaciousness and could, and often did, buttonhole Ewan for ages. Although he had been in the force for five years he had yet to develop the art of deflecting folk. Morag scowled at him, and then turned to Annie with a look of sadness, as if she was the reluctant messenger of bad tidings. 'Not a single offer I am afraid, Annie. You know you could — '

Annie McConville stopped her short as if divining what Morag was about to suggest. 'I could do nothing other than I am already doing! No dog under my care will ever be put down unnecessarily. No, Sheila, Zimba and I will just keep looking after the poor doggies — especially after all they have been through, what with the murder and suicide of their mistress and master.'

'I know that they have been through it, Annie,' said Morag, 'but we can't say that there was any murder involved. At the Fatal Accident Inquiry the sheriff said that culpable homicide of either Esther or Rab was not proven. He felt that it could have been a bizarre suicide pact.'

Annie McConville snorted derisively. 'Well, as good old Sir Walter Scott would have said, if that was the sheriff's decision, it was a 'bastard verdict'. I think it was otherwise and so does our local newsman, Calum Steele. Rab Noble killed his wife and then committed suicide.'

Morag was about to remonstrate further when the doorbell rang again and the dogs started up a cacophony of barking and howling. Then the door opened and another sprightly seventy-something woman entered the fray. Miss Bella Melville, the retired head teacher of the Kyleshiffin School had taught

18

half of the adult population of the island and was therefore treated with deference by most of the islanders. She was an elegant lady with platinum-coloured hair, dressed in tweeds and a rust-coloured shawl. With her hands sheathed in prim black leather gloves she exuded a no-nonsense persona.

'Morag Driscoll,' she said, above the noise of the barking dogs. 'What exactly is that noxious effluvium? Did you not learn anything about aesthetics in my class?'

Morag had groaned silently upon seeing the apparition of her former teacher advancing towards the counter. She smiled nervously. 'It is the inspector, Miss Melville. He is seasoning his bagpipes on police property!'

She had deliberately raised her voice so that Torquil could hear her. Out of the corner of her eye she saw his office door silently close and she allowed herself a subtle smile. She intended to have further words with him later — after she had got rid of the esteemed head teacher and the equally celebrated dog saviour.

Miss Melville went on severely, 'Will you just tell the inspector that I am not pleased with him. Dereliction of duty might not be too strong a — '

'Excuse me!' snapped Annie McConville, turning squarely to face Bella Melville. 'But I

19

was talking to the sergeant when you butted in.'

Morag took a sharp intake of breath. No one was used to seeing anyone stand up to Miss Bella Melville, but then again, Annie McConville was a law unto herself.

'I am sorry, Annie, I did not realize that — '

'You did not realize what, Bella Melville? That I was standing here talking to the sergeant with my dogs barking louder than the Hound of the Baskervilles?' She shook her head and eyed Miss Melville with an accusatory glare. 'You were just like this — overbearing — when we were in the same class at school.'

Despite herself, Morag let out a half snigger which did not go unnoticed by Bella Melville.

'I was never overbearing, Annie McConville. Why, you were just — '

The doorbell rang again, causing the dogs to raise their barking to another level. The door opened and a striking woman dressed in a pin-striped trouser suit entered. PC Ewan McPhee had just ventured out of the kitchen with a tray of mugs. He spied the new arrival immediately and asked above the protesting dogs, the arguing septuagenarians and his own, by now, fraught sergeant, 'What can I

20

do for you, my bonnie lassie?' Then realizing that he had uttered his thoughts rather than the professional question he had intended, he blushed to the roots of his red hair. 'I mean, what can I do for you, miss?'

She was about twenty-seven, pretty with a tidy nose, hazel eyes and copper Titian locks that tumbled about her shoulders. She smiled at him without any obvious warmth. 'My name is actually Sergeant Golspie,' she said. 'And you must be Constable McPhee.'

Before Ewan could reply she had wrinkled her nose, delightfully wrinkled it, Ewan thought. She glanced at the dogs, and at the arguing women then held up her briefcase and leaned towards Ewan. 'Actually, if you could just let me through to the back office then I would be grateful.' She tapped the briefcase. 'I have something here that I have to give Inspector Torquil McKinnon.'

As Ewan raised the counter flap for her she whispered up to him, 'What is that awful smell, Constable? It isn't a dog smell, but it is quite disgusting.'

'That is just something the inspector is doing, Sergeant,' Ewan explained cryptically. 'You had better come through to the kitchen for a while. I'll take you through to the boss when World War Three out there has finished.'

III

Five minutes later in Torquil's office, when Morag had managed to persuade Annie McConville and her dogs and Bella Melville to leave, Torquil had a word with Morag. 'What was Bella wanting? I couldn't hear above the noise of those yapping dogs.'

'Your blood, I think,' Morag returned. 'She thinks that you should be doing more to prevent 'undesirables' from coming to West Uist.'

'Undesirables? Who does she mean?'

'The flower folk among others. I don't think she appreciates people coming to celebrate at the Hoolish Stones.' She smiled, then told him about the two gorgeous representatives of The Daisy Institute who had accosted her on Harbour Street just a few minutes before. 'They were both good adverts for whatever it is they are studying. I don't think you could call either of them undesirable. I think Miss Melville is just getting even more strait-laced and territorial the older she gets.'

Torquil gave a short laugh. 'Goodness, what does she think we are? Passport controllers?'

Ewan tapped on the door and popped his head round. 'Torquil, I have a Sergeant

22

Golspie here to see you. She says she has something to give you.'

Torquil laid his bagpipe bag down on his desk and indicated for Ewan to show her in.

'And what can I do for you, Sergeant Golspie?' Torquil asked, rising from his chair as she came in. By his body language Morag could see that Torquil was impressed by the sight of his visitor.

'My name is Lorna Golspie, Inspector,' she said, producing her warrant card with the dexterity of a conjurer. 'I have been seconded to you from Superintendent Lumsden's office.'

Torquil nodded dumbly as Morag introduced herself and invited Lorna to sit down. Ewan had the tea tray at the ready and handed out mugs of his freshly brewed tea.

'I warn you that Ewan likes his tea strong,' said Morag with a grin at the big constable. 'Stewed, even.'

'So, what does the good superintendent want me to see?' Torquil asked cautiously. Indeed, at the mention of the name Lumsden all three members of the West Uist division of the Hebridean Constabulary had felt a tinge of apprehension. It had only been few months earlier that Superintendent Lumsden had been suspended from duty pending an investigation that arose from a case that

23

Torquil had been handling.[1] And some months before that Superintendent Lumsden had himself suspended Torquil during a murder investigation.[2] To say that there was little love lost between them would have been an understatement of the situation. Since the superintendent's reinstatement the week previously, they had been awaiting a first contact.

Lorna Golspie opened her briefcase and drew out a manila envelope. She looked distastefully and suspiciously at the bulging bagpipe bag lying on Torquil's desk like the corpse of some grotesquely skinned animal. 'Do you mean he hasn't discussed this with you in person? I rather assumed that he would have talked it over already.' She shrugged and handed the envelope over. 'His orders are in there.'

It was Torquil's turn to look suspicious. He cast a glance at his two friends then slit the envelope open with his thumb. They watched him read, his eyes slowly widening. He handed the document to Morag, then leaned forward and casually picked up the sheepskin bag which he began kneading between his hands.

---

[1] See *Deathly Wind*
[2] See *The Gathering Murders*

'So, you have been seconded to work with us,' he said. 'And I am to show you around the island and give you an area of responsibility, while you conduct an internal audit.'

'I am not sure that I am understanding about an internal audit?' queried Morag, knitting her brow as she reread the superintendent's orders.

The outer doorbell rang out and a moment later the door was pushed open to the sound of two male voices singing merrily away. Then there was a hammering of fists and a slapping of palms on the front counter, followed by the sound of the counter flap being raised and then dropped down as two lots of heavy feet came through.

'Gosh, Ewan McPhee, what are you doing in here drinking tea? We could have been a couple of real desperadoes,' said an extremely large man dressed in yellow waterproofs and heavy seaman's boots, as he unceremoniously barged into the office. A step behind him was a similarly dressed man of equal height and build. Both of them were wearing bobble hats.

'You ought to be having a word with the big PC, Torquil,' said the second. 'Discipline, that's what he needs.' He winked at Morag, then seeing Lorna Golspie his face burst into a welcoming grin. 'But I am sorry. We did not realize that you were entertaining.'

Torquil continued to work his bag. 'Sergeant Lorna Golspie,' he introduced, 'Meet Wallace and Douglas Drummond. Our two special constables.'

'We fish for our living,' Wallace, the second of the twins explained.

Lorna gave them a wan smile. 'I think I might have guessed that.'

'The sergeant will be joining us,' Torquil said unenthusiastically. 'Superintendent Lumsden seems to be concerned with the way we run the station here.'

Lorna Golspie coloured slightly as she looked around the office. 'The superintendent has expressed reservations about discipline, procedures and efficiency levels,' she said. 'My orders are to observe and report back to him.'

Douglas Drummond slipped an arm about Morag's shoulders. 'No worries then, eh, folks? We are just one big happy family here.'

Sergeant Lorna Golspie did not seem to be smiling.

IV

At Torquil's behest, Morag took Lorna off for a walkabout tour of Kyleshiffin while he got on with what he claimed to be pressing official business. When they returned at one o'clock they both sniffed upon entering the station, for the odour of Torquil's bagpipe seasoning still hung heavily upon the air. The bag itself was hanging like the corpse of some nondescript animal from a coat-hook inside the rest room, with a spread-out newspaper on the floor beneath to catch any drips of the seasoning fluid.

'The boss is out, Morag,' Ewan called through from the kitchen where he was busily cooking kippers and significantly adding to the aroma.

Throughout the tour Lorna had made intermittent notes in a small notebook, and she added a few more upon entering the rest room.

'The inspector is the piping champion of the Western Isles,' Morag hastily explained, jabbing a finger in the direction of the bag. 'He doesn't usually bring it in here to smell out my station. I expect his uncle has told him not to do it at home.'

Lorna Golspie flicked pages in her notebook. 'That will be his uncle, Lachlan McKinnon. He's a church minister, isn't he?'

Morag nodded. 'He's known as the Padre around here.' She pointed her chin at the book in Lorna's hand. 'How come you have notes about him? Has Superintendent Lumsden given you a rundown on everyone?'

Lorna smiled and snapped the notebook closed. 'Just some useful background.'

Morag eyed her suspiciously for a moment, then, 'Have you made arrangements about staying in Kyleshiffin?'

Lorna nodded. 'Yes, I'm booked into the Commercial Hotel.'

'You won't want to be there too long then,' Morag said. 'They know how to charge at the Commercial.'

'Oh the Force is paying,' Lorna volunteered.

Morag raised her eyebrows. 'Really? Then I guess the superintendent won't plan on this being a long secondment.'

Lorna shrugged noncommittally. 'Actually Morag, there is no time limit on it. I think that is why he wanted Inspector McKinnon to give me an area of responsibility. He sees me being here quite a while.'

'Oh,' Morag returned. 'So tell me, what exactly does — '

The front door had opened and Torquil's voice called through. 'Ewan! Good grief, man, what are you cooking? Morag will go spare when — '

He popped his head round the door and grinned sheepishly when he saw the two sergeants.

'Ah! Ewan just reminded me that it is lunchtime. I hoped you'd be back,' he said. 'I thought I would take our new member of the Force for lunch.' He nodded his head in the direction of the kitchen, where Ewan was tunelessly whistling away as his kippers sizzled in a pan. He crooked his finger at Lorna. 'Come on, Sergeant Golspie; let me take you away from this unwholesome smell.'

Then, as he held the door open wide for Lorna Golspie to pass, he added in a hushed tone to Morag, 'See that Ewan opens the windows afterwards, would you, Morag? We can't have the station smelling like a fishmonger's.'

V

The Bonnie Prince Charlie Tavern on Harbour Street was busy as usual. The aroma of freshly cooked seafood assailed them as soon as Torquil pushed open the door. Mollie McFadden, the doughty landlady and her staff were busy pulling pints of Heather Ale and serving the lunchtime clientele. Mollie blinked myopically at them as they entered and, recognizing Torquil, waved at him.

'Mollie, this is Sergeant Lorna Golspie,' Torquil introduced. 'She is joining us for a while.'

Mollie, a woman in her early sixties, beamed and took Lorna's hand in a firm grip, for her forearm muscles were well built from having pumped a veritable sea of beer over the years. 'Pleased to meet you, Lorna. But aren't you going to get a bit crowded with two sergeants?' Then a suspicious look flashed across her face. 'Don't tell me that Morag Driscoll is leaving us?'

Torquil grinned. 'Nothing like that. Lorna here is — sort of an observer.'

Lorna pursed her lips and smiled at Mollie. 'Well, until I have seen the ropes.' Then she gave Torquil a mock scowl. 'You will be giving me some responsibility, won't you, Inspector?' she added. 'Just like Superintendent Lumsden ordered.'

Torquil held her eyes for a moment then gave a noncommittal smile.

'Maybe the sergeant would like a wee job now then,' Mollie said. And she pointed to the far corner of the bar where a group of men were standing, their voices getting louder and louder. There were about ten of them, a motley group of various ages and builds. Some were dressed in tweeds, others in outdoor working clothes.

'It's the Farmers' Collective Day at the Duncan Institute,' Mollie explained to Lorna. 'The local farmers have a meeting every fortnight and then they lunch either here or at The Bell at the other end of the street. They are usually a noisy crowd, but they don't normally cause trouble.'

A heated argument was going on between two men in the middle of the crowd. One was a middle-aged man with a bushy, iron-grey moustache. He was dressed in a tweed suit with a canary-yellow waistcoat and a cravat. The other was a small, portly, bespectacled man in a yellow anorak. The bigger man was prodding him in none-too-friendly a manner.

'Calum has been in for his lunchtime drink as usual,' Mollie went on with a sigh, 'but you know how argumentative he can be. Well, he has seemed to inflame them all against him. Especially, that Tavish McQueen chap.' She leaned closer. 'I think it's something to do with one of his pieces in the *Chronicle*.'

Torquil gave Mollie a long-suffering smile that spoke volumes. He and Calum had been friends all their lives and Torquil had pulled his friend from enough scrapes no longer to be surprised to find him in yet another. If Calum Steele had a talent it was his gift for putting people's backs up. Torquil nodded to Mollie and began moving through the crowded bar.

'You little bugger!' came the voice of the man called McQueen, as he grabbed hold of

31

Calum's anorak. 'You just keep out of my affairs.'

Calum Steele, the editor of the *West Uist Chronicle* pulled himself up to his full five foot six inches and flicked the man's hands off his anorak.

'I am a journalist and I will not be intimidated. You can just — '

A third man, who looked a younger version of McQueen, except that he was dressed in jeans and a nondescript rugby shirt, cursed and drew back his hand. But before he could bring it forward to strike the *Chronicle* editor, Torquil had grabbed his wrist in a vice-like grip.

'Police!' he snapped. 'Make one move and I'll be booking you folk for causing an affray in public.' He tightened his grip on the man's wrist and turned him round. He looked from him to the older man. 'You are the McQueens, who bought the Hoolish Farm, aren't you? I don't think you've had dealings with the police before,' he said, 'but that could all change.'

'Take your hand off me!' the other growled. He was in his late twenties and clearly had a hot-headed temperament. 'Or do you want me to make you.'

Before he could finish, Lorna had taken his other arm and deftly pinned it behind his back, exerting enough pressure on his wrist to subdue him. 'Shall I cuff him, Inspector?'

The crowd of farmers began shuffling back.

'You take your hands off my son right away, or I'll be having words with my solicitor,' said the older McQueen.

Torquil eyed the man sternly, then a thin smile passed over his lips. 'You may need to if I book you.' Then, to the son, 'Brawling in public is not tolerated on West Uist. Do I make myself clear?'

The other gave a grudging nod.

'Do you want to press charges on these men, Calum?'

Calum grunted and shook his head. 'Don't waste your time, Torquil. Just throw them out. The press will not be intimidated and it does not need the help of the police.'

Torquil nodded to Lorna and released his own grip. 'You heard the man. Now off with the pair of you. Take this as a warning.'

The older McQueen's face had turned puce and he took a pace forward, only to be stopped by a touch on his arm from another man with short cropped hair and a slightly cauliflower ear. 'I think you ought to leave it, Tavish. Why don't we all go along to The Bell?'

There were murmurings of agreement

from the rest of the group.

'I will remember you,' Tavish McQueen said angrily to Torquil. 'You had no call to interfere with us. We were just warning this little pipsqueak. I may take this further.'

But his companions started to move him through the crowded bar, which opened up before them.

'Thanks for that, Torquil,' Calum said, his voice seeming for the first time slightly slurred. He stared quizzically at Lorna.

'Calum, meet Sergeant Lorna Golspie. She's joining us as an observer for a while.'

'An observer?' Calum repeated incredulously. 'If what she did to that gorilla was observation I'd hate to see what she does when she gets started.'

He raised his hand to attract Mollie McFadden's attention. 'But for now let me buy you both a drink. What will it be, Heather Ale as usual for you, Torquil? And what about the sergeant?'

Torquil caught Lorna's questioning look and shook his head emphatically. 'We are on duty, Calum my man. We are just here for a spot of lunch.' He smiled at Lorna. 'I suggest you try the local mussels and wash it down with some of Mollie's homemade lemonade. It is the best in the islands.'

Calum winked at Mollie. 'You heard the

inspector, Mollie. Make that two lemonades for the police people, a pint of Heather Ale for me — and a whisky chaser.'

'Are you going to tell me what that was all about anyway, Calum?' Torquil queried, after he had given their orders for food.

The *Chronicle* editor shook his head and tapped the side of his nose. 'Just newspaper business, Torquil. Nothing for you to worry about.'

Torquil nodded, having half expected some such response. He was all too aware that his old friend liked to play his cards close to his chest.

A few moments later with their drinks in their hands, they chinked glasses.

'Cheers,' said Lorna.

'*Slàinte mhath!*' said Torquil, 'Good health.'

He winked at Calum Steele. He had a feeling that he would have to watch Lorna Golspie pretty closely.

2

I

The Reverend Lachlan McKinnon, known throughout West Uist as the Padre, crunched his way down the gravel path from the manse with his golf clubs slung over his shoulder. He had spent a couple of hours writing a sermon and planned to pop into the church to have his morning conversation with the Lord before meeting Finlay MacNeil, the Black House Museum curator for their usual nine holes.

The Padre was a good-humoured man of sixty-four years with the ruddy cheeks of the outer islander, a pair of thick horn-rimmed spectacles perched on his hawk-like nose and a veritable mane of silver hair that perpetually defied brush or comb. As usual, he was wearing his clerical dog collar and a West Uist tweed jacket, his usual wear for both pastoral care and the golf course. He pushed open the iron gate and stopped a moment to light his briar pipe before striding along the metalled road to St Ninian's Church, a walk of a couple of minutes. There he propped his bag up in the porch, tapped his pipe out on his heel then let himself into the church.

A solitary figure in a white hoodie was sitting in the first pew, head bent as if in prayer. The Padre walked silently up the aisle and nodded at a pretty blonde-haired young woman who looked up sharply as he stopped to genuflect before the altar.

'I . . . I am sorry, sir. I did not mean to trespass on your church,' she said tremulously, in a voice so devoid of an accent that the Padre suspected she was from one of the Scandinavian countries.

He put up a restraining hand as she shot to her feet. 'Everyone is welcome in the Lord's house. Please, carry on with your prayers or your meditation.' He smiled as he pointed to the flower logo on her hoodie. 'You are from The Daisy Institute, I perceive.'

She returned his smile. 'I am one of the acolytes. I am Johanna Waltari, from Helsinki in Finland.' She pointed to the altar with its wooden cross and the large stained-glass window behind it depicting St Ninian. 'I love your church, Father. It is simpler than the ones we have at home. It is good for sitting and talking to God.'

'That is just what I think, Johanna,' he returned, extending his hand. 'My name is Lachlan McKinnon, but folk round here call

37

me the Padre. I like to think that the Lord enjoys coming to simple places like this.' He grinned then added with a merry twinkle in his eye, 'I am sure he needs a rest from cathedrals sometimes.'

Johanna giggled at his joke, immediately warming to him. She pointed to the ancient stone with its peculiar ancient markings that stood behind the baptismal font. 'It seems old this church of yours. But I think that stone is older.'

'Aye, you would be right there, Johanna. The church was built in the eighth century, but the stone was here long before that. They just built the church around it. It was a common enough practice to build churches on top of old pagan sites. We call this one *Eilthireach*, the Pilgrim Stone.'

Johanna rose and crossed to the large obelisk-like stone which stood ten feet tall. It was covered in ancient carvings; a mix of curls, wavy lines, straight lines and with one or two carvings suggestive of human forms.

'The markings look like runes,' she said, running a finger over the surface. 'We have many of them in Scandinavia. Our founder and president, Dr Logan Burns, is an expert on all sorts of ancient religious writings. He tells us that many of the standing stones in the Hebrides are covered in a type of script

38

that is older than runic or Ogham.'

'I have heard that he is some sort of an expert,' Lachlan returned. He pursed his lips thoughtfully. 'But as to exactly what language they are written in, I don't know if we will ever find out. Many a scholar has studied them and failed to come to a conclusion.'

Johanna seemed about to say something then thought otherwise. She pushed her hoodie back and shook her head to let her blonde hair escape. She ran a hand through her hair and smiled. 'Well, I had better get back. I have duties to perform and I am behind schedule. I have to take a class with some of our newest inceptors.'

Lachlan's eyes narrowed and it seemed as if he was about to say something before thinking otherwise. And indeed, it troubled him that The Daisy Institute had recruited several islanders over the last few months, much to the distress of several of his parishioners, for they had not seen their families since.

'I think I know what you were thinking, Padre,' Johanna said. 'You are concerned about the institute's policy of seclusion for three months.'

Lachlan gave a short laugh. 'Do they teach you to be mind readers at the institute? Actually, you are quite right, Johanna, I was.

It seems . . . over-strict to me.'

She smiled. 'It is time for contemplation, that is all. Three months of intense meditation and contemplation on the wonders of the universe. It makes you find joy. Real joy.' She laughed, a spontaneous ripple of pleasure that seemed to bubble up from within. 'That is why we are all so happy. Logan Burns is a genius, Padre. A genius.'

She shook hands and left quietly.

The Padre bit his lip. 'It seems a bit more like brainwashing to me,' he said worriedly. And he was not so sure that she really did feel as joyful as she suggested. He had the distinct impression that she had been crying when he came in.

II

Two hours later the Padre was on the ten-acre plot of undulating dunes and machair that he and several other local worthies had years before transformed into the St Ninian's Golf Course. Using the natural lie of the land they had constructed six holes with billiard smooth greens surrounded by barbed wire squares to keep the sheep off, in contrast to the coarse grass fairways where they were allowed to graze

40

freely. Each hole had three separate tee positions, each one giving its route to the hole a special name in both English and Gaelic, thereby allowing players the choice of playing a conventional eighteen holes or any combination. The Padre was proud of telling people that while it was not exactly St Andrews, yet it was a good test of golf.

'Good shot!' he cried, as he watched Finlay MacNeil's tee-shot on the long eighth hole. The ball started left, heading towards the gorse bushes that abutted the fairway then gradually faded back into the fairway to roll on to about 250 yards. 'And that is despite the atrocious noise that newfangled travesty of a club makes. It sounds as if you are hitting the ball with a tin can.'

Finlay MacNeil, the Black House Museum curator and an old golfing buddy of the Padre's, shook his head. He was a stocky little fellow with pebble-thick spectacles and a small goatee beard, minus the moustache. His cheeks had a network of dilated blood vessels that betokened a bucolic nature. 'Ach, Lachlan, old-fashioned you are. You must be about the only single-figure handicapper in the islands who still plays with woods. One day we shall drag you into the twenty-first century.'

'I will be kicking when you do,' returned

Lachlan, bending to push a tee peg into the turf and balance his ball on top. He straightened up. Then, mentally selecting a spot on the fairway to aim his shot, he took a couple of practice swings before setting up over the ball. He swung freely and effortlessly. There was a satisfying click of wood on the ball and he held his follow-through as he watched the ball start right then draw back to bounce a yard ahead of Finlay's ball and then bob and roll along the fairway for another thirty yards.

'And another fine shot to you, Lachlan,' said Finlay. 'You should be on the green in two with a chance of an eagle. A birdie at the least.'

'Which I will be needing the way you are playing,' replied Lachlan, as he stowed his trusty old two-wood into his bag and pulled out his pipe. He struck a match to it and puffed it into action.

He waited while Finlay put the finishing touches to a roll-up cigarette and snapped a Zippo lighter into flame to light it. Then they walked on together, waving to another two-ball on the adjoining fairway.

'So tell me how are things going with your book?' Lachlan asked.

Finlay exhaled a stream of smoke then stopped with a scowl and reached into his hip pocket and drew out a hip flask. It was the fourth time that it had appeared during the round and he proffered it to Lachlan, who refused, since he restricted himself to a single dram during the course of a round, and that preferably well into the second nine. Finlay shrugged his shoulders and took a hefty swig.

'It was going well enough for a few weeks, but I have hit a block.'

'Writer's block?'

'You could say that. But really, it is more to do with this bloody Logan Burns and his Daisy people.'

Before Lachlan could say anything the museum curator had stomped off to his ball, grabbed a five-wood from his bag, then without a practice swing thrashed at the ball. The result was almost inevitable. He scuffed the ball off the heel of the club and it shot off diagonally to the left, sliding a mere twenty yards through the grass to come to rest at the foot of a standing stone that rose out of the rough and gave the hole its name of *Carragh*, the Pillar.

'*Luinnseach mhor*,' Finlay cursed. 'Clumsy lump that I am!' He shoved the five-wood back in the bag and strode on to check his lie. 'And now I will have to hit it sideways, back into play.' He pulled out a pitching wedge and chipped the ball back into the fairway.

43

Lachlan waited until he played his next shot on to the edge of the green, before taking a mid-iron himself and popping a shot into the heart of the green.

'Do you see what I mean, Lachlan?' Finlay said, as they walked up to the green and climbed over the barbed wire to reach the putting surface. 'That is my block. I get so cross at the garbage that man is peddling, it even unsettles my golf swing!'

'Peddling garbage about religion, do you mean?' Lachlan ventured. He thought about the young woman, Johanna Waltari that he had met that morning.

Finlay had pulled out his putter and was lining up his long put while Lachlan walked to the hole and attended the pin.

'No. It is the rubbish he talks about the Hoolish Stones and the inscriptions. It is all New Age nonsense in disguise and is no help to serious researchers like myself. And as for all this media attention that he has brought to the island!'

He putted and the ball rolled up to a couple of feet.

Lachlan bent and picked up the ball and tossed it back. 'Give you that putt,' he announced magnanimously. 'But he has certainly not had an easy press from Calum Steele in the *West Uist Chronicle*.'

'That was a wee bit generous with that putt, but it is only a six at that.' Finlay reached for his hip flask and took a swift nip. 'No, you are right there. For once Calum Steele has got it right. But it wasn't the local press I was talking about; it was this Scottish TV coverage that he is getting each night.'

'Ah!' Lachlan said in understanding. He lined up his own putt and smoothly stroked the ball to the hole, where it fell in with a welcome tinkle. He walked over to retrieve it and replaced the flag in the hole. 'But Calum is not giving the television programme much praise either.'

Finlay shrugged. 'I saw him the other day and from what I can gather that is personal. He doesn't care for the broadcast journalist. Anyway, he's a local man and he doesn't like people capitalizing on our Hoolish Stones, whatever the inscriptions are about.'

They walked on to the next tee. As they did so, Lachlan looked into the distance where he could just see the tops of the megalithic Hoolish Stones. Strange, he thought, how much of an enigma they had proved over the years. And equally puzzling was the fact that those strange carvings seemed to stir strong passions within people.

Calum Steele had left the Bonnie Prince Charlie a little after three o'clock, after he had partaken of another couple of pints of Heather Ale with Glen Corlin chasers to calm his temper down.

'Those bloody *teuchters*! I will show them,' he muttered to himself, as he walked to the *West Uist Chronicle* offices. 'The cheek that they have, accusing me of interfering with them. Well no one interferes with the *Chronicle*. Wait till I get to the newspaper offices.'

In fact, 'newspaper offices' was a somewhat grandiloquent title, for although there was a large printed sign attached to the wall beside the door, the newspaper offices consisted of two floors, both of which were exclusively used by Calum. The actual news office itself where Calum interviewed people and took orders for photographs which appeared in the paper occupied the first room on the ground floor, with the archives of back issues in the room at the back. Upstairs was where the actual work took place. At the front was the room with a cluttered old oak desk where he wrote his articles and columns on a vintage Mackintosh computer or on his spanking new laptop. Sitting between the two computers was a dusty old Remington typewriter, which served no real purpose other than to help him feel the part of a writer. The rest of the room was occupied with his digital printing press, paper and stationary supplies, and in the corner was the space where he stacked the next issue of the newspaper ready for distribution. Across the landing was a larger room which had been divided up to form kitchenette, a shower, a toilet, and a room containing a battered old settee and a camp bed, which Calum used when he was either working late, or when he felt too inebriated to return home. As the editor, printer and sole reporter of the paper he worked flexible hours, his only rule being that however he managed it he would produce a paper every Tuesday and Friday. Sometimes he even produced extra editions, which he called 'specials' when there was something of significant newsworthiness that he felt the good folk of West Uist needed to know about. With the interest generated in the summer solstice and the population of the island suddenly swelled with holidaymakers and solstice-followers he had effectively been producing a daily *Chronicle* for the past fortnight.

Such was the popularity of the paper, albeit that at times it was merely a gossip press and a local advertiser, that not only did it generate enough money to fund itself, but it paid him a weekly wage, and sometimes also paid for an assistant.[1] More than that, over the years his pieces had often been taken up by the mainland newspapers, and on occasion he had been commissioned to report on news items for Scottish TV.

And that had been a bone of contention with him lately, especially since it involved a matter of the heart. The fact was that Calum had been infatuated with Kirstie Macroon, the pretty, large-breasted Scottish TV newsreader and anchorperson. His occasional contacts with her by telephone, when she had interviewed him for some of the more sensational stories that he had covered, had led him to believe that he might have stood a chance of asking her out. And one day he had actually telephoned to ask her, only to learn as he stood, with the telephone in hand, that she was engaged. Worse, she was engaged to an irritatingly handsome and affable television reporter called Finbar Donleavy, with whom Calum had a run in before he had known about the engagement.

Finbar and a cameraman had been sent to West Uist to do a regular feature on The Daisy Institute in the week running up to the summer solstice, to be slotted into the daily

---

[1] See *The Gathering Murders*

48

Scottish TV six o'clock news bulletin. Grudgingly, Calum had to admit that Finbar, a dark-haired Irish demi-god from Dublin, who had clearly kissed the Blarney Stone, was a good reporter. He had seen him before and marvelled at his knack for smilingly lulling interviewees into a feeling of false security before screwing them down with what seemed to be a barrage of innocent questions, but which were indeed extremely penetrating. On more than one occasion he had thus exposed a shady character.

'Bugger him!' Calum often found himself saying whenever he came to mind. And that was a more regular occurrence than he would have liked, since he always saw him on the six o'clock news, as well as when he bumped into him and his pint-sized peroxide-blond cameraman, who all too clearly hailed from the London area. Somewhat maliciously, Calum had nicknamed them as *Ebony and Ivory, the piano-men* in one of his review articles on the Scottish TV programmes.

Calum mounted the stairs two at a time and went straight to the toilet to relieve his bladder from the diuretic effect of the Heather Ale and Glen Corlin chasers. Then he brushed his teeth, tossed off his anorak, tumbled into the camp bed and closed his eyes.

'Time for a think, Calum, lad,' he said, as

he swiftly sank into one of his bleary moments before sleep arrived. He firmly believed this state was when he composed his best pieces, when his unconscious mind assembled the information in readiness for his conscious self to dredge it back in a vague semblance of order upon waking.

He had dropped into a doze and was enjoying the hinterland between sleep and wakefulness when he became dimly aware of a strange warbling note from somewhere close by. 'Bloody phone!' he groaned, mechanically reaching for the receiver and pulling it up to his ear. 'West Uist Chronicle. Steele here. What can I do — ?'

'You bloody little guttersnipe! Mind your own business or — you — will — be — '

Calum's eyes blinked and he shot up, immediately aware that he was not dreaming. He was listening to an obviously disguised voice that was slowly and emphatically enunciating a threat.

' — a — dead — man. Butt out!'

There was a click as the phone was put down.

Calum unconsciously ran the back of his hand across his brow, all too conscious of the film of perspiration that had suddenly appeared.

He cursed himself for not having a recorder attached to the phone. 'Who on earth was that? Surely not those *teuchters* in the pub.

They wouldn't be so stupid, would they?'
And, as he thought about the threat as his
mind began to climb further into wakefulness, a slow smile spread across his face,
despite the cold sweat that had moments
before engulfed him.

'So it is death threats I am getting, is it?' he
mused to himself. 'Well, whoever you are you
can just bugger off. I am a newspaperman,'
he said proudly. He opened a cupboard and
took out a can of lager. He tugged the
ring-pull in a defiant mood and took a hefty
swig. 'The editor of the West Uist Chronicle
will not be intimidated. Whoever you are.'

IV

Logan Burns could never have been accused
of being camera-shy. Conscious of his good
looks ever since the first stirrings of
adolescence, he had capitalized on his ability
to charm and captivate members of both
sexes. As a young divinity student in Glasgow,
then years later as a researcher for an
evangelical preacher in the USA, he had
realized that people were fascinated by
spirituality. After flirtations with Zen Bud-
dhism in Japan, time in an ashram in
Southern India and a gruelling four years

51

writing up his Ph.D. at one of the minor American universities, he set off on what he believed was his life's work by setting up the DSY Institute.

He had always been careful to adopt the right image for the time. Part of him relished the role he had adopted as a cultural chameleon. Still a handsome man in his mid-forties, with a full head of distinguished-looking pepper and salt hair, a clean-shaven lantern jaw and a trim waist, he exuded the air of a man who had studied the world's mysteries and now felt at peace with himself. The silver, wire-framed spectacles that he wore perched halfway down his nose when reading lent him the intellectual air which was exactly the image he felt was needed as the director of the quasi-academic institute. In his yellow hoodie he looked like a slightly eccentric yet laid-back professor.

'Could we just do a sound check, Logan?' Finbar Donleavy asked, nodding to Danny Wade, his diminutive cameraman.

Logan winked at the two white hoodie-clad young acolytes, Peter Severn and Henrietta Appleyard, who were standing on either side of the central chambered cairn at the centre of the towering Hoolish Stones. 'Anything you want, Finbar. The three of us will just chat away about the nature of life.'

And although he sounded as if he was teasing, The Daisy Institute director began giving a mini-lecture on the tenets of Jainism.

'That is spot on, Finbar,' said Danny Wade, as he checked his sound meter. 'The wind is no problem at the moment and we can start shooting whenever you are ready.'

Logan pulled up the hood of his yellow hoodie. 'Good. But, Finbar, before we start I suggest that you take a shot of us with our heads dipped, as if in contemplation. Peter and Henrietta can do a Gregorian chant and then you can count me in. I will slowly lift my head and pull back my hood while you home in on me.' He smiled. 'Then I will do my preliminary spiel.'

Finbar suppressed a grin. Logan Burns was as polished a performer as any of the actors, politicians and celebrities he had worked with over the years, yet he thought that there was something of the snake-oil salesman about him. They had filmed every evening for the past four days in the run-up to the summer solstice, each occupying a mere four minutes. So far they had gone out completely unedited, and most of them had been stage-managed by Logan Burns himself. Other reporters might have been resentful of that, but Finbar believed it was always best to give someone a lot of rope. If they wanted to hang themselves that was their affair.

And so, having agreed upon the introduction, they began filming.

Danny Wade was equally used to working with all sorts and had formed a similar opinion of The Daisy Institute director. He focused on the job in hand, sure in the knowledge that if he was a con-merchant, Finbar would find the weakness and hang him out to dry live on Scottish Television.

V

Torquil arrived home at the manse earlier than usual to find his uncle, the Padre, wiping his hands on an apron, having just replaced a casserole in the simmering oven of the Aga.

'Rabbit stew and dumplings followed by apple pie,' the Padre volunteered in answer to Torquil's unspoken question. Then, 'Time for a dram?'

They passed through the hall where carburettors and various motorcycle parts lay on spread-out newspapers along the wall, testimony to their mutual interest in renovating classic motorcycles. The two men had lived in the manse ever since Torquil's parents, Lachlan's brother and his wife, had died in a boating accident when Torquil was a youngster. Torquil had grown up under Lachlan

McKinnon's guardianship, inevitably absorbing and sharing interests, such as the bagpipes, golf, classic motorcycles and politics. Over the years there had been two or three housekeepers, but none had stayed for long, either because they could not put up with the staunch masculinity of the manse, or because they just could not impose order amid the eccentric clutter of books, motorcycle parts or stray golf clubs and bagpipe chanters that somehow seemed to explode into every room.

The Padre poured a couple of drams and added water to two glasses while Torquil switched on the television before slumping into one of the armchairs.

'Tough day, laddie?'

Torquil grimaced, and then told his uncle about the coming of Sergeant Lorna Golspie. He smiled wryly. 'You could never accuse Superintendent Lumsden of subtlety.'

Lachlan nodded sagely. 'You are thinking that he blames you for his suspension.[1] And if that is so then it is possible that this Lorna Golspie has been sent to spy on you. What is she like?'

Torquil pursed his lips in thought. 'I have to admit she is dynamic enough.' And he described the speed with which she had

_____
[1] See *Deathly Wind*

55

restrained one of Calum's interlocutors at the Bonnie Prince Charlie.

'Is she pretty?'

Torquil frowned. 'As a matter of fact she is, but that is hardly relevant, is it? I mean, she is just a colleague.'

Lachlan grinned. 'Just teasing, laddie. And that is the right answer, of course. It shows that you are not going to be taken in by a bonnie lassie.'

The musical jingle of Scottish TV's *Six O'Clock News* diverted their attention towards the television. Kirstie Macroon's familiar silky voice read out the headlines in neat staccato sound bites:

'ANOTHER SCOTTISH MINISTER ADMITS THAT HE SMOKED CANNABIS.'
'MORE TROUBLE OVER SUNDAY FERRIES TO THE HEBRIDES.'

The inter-slot jingle sounded, then:

'But first we go to West Uist for our usual look at the run-up to the summer solstice. We have an interview with Logan Burns of The Daisy Institute at the famous Hoolish Stones.'
'So it is over to Finbar Donleavy — '

The link went like clockwork. The sound of seagulls and a light breeze merged into a melodic chant as the picture changed to give a distant shot of the Hoolish Stones. The shot then panned into the circle of megalithic standing stones arranged in three perfectly concentric rings and what seemed to be an aisle up the middle. Three hooded figures, two white ones flanking a taller one in yellow, were standing behind a central chambered cairn and before a towering column which was covered in weird carvings. All three had their heads bowed and two were chanting.

Then Finbar Donleavy's pleasant Irish brogue broke in as a voice-over.

'The Hoolish Stones! Possibly older than Stonehenge itself are the scene for tonight's coverage of The Daisy Institute. This evening we have come to the ancient stone circle where, in a few days, we shall see how Bronze Age folk used these stones, just as they did other rings like Stonehenge, to celebrate the summer solstice.'

The crescendo of chanting stopped abruptly as the view homed in on the central yellow-hooded figure. Very deliberately, Logan Burns raised a hand and pulled back his hood to reveal his distinguished mane of hair.

The shot panned out slightly and Finbar stepped forward with a microphone in his hand. 'And this evening,' Finbar continued, 'we have the director of The Daisy Institute himself, Dr Logan Burns. Good evening, Dr Burns.'

Logan Burns's lips moved in the subtlest of smiles and he nodded, much as one might have expected from a medieval abbot. Then he spoke. 'I prefer to be called simply, Logan.'

'OK, Logan it is,' Finbar said, returning the smile. He turned to the camera and continued, 'We are at the very centre of the Hoolish Stones with its chambered cairn here before us and the famous Runic Stone behind us.' He inclined the microphone slightly towards Logan Burns.

'These strange carvings have been here for centuries, haven't they, Logan? Can you tell us something about them?'

Logan Burns nodded, like a professor acknowledging his introduction. He looked directly into the camera, as if aware that he was peering into innumerable television sets across the islands and the mainland. 'Yes indeed, Finbar. These are ancient carvings, similar to scores of other ones that I have studied around the world. I should say in beginning that I have a doctorate in epigraphy and am considered one of the world's foremost experts on ancient inscriptions.'

He turned and ran a finger over a carved whorl. 'Beautiful, are they not?' he said, as if overcome by the beauty of the markings. 'Some academics, misguidedly and naïvely, believe these to be runic in origin.'

Finbar nodded. 'I believe it is called the Runic Stone. As I understand it, that implies a Viking origin?'

Logan Burns smiled enigmatically. 'Others would have us believe that they are Ogham scripts.'

'Could you explain that, Logan?'

'Ogham is basically tree language. Some call it Celtic Tree language. It is another ancient script, but whereas runes represent a definite language of symbols, Ogham is made up of notches, coming off an edge or off an axis. It was originally used on wood, on trees, so you can see one simple flaw in that hypothesis straight away.'

'And what is that, Logan?' Finbar asked, with a quizzically raised eyebrow.

'West Uist has practically no trees.'

'So what does this all mean?'

Logan Burns again peered directly at the camera, directing himself to the viewers rather than the reporter beside him. 'I believe that these carvings are far older than either Runic or Ogham script. Indeed, I think there is good evidence that the Runic and Ogham are derived from these, rather than the other way around.'

'I am afraid I do not follow.'

Logan Burns smiled, like a benevolent schoolmaster explaining to a bright pupil.

'The usual thinking is that Runic and Ogham scripts were brought west by invaders from Scandinavia. I think the reverse may have happened. People from here travelled east, taking with them this proto-Runic or proto-Ogham writing.'

'But surely that can't be right!' Finbar exclaimed. 'Are you seriously suggesting that people from West Uist invaded Scandinavia?'

Again Logan Burns smiled. 'I didn't say invaders. No, that would hardly be the case, for a small island like this would not have been the home of a great warrior people. The population would never have been large. But travellers, possibly priests and scholars could have left here carrying knowledge. Ancient knowledge.'

Finbar knotted his brows. 'Ancient knowledge, you mean as in knowledge from an ancient civilization?'

'Exactly. And I refer to the lost continent of Atlantis. My researches have revealed that these stones form a direct link to Atlantis.'

Before Finbar could interject, Logan Burns had returned to the Runic Stone and pointed out several carvings. 'These markings are remarkably similar to some of the ancient carvings that come from the Mayans of South America. They also look similar to the pre-cuneiform script of the Sumerians and some of the very earliest Egyptian hieroglyphics.'

'But you said Atlantis. Surely that is just a myth?'

Logan Burns looked at his two companions who both smiled knowingly for the camera, as if all three were aware of a great secret.

'Atlantis is no myth,' Logan replied at last. 'It is well established that before the great natural disaster that destroyed it, priests were sent out to all corners of the earth to establish sun and moon temples.'

Finbar nodded his head, yet did not look convinced. 'And do these barely discernible markings make any sense?'

Logan Burns smiled knowingly. 'Oh, I have a very good idea what they mean. As I said, I have studied inscriptions from all over the world and I have gone further than any previous scholar in understanding the origins of writing. Here we have a direct link to Atlantis, just as the ancient civilizations of Mu and Lemuria are linked to the civilizations that they spawned in China and India. Many of the major religions and philosophies in the world can be traced back to them, which partly explains The Daisy Institute's purpose. And these great peoples were all highly skilled in astronomy and astrology, which is why the solstices are so important.'

'And?' Finbar asked, hopefully. Although looking unconvinced, he certainly was at least intrigued.

'And it is too early to reveal all,' Logan Burns replied, pulling up his hood. 'But as we approach the great summer solstice, it will become clear.' He nodded to Peter and Henrietta, his white hoodie-clad companions and all three turned and walked past the Runic Stone up the aisle of stones.

'All very exciting,' said Finbar Donleavy to the camera. 'Perhaps we will indeed learn more as we approach the summer solstice. This is Finbar Donleavy bidding you goodnight from the Hoolish Stones in West Uist.'

The picture shifted to Kirstie Macroon in the Scottish TV studio as she did a link with the story about the Sunday ferries debate.

'All bonnie-looking folk,' the Padre remarked, as he drained his whisky and rose to his feet.

'Aye, I suspect that young blond-haired fellow is the one that Morag was going on about this morning,' Torquil said. 'Fair smitten with the young man she was.' He grinned as he finished his own whisky. 'Which is more than she was with Sergeant Lorna Golspie. There could be friction there, I am thinking.'

Lachlan McKinnon clicked his tongue.

'Just as I am thinking there will be between Finlay MacNeil and that Logan Burns. Finlay is not at all happy with all the publicity that The Daisy Institute people are getting. He is feeling pretty territorial over the Hoolish Stones.'

Torquil followed him through to the kitchen. The aroma of rabbit stew was starting to stir up his gastric juices. 'It is to be hoped that he wasn't watching the news, just now.'

VI

Finlay MacNeil had indeed been watching the news. After leaving the golf course he had gone back to the Black House Museum which stood on one side of a narrow metalled road about quarter of a mile off the coastal road from Kyleshiffin, with a fine view overlooking Loch Hynish. Beyond it was moorland leading to the clifftops. It was typical of the traditional dwelling of the islands and was at least 400 years old. Chimneyless, with a peat fire smouldering continuously through a central hole in the roof, it had in days gone by been home to generations of families and their livestock. Finlay had lovingly cared for it for twenty years as the island's museum curator. In the holiday season it had a fair amount of trade, and in the less clement months he was frequently visited by scholars, students and researchers. He had put the finishing touches to a small exhibition he was working on, then retired to his own home, a modern log cabin on the other side of the lane. While he waited for a pan of potato broth to heat up he had sat nursing his umpteenth whisky of the day as he stood watching his ancient black and white television.

'Bloody charlatan! You have no idea what the stones say — you and your New Age nonsense about Atlantis and Lemuria.'

Then his hand fell on his diary that he had left on the arm of the chair and he felt the usual old surges of guilt. Then his temper boiled furiously, just as his broth bubbled over the hob to make a sizzling noise that he barely noticed. 'I'll teach you, you — bugger!'

VII

Ever since The Daisy Institute had taken over Dunshiffin Castle only one television set was allowed for the inceptors and acolytes. It was a pitifully small second-hand set that looked ridiculous in the great hall in which it had been installed atop a cheap set of stepladders.

And that was precisely how it was intended, for it was only switched on for the news bulletins, and only then because of the exposure that the institute was receiving. For many of the new inceptors it was the only sight they were permitted of the outside world during their period of three months' contemplation.

There were about thirty people in the room, all wearing the same style of hoodies. Two wore yellow ones, ten wore white and the rest pale-pink. The pink ones, supposedly representing the pale-pink tips of the petals of a daisy, represented the inceptors, the students of the institute. Everyone watched The Daisy Institute slot at the Hoolish Stones with evident interest.

There was much muttering around the hall. Mainly the mutters were of approval and awe. Veneration even.

Yet one person seethed with internal, well-disguised rage. The unspoken thoughts were anything but full of approval.

You lying, sanctimonious bastard! I would start counting my time, if I were you.

3

I

Finlay MacNeil woke at half past four in the morning, his habitual time to return to consciousness as the paradoxical action of his whisky-drinking kicked in. Dehydrated, with his tongue stuck to the roof of his mouth, yet with a full bladder that felt as if it could burst, he cursed his dependence on the *uisge beatha*, the so-called water of life. His head began to pound as he flung back his quilt and he began his habitual mantra 'never ever, never again', as he sat for a moment on the edge of the bed mentally reviewing his actions of the day before to ensure that he had done nothing too embarrassing. He spied his diary on his bedside table and flicked through it to his habitual last entry of the day. As usual, the handwriting showed the cumulative effects of his daily intake of alcohol. He ran a finger down the page, using his notes as a memory prompt to recall what had happened. He sighed with relief when he got to the end, and then absently let the pages flick backwards, his sore dry eyes threatening to produce tears.

And then with a tide of self-loathing he lay the diary down and sighed deeply.

'You bloody old fool!' he said, cudgelling the sides of his head with his knuckles. 'Guilty you are feeling, and guilty you should be for having no gumption.'

Padding barefoot to the bathroom he relieved himself then sluiced cold water from the sink into his face. He poured water into his toothbrush glass and went through to the spartan sitting-room with his desk in the writing recess. He sipped the water then immediately gagged, as the taste of old toothpaste in the bottom burned the back of his throat. He dropped into the chair and eyed the ashtray on top of the desk with several stubbed out roll-ups and his tobacco pouch lying beside it. Inside it was half an ounce of Golden Virginia and a small packet containing the same amount of cannabis. He winced at his own weakness for the weed, and deliberately shifted his attention to the quarter-full bottle of malt whisky and the empty glass beside it.

'Ach, what the hell!' he said, grabbing the bottle and pulling out the cork to pour a finger in the whisky glass. 'A hair of the dog never hurt anyone. Better than the weed at this time of the morning.'

He swallowed it in one, relishing the liquid

as it went down with an altogether more pleasant fiery sensation than the old toothpaste. He pressed the empty glass to his forehead and within seconds the pounding stopped. And as it stopped so did the self-loathing for his own weakness. Yet he was still angry.

The sun had already risen and rays were streaming through the gap in his curtains.

'It will be the solstice in a few days,' he mused. His glance fell on the piles of papers on his desk, on the half-open books and the screeds of handwritten notes he had made as he prepared the next chapter of his next book, entitled *The Hoolish Stones — the most westerly stone circle.* His computer stood on a neighbouring table, a fine patina of dust covering it, for he only used it once he had drafted the entire manuscript of whatever book he was working on. He had written thirty-two books so far, mainly small monographs for a quasi-academic publisher who specialized in archaeology, history and rural crafts. His work barely kept him in whisky, yet it helped to satisfy his literary aspirations and his belief in himself as a local scholar.

He was proud of the introductory chapter on *The Archaeo-astronomy of the Hoolish Stones*, and of the chapter he was currently working on, *The Ancient Stone Carvers of West Uist*. He believed the book to be a valid and well-researched piece of work that made a genuine contribution to the enigma of the Hoolish Stones and the scattered monoliths that dotted the island. Just thinking about it made his ire rise again as he thought back to the previous evening's news programme with The Daisy Institute slot.

'I wonder what garbage that charlatan will be peddling to folk today.' And with a sudden snort of disdain he snapped the glass on the desk, tightened the cord on his dressing gown and went through to shave and dress. 'He pretends to be an expert. Well, maybe I'll just put him to the test.'

II

Pug Cruikshank was also an early morning riser. As a farmer he had little choice. He never needed an alarm, being used to waking at about five o'clock. Breakfast was usually limited to a couple of roll-ups and a jug of thick black coffee while he listened to *The Farming Programme*. Then it was out to the milking parlour by six, by which time his brother Wilfred would have herded the cattle into the collecting yard and started milking

69

their small dairy herd of thirty Ayrshires, which had been swelled to fifty since they had bought Rab Noble's herd after the tragedy.

No one on the island, except for his brother, knew exactly why he was called Pug, although most folk assumed that it had something to do with being pugnacious. Indeed, pugnacious summed him up. He was a big unattractive man with a cauliflower ear and the physique of a light-heavyweight boxer, which in fact was what he had been in his youth before he opened a small debt-collecting business in Glasgow, prior to moving with his brother to West Uist to look after the farm when his uncle died two years previously. It had been a return to the life he had been brought up to in his native Galloway, where his father had been a tenant on a 200-acre dairy farm.

He crossed the yard into the parlour and glowered at Wilfred, his younger brother by five years. In many ways Wilfred was just a slightly smaller version of Pug, except that he had two missing front teeth, a legacy of arguing with Pug when they had been teenagers. From that day onwards, Wilfred, lacking in guile and cowed by his elder brother, had done virtually everything Pug had asked of him. He had enjoyed the physical aspects of the particular method of debt collecting that they had used in Glasgow.

'You still angry at that newsman, Pug?' Wilfred asked, as he attached the cluster, the four-cup unit, to the teats of one of the six Ayrshires that stood in the six-bay-abreast milking parlour.

'Aye, the jumped up little toe-rag. McQueen had every right to be pissed off at him. But if it had been me — ' He pointed his thumb at his Adam's apple and made a choking noise in the back of his throat.

'I know. We'd have had him. You handled the situation well though, Pug. You got McQueen out of there pretty quick.'

Pug nodded. 'Tavish McQueen is a shrewd businessman, but he and his boy are hot-headed fools.'

'What did you think of that copper, what's his name — McKinnon and his tart?' Wilfred leered. 'She's a pretty piece, though. I wouldn't mind — '

'I don't want to hear what is on your dirty wee mind, you bugger!' Pug snarled. 'You know I don't like people talking like that. When I think of what happened at Hoolish Farm, it makes me feel sick.'

Wilfred bit his lip and straightened up, then moved over to start the milking machine.

Pug sighed and patted his brother's shoulder. 'Sorry, Wilf, I'm just a bit frazzled, that's all. I have a lot on my mind, what with all these complications. Let's just get these cows milked then go and see how Tyler is getting on with the pigs and the training.'

Wilfred grinned. 'That's OK, Pug. I don't know how you manage to keep all of these fancy business schemes in your head, really I don't.' He grinned even more broadly. 'I am always here to help though, you know that, don't you, Pug?'

Pug smiled absently and they lapsed into silence as they got on with the process of milking the herd. Doing six animals at a time, each milking taking five minutes, by the time they had disinfected each animal's udders, cleared them out and installed the next lot it took the better part of an hour and a half.

Once they had finished they returned to the farmhouse kitchen where they ate a bowl of porridge each before heading out in their old Land-Rover to the fields at the far end of the Goat's Head where they kept their saddleback pigs. Half-a-dozen corrugated arcs with fresh straw strewn outside each dotted the churned-up fields.

'Tyler has done his work already,' said Wilf, eyeing the contented pigs and piglets noisily mooching about. 'I reckon he's already working in the barn.'

Pug nodded as he slammed the door shut and started along the track towards the remote building perched not far from the cliff tops. It was a large, aesthetically unpleasing brick building that had deliberately been erected far away from prying eyes, and better still as far as they were concerned, from curious ears.

'I am looking forward to having this proper meet at the solstice eve,' Wilfred said with a grin, as he rubbed his hands together.

Pug grabbed the handle of the barn door and slid it open. Immediately a cacophony of howling and barking filled the air. 'Shut up!' Pug snarled, kicking the door with his boot. Almost instantly, the noise abated.

Pug Cruikshank grinned at Tyler Brady, a tall man in his early thirties with close-cropped hair, who was standing beside a cage inside which a large mongrel with the look of a retriever and the broad shoulders of a boxer was running inside a metal treadmill.

'You scared me there, Pug. I was miles away.'

Pug looked down at the electric prod in Tyler Brady's hand and at the wild look in the mongrel's eye as it dashed on the treadmill, its ears pulled back and saliva dripping from its muzzled jaws. 'Has it been giving you trouble?'

In answer, Tyler Brady, the brothers' pig-man and long-standing business partner, shoved the long cattle prod into the cage and applied a shock to the dog's buttock. It yelped, then increased its speed.

All three men laughed.

Pug slapped Brady on the back. 'OK, good job, Tyler.' He looked round at the line of fifteen other cages where a motley assortment of fighting dogs, some pacing, others just sitting, stared out at them. Although several of them made half-hearted attempts at wagging their stubby tails, all of them had a look of ferocity that made it clear that they had not been bred as pets. Indeed, each and every one of them had been bred as a biting machine.

'I take it that the pregnant ones haven't produced yet?' Pug asked, pointing to the end two cages.

'Naw. Another day I reckon, then the boxer should drop hers and the Stafford maybe next week. Do you think we'll be able to sell them all?'

'Reckon so,' Pug replied. 'I've got orders from the other islands and the usual ones up and down the west coast.' He grinned. 'Each of these little buggers is worth a tidy sum, to the right type of folk. I've even got orders down in Yorkshire and the Midlands.'

'Regular entrepreneurs, aren't we?' Tyler said. 'What with this and Wilf's little cannabis crop.'

'Aye, it's doing well for us, as long as the law doesn't come sniffing around. That means we had best be careful.'

'Of course we're careful, Pug!' Tyler Brady exclaimed sarcastically. 'We're a careful lot up on Goat's Head Farm. Ask anyone who dares come up here.'

Wilfred guffawed and was rewarded by a censorious glower from his elder brother.

'Get the food out of the Land-Rover, Wilf,' Pug ordered. He pointed to the circular wall that enclosed the pit that had been sunk in the middle of the barn. 'We'll give a couple of the younger ones a roll with their muzzles on. See if they can build up an appetite.'

'How about the Rotty and the mastiff?' Brady suggested, pointing to two of the cages.

'Suits me,' Pug returned.

Wilf returned with a large basin full of roughly chopped raw meat and bones. He walked down the line of cages depositing hunks of meat and a bone in each one, except for the cages with the young Rottweiler and what looked like a bull mastiff. The two animals inside stared at him and began barking at their omission from the food chain. And then they looked at each other and, as if knowing what was about to happen, they began growling menacingly at each other.

'Maybe a little wager?' Tyler suggested with a grin, as Wilfred returned with choke chains. He reached into the front pocket of his dungarees. 'And how about a smoke?'

'Of course,' Pug returned, and once again the three men dissolved into unpleasant mirth. 'A smoke is always good when the bets get high. And then we can talk about how we're going to settle some outstanding debts.'

III

Dunshiffin Castle had been the stronghold of the Macleod family, the hereditary lairds of West Uist since the thirteenth century up until the preceding two years when it had fallen into private ownership. The liquidation of the last owner's assets had once again put it on the market, only for it to be snapped up by The Daisy Institute and transformed into a residential centre for spiritual education.

At eleven o'clock, Logan Burns was sitting in the lotus position on a large nineteenth-century Persian rug in the centre of the castle library, which he now used as his private office. Opposite him, also in the lotus position, was a young woman dressed in a pink hoodie. A mere six inches separated their knees, as also was the gap between their outstretched palms. The girl's eyes were shut, a smile hovering over her lips as she breathed deeply in and out at his command. Logan Burns watched the rise and fall of her pert breasts as he talked.

'Feel the energy flowing between us, Eileen. It flows from my hands, to your hands, and from my knees to your knees.'

Eileen Lamont's smile deepened and her attractive little snub nose wrinkled with pleasure. 'It . . . it almost tickles, Dr Burns.'

'My name is Logan, Eileen. We have no sense or need of hierarchy here. Just concentrate on the energies. Become aware of your aura and of how it meets with mine. And yes, it will tickle. It will feel pleasant. You are starting to become aware of your higher self.'

He smiled as she sighed, her breasts rising as she did so.

'Now, just let yourself relax, feel yourself become aware of the heaviness of your physical body as I count backwards from five.' He paused, and then closed his eyes as he counted aloud. 'Five . . . four . . . three . . . two . . . one! Now just let your eyes open and feel yourself returning to the here and now.'

Almost reluctantly Eileen slowly opened her eyes, just as the director timed the opening of his own.

'Did you enjoy that?' he asked.

She nodded eagerly. 'That was fantastic, Doctor . . . I mean, Logan. I have been so looking forward to my first session with you. The first couple of weeks had begun to drag.'

'The contemplation and meditation times are important, Eileen. You have to feel that you want to belong to our institute.'

'I almost asked to leave last week. Then Henrietta, Johanna and Peter, the senior inceptors, advised me to stay. They have all been a great help.'

Logan Burns nodded. 'Yes, they are all going to be great assets to the institute in time.' He clapped her hands in his and squeezed. 'As will you, I am sure. We need young people like you. You are the future.'

He rose effortlessly to his feet and helped her up. 'Time to go and study now.'

He watched her leave then locked the door and crossed to the window which he slid wide open.

'Yes, she will do very well,' he mused to himself as he slumped into the leather chair behind the desk and pulled open a drawer.

With practised hands he rolled a spliff and lit it. He inhaled deeply. 'Very well indeed.'

IV

Saki Yasuda, known to all of the inceptors at the institute as Miss Yasuda, was in the middle of her Kiko bodywork class when Eileen Lamont pushed open the squeaky door of the great hall and sidled into the back of the class.

'Sorry . . . sorry, Miss Yasuda,' Eileen stammered, her face flushed. 'I was with Dr Burns . . . I mean, I was with Logan. He was — '

Miss Yasuda was thirty-two years of age, but looked ten years younger. A mere five feet tall with the lithe supple body of a gymnast, she stopped, momentarily balanced perfectly on one foot and acknowledged Eileen with a smile of ruby-red lips and a slight inclination of her head.

'Please join the class, Eileen. I know that you were having your induction with Logan. Please, watch with the others and join in.'

She lowered her foot to the floor to stand with her feet together and with her hands raised perpendicularly above her head, fingers together.

'So now you ground yourself,' she said, as her dark eyes darted round the class of twenty inceptors and acolytes in their respective pink and white hoodies, and she suppressed a smile as she watched the less adept struggle to maintain their balance. Eileen Lamont certainly was not in that category. The thought that Logan Burns had kept her longer perhaps than was necessary, briefly intruded upon Miss Yasuda's mind before she instantly swept it away.

'And as you breathe in, please become aware of the energy within you. Draw that energy, your *ki*, down into your tummy.' She lowered her hands slowly and rested them on her own flat abdomen. 'This is your *hara*.' She moved her hands in a circular movement around her abdomen. 'Feel the energy, feel your *hara*.'

One or two giggles went round the room as people became aware of the strange butterfly sensation that Kiko bodywork often induced. The *hara* was so real, Saki Yasuda knew, a reassuring self-proof that there was more to life than just the chemistry of cells that modern science taught. And in that moment she felt the usual immense sadness when the image of her father crept into her mind. Doctor Toshiko Yasuda, one of the finest scientists of his generation, had been brought

80

low by his own depression, that awful negativity that forced him to take his life by *hara-kiri*, the traditional ritual suicide of the samurai. *Hara-kiri*, which literally meant cutting the *hara*, the life force. She expelled the thought from her mind and swiftly finished the class.

She bowed to the assembly and they bowed back, then she left swiftly.

And then in the safety of her locked bedroom in the west wing of the castle she kicked off her trainers, peeled off her hoodie and joggers and flung them on to a chair. She stood naked before the mirror wincing at the scars on her arms, the old scratches where she cut herself when the need arose. Just as it was arising now, like a head of steam that needed venting.

Logan Burns! The thought of him would drive the bad thoughts from her mind. She closed her eyes and conjured up the picture of him as she liked to see him in her mind's eye — naked. She shivered, smiled and felt guilty. But then she saw Eileen Lamont's face and the spell was immediately broken.

Why did the thought of the director do this to her? Why did he send her into a spin? And why did she always feel so jealous? With a sigh she opened her bedside cabinet and took out the bag containing the scarifiers. And the bottle of vodka which helped her to reduce the tremor that even now was starting as she unzipped the bag and drew out the blade.

V

Drew Kelso was also sitting in his locked office, the former laird's billiard room. The table itself had been removed to one of the cellars and replaced by a large desk that was covered with books, ledgers, student files and a large laptop. The walls were covered with prints and posters of other Daisy Institute locations around the world. Immediately behind the desk was a clip frame containing the photographs of all of the inceptors and acolytes.

Drew was a well-built, dark-curly-haired man with an olive skin and pleasant, if not handsome features. He had high cheek-bones and hazel eyes, above which slightly drooping eyebrows gave him a faintly melancholic, puppy-dog appeal. He was drumming his fingers on the table as he pored over a sheaf of figures, his expression decidedly one of anxiety.

'Damn Logan!' he exclaimed to himself. 'The man has no idea about business. He could screw everything up — '

Something seemed to click in his mind and he thumped the desk, knocking over a glass of water in the process. He ignored it and, standing up, proceeded to pace the room.

'There has to be a way. He'll have to be — chained back, somehow.'

VI

Torquil arrived at the station in the middle of the morning after a couple of meetings with various local worthies. He was met with stone-faced silence from PC Ewan McPhee and with a curt nod of the head from Sergeant Morag Driscoll.

'A word in your office please, Inspector McKinnon,' Morag said, through tight lips.

Torquil held open the door for her and followed her in. She turned and sniffed the air with a scowl. 'I am not happy, Torquil.'

'I know, I know, Morag. The bag seasoning is a bit strong, but I'll get some air-freshener and it will soon — '

'I am not talking about your bagpipes, Torquil. It's her!' she said, nodding her head sharply in the direction of the office wall.

'Her?'

'This Sergeant Golspie of yours. She's a nightmare.'

Torquil opened his mouth to reply, but she went on, 'It is like having a time and motion woman on my back. She's ticked off Ewan for the number of cups of tea he makes. She complained about the way he makes it.' She saw the start of a smile cross Torquil's lips and shrugged. 'OK, so the poor lamb always stews it, but that's the way Ewan makes tea, we all know that. She has gone over the times the Drummond twins have signed in for and queried them. She has gone through all of the files, grumbled about the way that I organize them, about how I draw up the duty roster, how I pin things to the board and even how I answer the telephone.' All of this had tumbled out in an exasperated manner in gradually increasing volume. She stopped, hands moving emphatically to her hips. 'You'll have to get her off our backs, Torquil, or I will — '

There was a tap on the door and Lorna Golspie pushed the door open, a file under her arm. She looked from one to the other.

'Excuse me, Inspector McKinnon. I thought I heard you come in and I just wanted to catch you to have — '

Out of the corner of his eye Torquil caught Morag's lips firming up.

' — a word?' he interjected. 'Of course. In

fact, I'll do better than that, Sergeant. I'll take you for a wee outing.'

And, taking the file from under her arm, he handed it to Morag and deftly shepherded the sergeant out of his office.

VII

Finbar Donleavy and Danny Wade had been waiting for half an hour up at the Hoolish Stones. One of the typical Hebridean sea squalls had passed over and they had sheltered inside the chambered cairn under one of the large umbrellas emblazoned with the Scottish TV logo until the worst of it had passed over.

Danny was the first to emerge into the fine drizzle. 'I think it will be OK, Finbar,' he said. 'I was worried that the lens would just get wet-speckle. What is the main theme of the slot going to be tonight?'

'Just a bit more about the geometry of the place, I think. Logan Burns wants to explain about the positions of the stones and the way the light will fall at the solstice.'

Danny had lit up a cigarette and was smoking it cupped inside his hand against the drizzle. 'What do you really make of him, Fin?'

Finbar looked about him then leaned forward with a grin. 'Now what sort of a question is that, with the man himself about to appear?'

'Come on, you've been as nice as ninepence with him all the way along. That's not like you.'

Finbar aimed a playful cuff at the cameraman's ear. 'Watch it, you wee tyke. I am being a responsible broadcast journalist, nothing more.'

'That's not what that little pot-bellied newsman called you in the pub the other night.'

Finbar guffawed. 'Calum Steele is jealous.'

'Of you going out with Kirstie?' Danny grinned. 'But so are half the men in Scotland. Come on, Fin. There's more to it than that, isn't there. He's not happy about you for some reason.'

'Well he's just going to have to lump it, isn't he? Anyway, here come Logan and his two side-kicks.' He held his hand out and gave a short laugh. 'And wouldn't you know it, the rain has gone for him. Maybe he is a bit of a shaman.'

Logan Burns greeted them effusively and, as before, outlined how he would like the slot to be filmed.

VIII

The sea had been choppy all afternoon and Lorna Golspie was looking decidedly green about the gills as Torquil put the West Uist Police *Seaspray* catamaran through its paces. After leaving the station that morning he had taken Lorna on his Royal Enfield Bullet classic motorcycle for a trip around the island, showing her the main features, the larger villages, hamlets and crofting communities. Then he had bought her lunch at the Bonnie Prince Charlie before heading off for a trip around the island and out towards the Cruadalach Isles.

'Don't be surprised if I go a bit peaky, Inspector,' she had jokingly protested as they left the crescent-shaped Kyleshiffin harbour.

He had thought that she was joking until they started back from the largest of the isles and she had suddenly dived for the side of the vessel, losing her lunch over the side.

'You'll be fine, Sergeant,' he said encouragingly, 'just keep your eye on West Uist and you'll be — '

'You . . . did that on purpose, didn't you?' she blurted out, her eyes red and her face as white as a sheet. 'Sergeant Driscoll told you to give me a hard time.'

Torquil looked at her in horror. 'I did

nothing of the sort! I just thought — '

She bent over the side and retched again.

Torquil slowed down and patted the back of her life jacket. 'Can I do anything?'

'Get me back to dry land, please,' she returned, pleadingly.

'Aye, lass, I will that,' he said soothingly. He glanced at his watch, surprised to see how late it was. 'But like I said, you might feel better if you stare at the horizon. Look, you can see the Hoolish Stones from here. I am guessing that they will be filming again now.'

'I don't care! I think . . . I am going . . . to die!' groaned Lorna.

IX

The Padre was watching the evening news, a whisky in his hand, his long legs stretched out in front of him.

'And so here we are again at the Hoolish Stones on West Uist. A rainy day on West Uist as it happens,' said Finbar Delaney to the camera. 'I am once again joining Dr Logan Burns and two of his young colleagues at the ancient Hoolish Stones on West Uist.'

Logan Burns walked into the picture flanked by Henrietta and Peter.

'Thank you, Finbar,' Logan said. 'This

evening I want to give the viewers a brief description of these fabulous stones which were clearly constructed four thousand years ago as a temple to — '

'Liar! Charlatan!' a voice off-camera screamed.

Danny Wade spun round and picked up the lone figure of Finlay MacNeil staggering across the heather towards the stones.

'You are a lying charlatan, Burns,' Finlay cried, his voice slurred and his eyes threatening to go slightly crossed.

The Padre sat forward with his glass halfway to his lips. 'Oh, Finlay, my man, what are you playing at? You are fair sozzled.'

Finbar interposed himself between The Daisy Institute director and the advancing museum curator. He spoke into his microphone. 'It — er — seems that we have a heckler.'

'Ask him what his credentials are!' Finlay demanded. 'He is no scholar. He has no genuine academic background.'

A nervous, fixed smile had come to Logan Burns's lips. 'I assure you sir, I have impeccable qualifications.'

'Shall I help the gentleman away, sir?' Peter asked.

'Don't even think about touching me, laddie,' Finlay snapped belligerently.

Finbar tried to defuse the situation. 'Yes, well, if you would just be a bit calmer. It is Mr MacNeil, isn't it?'

'You know that well enough, Mr News,' Finlay replied sarcastically. Then turning directly to face the camera, which Danny Wade kept trained on him, he said, 'All this Daisy Institute and solstice nonsense has gone too far. It is dangerous nonsense this man is peddling. I know exactly what is going on here. I know all about you and your Daisy Institute, I tell you.' He stopped and glared at the bemused Logan Burns. 'I have studied these stones for years. I know all about them and I know all about the solstice. And I know all about the winter solstice as well.'

The television picture was suddenly cut and Kirstie Macroon appeared in the Scottish Television studio.

'Well, unfortunately we seem to be having technical problems in our item from West Uist. So now we shall go to Alistair MacIntosh who is outside the Scottish Parliament with more news about another cannabis smoking MP.'

The Padre sighed and stood up. He cast a sour glance at his untasted whisky and put it aside. He had suddenly lost the desire for it.

X

Finlay MacNeil woke with a start to find himself sprawled across his settee, an empty glass on his chest and whisky fumes rising from his sodden clothes. It was dark.

'Oh man! What time is it?' he mumbled to himself, as he strove to sit up. 'What have I done now?'

He had the vague recollection of having gone to the Hoolish Stones to confront Logan Burns, of the television camera and the rain.

'It is late!' came a voice from the darkness. 'Perhaps a little too late.'

Finlay gasped and shot upright.

'Who's there?'

He fancied he heard a short laugh.

Then, before he knew it, something dropped in a loop about his neck and suddenly he was gasping for air.

4

I

Ewan McPhee had been up since five in the morning in order to practise his hammer-throwing technique. Having virtually demolished his mother's outside shed roof he had taken to going for an early morning run up to the moor above Kyleshiffin where he could hurl his highland hammer with abandon. He had won the Western Isles heavy hammer championship for five years in a row, breaking his own record on each occasion and had even contemplated converting discipline to throw the Olympic hammer. Yet to do that filled him with a degree of anxiety, since it would necessitate trips to the mainland and beyond, a journey that he had only made twice before in his twenty-five years.

'Ewan my man, you are a poor specimen. A real timorous beastie!' he chided himself, as he stood just in front of the twelve-foot-tall ancient standing stone, knee deep in the heather, in track suit bottoms and vest, with the twenty-two pound steel ball on the end of a four-foot wooden cane at arm's length on the ground. 'You are lacking in gumption and no mistake.' He hefted the cane, tensing his muscles, then swung the ball up and around his shoulders three times, picking up momentum all the time, before hurling it over his shoulder on the fourth revolution.

He turned to look after it as it sailed away. Then he saw a flash of movement as the runner appeared from behind one of the undulating mounds.

'Look out!' he screamed.

The female runner stopped abruptly, looked round as the great hammer came hurtling towards her and with a cry of alarm threw herself on to the ground. The hammer sailed over her head and embedded itself in the heather ten feet away.

'Are you all right?' cried Ewan, jumping through the heather for all he was worth to get to her.

'You bloody maniac!' the woman cried, staring in horror at the cane sticking up at a forty-five degree angle from the heather. 'You could have — '

She turned as Ewan came bounding towards her, then:

'You! You great, red-headed baboon!'

Ewan stopped and stared down at Sergeant Lorna Golspie. 'G-Good morning Sergeant. N-Nice morning, don't you think?'

'What is it with you lot on West Uist?' she asked, declining his outstretched hand and pushing herself to her feet. 'Are you determined to kill me?' Then, after dusting down her track suit she set off on her jog again and called over her shoulder, 'I will see you at the station later this morning . . . *Constable.*'

II

Annie McConville was up with the larks as usual and out walking her beloved German shepherd, Zimba, Sheila, her West Highland terrier and the three collies that she had taken into her care. She chose a different walk every day, sometimes going entirely on foot and sometimes, as on this morning, heading further afield in her ancient Hillman Imp. She had driven up to the Goat's Head, a peninsula at the north of the island that jutted into the sea and had started walking them up past the pig farm with its corrugated iron arcs, towards the cliff tops. Several dozen saddleback pigs were foraging about in their enclosures.

The collies began barking first, followed by Zimba when they saw the old green Ford van cross the rough ground from an ugly brick barn perched near the top of the headland.

'Wheesht, the lot of you,' Annie called, tugging on the collies' leads as the van passed them then described a complete U-turn and stopped beside her.

Annie smiled as the window was rolled down. '*Latha math*,' she said, 'Good morning to you. It is a good — '

'This is private property, woman! Did you not see the sign?' snapped Tyler Brady. Immediately, the large head of a Rottweiler appeared in the window behind him, its teeth bared.

'We are only walking,' Annie replied, undaunted. 'We will not be harming any of your animals. These dogs used to belong to Rab Noble at Hoolish Farm and I have them under control. I am Annie McConville and I am — '

'I don't care about the dogs and I don't care who you are. This farm is private! Now get off the land before I get the police on to you.'

The dogs under her care seemed to sense the animosity and renewed their barking, matched by a clamour from the Rottweiler.

'Oh, I will be going, don't you worry,' Annie replied, not in the least intimidated. 'But I will be remembering you, you impudent lump. You and your impertinent animal there.'

Tyler Brady's upper lip lifted in an ugly sneer and he gunned the engine. 'You and me both, sweetheart. Now, bugger off.'

The van wheels spun, spraying Annie and the dogs with mud and he sped off.

III

Torquil had slept poorly. The image of Lorna Golspie retching over the side of the *Seaspray* had haunted his dreams and he had spent half the night struggling with a feeling of mounting guilt. She had looked so ill when he took her back to her room at the Commercial Hotel, and her grudging thanks belied the impression that she had given him previously; that he had deliberately set out to give her a rough time, literally by making her seasick.

He welcomed the coming of dawn, rose and dressed quickly. As usual his Uncle Lachlan was up and was himself preparing for a busy morning of pastoral visiting. As they ate a swift breakfast of porridge, soda-bread toast and half a pint of tea each, the Padre brought up the subject of the fiasco over The Daisy Institute slot on the news the previous evening.

'I fear that Finlay MacNeil is his own worst enemy,' said Torquil, as he pushed away his porridge bowl and began spreading marmalade over his toast.

The Padre shook his head. 'A great shame it is, since he has a great mind. The whisky is his weakness. I shall pop in to see him at the end of my visits. He may have sobered up by then and may be feeling a touch repentant.'

Ten minutes later, Torquil emerged from the manse in his leather jacket, with his tartan scarf tied about his neck, his Cromwell helmet dangling from his wrist and his bagpipe carry case in his other hand. Stowing the bagpipes in the pannier of his Royal Enfield Bullet, he donned his helmet, snapped on his goggles and gauntlets, then kicked the Bullet into action. Moments later he was on his way to St Ninian's Cave, the great basalt-columned sea cave that he used, as generations of pipers before him had done, to practise his piping.

Normally, a good blow on his pipes raised his spirits and helped him to clear his mind, so he approached his practice in the huge cave with enthusiasm. Yet when he got there and stood playing a decidedly poor *piobaireachd*, a pibroch, he gave it up as a bad job and headed off to the station at Kyleshiffin.

The pleasing aroma of freshly baked butter rolls and newly brewed tea greeted him as soon as he pushed open the door. Ewan and Morag were standing leaning against the counter, each with a roll in one hand and a mug of tea in the other. Knowing them both so well, a single look at the expressions upon their faces told him that they had been in the middle of some sort of counselling session.

'Trouble?' he asked.

Ewan drew himself up to his full six foot four inches and winced, his cheeks flushing with embarrassment. He put down his mug and self-consciously ran his fingers through his mane of red hair, then he cleared his throat. 'I am thinking that Sergeant Golspie will want to have a chat with you, Torquil. She and I had a — er — run-in this morning. That is . . . we were . . . both out on runs. Well, I was out practising the hammer up on the moor by the old standing stone and I — er — almost hit her.'

'Och, I am sure you did nothing of the sort, Ewan!' Morag interceded. 'She just wouldn't have been looking where she was going. How were you supposed to know she was skulking about up there?'

The big constable hung his head. 'I ignored the first rule of the hammer, Morag. I hadn't made sure it was safe to throw. I just kind of assumed that I had the whole moor to myself.' Almost absently he took a bite of his roll and chewed mechanically.

Torquil laid his bagpipe case on the filing

cabinet and deposited his helmet and gauntlets beside it. Spying the third mug placed in readiness for him on the tray he poured himself a cup of Ewan's strong tea.

'Actually,' he said, as he added milk and picked up a roll, 'I think that Sergeant Golspie's ire may be directed more in my direction, Ewan, my man.' And he told them of their trip in the *Seaspray*.

Morag barely suppressed a smile of glee while Ewan gave a forlorn sigh.

Torquil shrugged. 'Well, we shall see,' he said, picking up his bagpipe case and heading towards his office.

'Oh, have you seen this morning's *West Uist Chronicle* yet?' Morag asked, wiping a fleck of bread from her lower lip. 'I have put it on your desk. Calum has written a hoot this time.'

Torquil took a slurp of tea then pushed open his door with a toe of his Ashman boot. Dumping his bagpipe case in the corner he sat down with his tea and smoothed the newspaper as he read the headlines:

STONED AT THE HOOLISH STONES

He grinned at the fuzzy picture of Finlay MacNeil berating Logan Burns at the stone circle. Clearly Calum Steele had taken the picture off his television set. Yet although it was hazy and distorted, still it gave the impression that Finlay MacNeil was in a distinct state of inebriation.

He read the article:

'Our ancient stone circle, the Hoolish Stones, have probably gathered more media attention in the last six months than they have done in all their four-thousand-year history. The religious cult organization that calls itself The Daisy Institute, headed by a charismatic New Age mystic by the name of Logan Burns, has managed to grab national media attention as they gather to celebrate the coming summer solstice.

There is nothing wrong with that. The thing that does seem to rub people up the wrong way is their pseudo-scientific non-sense about the Hoolish Stones being an ancient temple of some sort, built by refugees from the mythical lost continent of Atlantis.

This in itself so incensed our local scholar, Finlay MacNeil, that he took it upon himself to interrupt a national television programme last night. Unfortunately, Finlay, who is known to like his cups as well as many, came up against a stone wall in the form of Finbar Donleavy, the heavy-handed inter-viewer from . . .

Torquil read the rest of the article with a grin. He was aware of Calum's admiration for Kirstie Macroon, the Scottish TV anchorwoman and his antipathy towards her Irish broadcaster boyfriend. A hoot, Morag had described it, but Torquil suspected that if Finbar Donleavy read it, then Calum could expect repercussions of some sort.

Sipping his tea and nibbling his roll he turned the page and read the headlines under a photograph of a lorry with the logo *McQUEEN'S REGAL EGGS — STRAIGHT FROM McQUEEN'S CHICKEN FARM.*

WEST UIST TAKES A BATTERING — DUBIOUS PRACTICES BROUGHT IN BY INCOMERS

There was an insert photograph showing Tavish McQueen, one of the men with whom Calum had the run-in a couple of days before at the Bonnie Prince Charlie.

He read the *West Uist Chronicle* editor's diatribe about the new battery farm at the old Hoolish Farm. It was a blunt piece denouncing battery farming in general and the McQueen Regal Eggs business in particular. He recalled the anger in the bar the other day and shook his head.

'Oh Calum, my man. You have a rare talent for putting people's backs up, so you have.'

101

The great dining-room of Dunshiffin Castle, which had been converted into a refectory when the institute took it over, was humming with whispered conversations about the previous evening's newscast. Outside on the balcony the three directors were eating breakfast.

'I tell you, Logan, you are going to have to be careful,' Drew Kelso said.

Logan Burns finished pouring himself coffee and smiled at the financial director. 'I think I have everything in hand, thank you, Drew.'

Drew looked at Saki for support. 'Tell him, Saki. The Daisy Institute can't afford to lose credibility. That programme last night was a fiasco.'

'The man was drunk, that's all,' replied Saki. 'I think Logan is right. Everything is going well. The inceptors and acolytes are all happy.'

'Are they?' Drew returned, nodding his head at the glass door to the refectory full of inceptors and acolytes. 'What do you think they are all so animatedly talking about right now?' He shook his head. 'I don't think everyone is happy. Especially not with the contemplation period we impose on them.'

'It is the way it has to be,' said Logan

firmly. 'It is the time they need to purge their minds of all the rubbish of consumerism.'

'There have been complaints from relatives,' Drew persisted. 'I field most of them. Maybe I field too many.'

'Complaints about what?' Saki asked, over the rim of her coffee cup.

'The usual thing. About not being able to see their darling young things. Accusations of being a cult.'

Logan Burns tossed his head back and roared with laughter. 'A cult! That is nonsense and you know it.'

Drew wiped his lips with his napkin. 'Of course I know that, Logan. But that's where you have to be careful about your Atlantis theories.'

'They are more than theories, Drew. They are firm conclusions based on solid research. I am the academic here, remember that if you will.'

'Yes but — '

'No buts, Drew. I am the founder of this institute and I shall steer the course that I see fit.' He swallowed the rest of his coffee then pushed his chair back. 'Now, if you will excuse me, I have work to attend to.'

Once he had gone Drew sat back in exasperation. 'That felt as if I was being told off by the headmaster.'

Saki gave him a wry smile. 'I think you deserved it a little. Logan is a genius.'

'You can see no wrong in him, can you? Well, all I can say is that we don't want another episode like Geneva. Have you seen how he is with that new girl, Eileen Lamont?'

Saki winced as if she had suddenly received a shock. 'Don't talk about Geneva like that, Drew. We still don't know what happened there. The police investigations cleared us entirely.'

Drew Kelso leaned forward. 'Let's just be clear on this, Saki. We can't afford to have another dead student. It would finish us.'

He turned at the sound of tyres crunching on the gravel of the castle courtyard. An old Land-Rover drew to a halt by the castle steps. He watched and frowned slightly as Pug Cruikshank got out and headed for the steps leading up to the front door.

'Speaking of the devil, this could be trouble,' Drew said, rising from the table. 'Just think about what I said, Saki. Logan may need to be saved from himself.'

He made his way through the refectory and was descending the main staircase as Pug Cruikshank came through the front door. 'Can I help you?' he said, descending quickly.

Pug Cruikshank stared at him for a

moment, then he shook his head emphatically. 'I've come to see the organ-grinder, not the monkey.'

'I think not!' Drew returned, reaching the bottom of the stairs and stepping towards the farmer. 'I deal with — '

He was stopped by Logan Burns's voice from an adjacent corridor. 'It is OK, Drew, we have an appointment.'

The director was standing talking to Eileen Lamont, who blushed when she saw Pug Cruikshank. 'If you don't mind, we'll talk later, Eileen,' Logan Burns said.

'Morning, Cousin,' Pug said, as he stood aside to let her pass. 'So this is what you meant when you said you were moving up in the world? To a castle. I am impressed.'

Eileen gave him a wan smile and sidled passed him and Drew Kelso.

Drew stood staring as Pug Cruikshank then walked past him with a sneer and shook hands with the institute's founder before they disappeared back along the corridor.

'Damn!' he cursed under his breath, as he turned on his heel and returned upstairs, forcing a smile he did not feel as he passed three white-hoodied acolytes and let himself into his office.

'Number Two is looking pretty peeved,' said Peter, opening the door to let Johanna and Henrietta pass him into the hall.

'I think there is trouble brewing among the directors,' said Henrietta. 'Did you see them at breakfast?'

'I did,' said Johanna. 'I passed Miss Saki as she left the refectory. I think they have been arguing.'

Peter laughed. 'I reckon it is all to do with sex. A love triangle, what do you reckon?'

Henrietta grinned. 'What's that, an offer?' She put a hand on Johanna's shoulder. 'What do you think, Jo?'

Johanna jabbed her in the ribs. 'You have sex on the brain!'

Henrietta giggled and swayed her hips coquettishly. 'You never know.'

But as they all three burst into hysterics, Johanna had other things on her mind than rolling in bed with her two fellow acolytes.

V

Calum Steele rode up Harbour Street on his Lambretta, its two-stroke engine screeching and its exhaust belching fumes. He coasted in to the kerb by Tam MacAlias, the butcher's, to buy a couple of freshly baked mutton pies for his breakfast. He had just overseen the deliveries of the morning's *West Uist*

Chronicle and he was hungry. He was still looking over his shoulder swapping a few words of good-humoured banter with the worthy butcher as he came out of the shop and almost tripped over a dog lead that was stretched across the doorway.

'Oh Calum Steele, you poor man!' exclaimed Annie McConville as Calum regained his balance, only to find his legs encircled by the collie on the other end of the lead. Before he knew it he was surrounded by three collies, a West Highland terrier and a large Alsatian, all of which began barking and salivating at the smell of fresh food. Calum hastily lifted the paper bag with one of the pies above his head and removed the other from his mouth, releasing a stream of juice that flowed down his two chins on to his yellow anorak.

'What the — ?' he spluttered. Then, recognizing Annie and the prim Bella Melville, his old teacher, standing beside her, he swallowed hard and grinned obsequiously. 'Ah, Annie. And Miss Melville. Both out enjoying the air,' he said limply.

'We are not!' Miss Melville replied severely. 'Annie here just had a run in with an obnoxious idiot up at the Goat's Head Farm.'

'Incomers!' Calum pronounced.

'Exactly!' Annie agreed with alacrity, all the

while expertly shepherding the collies from about Calum.

Calum eyed them suspiciously, holding his precious pie higher. 'These are the Noble dogs, aren't they?'

'They are that,' replied Annie. 'The poor souls miss their owners, I can tell.'

'Tragic business,' Calum agreed, a shiver running up his spine at the recollection of finding Esther Noble hanging from her banister. He had covered the story quite extensively and it still made him feel uneasy.

'And I don't even have Eileen to help me walk them any more,' Annie continued.

'Eileen?' Calum asked innocently, in his best journalistic manner, although he knew full well whom she meant.

'Eileen Lamont, as you know well enough,' Miss Melville interjected. 'You were always a nosy boy at school and I do not believe that you are any less so today.' She pulled her leather gloves up her wrists and Calum wilted before her withering glare, just as he used to when she was standing in front of the class.

'She is one of the four local folk who have gone and got themselves involved with the flower people up at Dunshiffin Castle,' Bella Melville went on, proceeding to tick them off on her fingers. 'Agnes Doyle, Nancy MacRurie, Alan Brodie and Eileen Lamont.'

'Aye, The Daisy Institute!' Calum exclaimed with a scowl. 'All incomers.'

'We are not happy about it at all,' Miss Melville said huffily. 'Eileen's parents have been going near frantic because they cannot get in touch with her. It is some sort of ludicrous rule they have. Stuff and nonsense!' She shook her head decisively. 'Well, we are going to report it all to the police.'

'About The Daisy Institute?'

'About our concerns over our local folk. We have no idea what they are up to at the castle. And all this business about the solstice; it smacks of cultism to me.'

Calum stroked grease from his chin with the back of his hand and absent-mindedly licked it. 'A cult, eh?' he mused, a twinkle coming into his eye. 'I think you could be right, Miss Melville. Reporting it would be your civic duty.'

'And I am going to have a word about that rude farmer,' said Annie McConville. 'I didn't like the look of him or his dog.'

Calum nodded sympathetically. 'There are far too many of these incomers to the island. They all seem to be interfering with the West Uist way of life.'

Bella Melville put a hand on his arm. 'You

have a point there, Calum Steele. I read your piece in the paper this morning about the egg man, McQueen. I do not think it is right having one of those battery farms on West Uist.'

'It is disrespectful to the Nobles, if you ask me,' added Annie.

Calum nodded, now eager to end the conversation. He was aware that his stomach was gurgling and that his pie was getting cooler by the minute. He knew that he would have to make the first move, so he stowed his barely touched pie into the paper bag with the other and took a step backwards towards his parked Lambretta.

'Well, if you will excuse me I had better be getting off. The press await — '

He felt himself bump someone then heard a curse as something heavy fell to the pavement.

'You bloody moron!' a voice cried. Then, 'You!'

Calum spun round to find himself facing Finbar Donleavy. Bending down beside him to retrieve a large black bag was Danny Wade.

'Bugger!' Danny Wade cursed, as he gingerly opened the camera case. 'I think you have broken it, you dozy fool! That camera is worth thousands of pounds.'

The glimmer of a smile passed over

Calum's lips. 'You should watch where you are going,' he said with a shrug.

Finbar Donleavy's eyes narrowed and he jabbed Calum's shoulder. 'You need to watch it, Steele. Especially the garbage you write in that rag of yours.'

'You have read my latest review of your programme then?' Calum asked with a smile of satisfaction.

Danny Wade wailed, 'It is broken, Finbar. He did it on purpose, I reckon.'

Calum looked round, expecting some support from Annie McConville and Bella Melville, but they had already departed, the five dogs now padding obediently along with them in the direction of Kirk Wynd.

Unruffled, he turned back to the irate duo.

'So why don't you sue me,' he said with a smile, as he stowed his pies in the carry-basket on the back of his scooter.

'Don't worry, tubby, we might just do that,' returned Finbar. 'And maybe Kirstie will say something about you trying to sabotage us on the next news.'

Calum winced inwardly at mention of the woman he so admired, but outwardly he maintained an air of unconcern. 'If you'll excuse me, I have urgent work to do.'

'We might let you go now,' snarled Danny Wade, 'but the police might be calling to see you after we report you for this.'

Calum started up the Lambretta and studiously ignored the twosome. Then, just before he was out of earshot, he shouted, 'Bloody incomers!'

VI

Morag was dealing with Finbar Donleavy and Danny Wade while Ewan was doing his best to placate an irate Bella Melville and an equally angry and voluble Annie McConville and her pack of animals when Lorna Golspie came in. Gone was the trouser suit, to be replaced by one of the West Uist Division's blue pullovers, yet still with smartly creased trousers rather than jeans like Morag's. She let herself through the counter flap and went straight to the back office where she removed a sheaf of neatly typed papers from her briefcase. She added a few notes to the last page in biro then stacked them in the fax machine. She dialled a number and pressed the send button before making herself a cup of weak tea. Then she sat down in one of the battered old easy chairs beside the table tennis table and sipped her brew. As she expected, her mobile phone went off within five minutes.

'Good morning, Superintendent Lumsden,' she said into the mobile phone. 'Yes, sir, you were right. It is a total shambles. And so far, in my experience, not the safest of places to be.'

VII

Above the cacophony of barking dogs and raised voices from the outer office Torquil heard the telephone ring. Moments later his own extension rang.

'Superintendent Lumsden for you Torquil,' Morag announced. 'He sounds . . . brusque.'

Torquil thanked her for the warning, for he had been expecting a call sooner or later. 'Good morning, Superintendent Lumsden, what can — ?'

The familiar voice snapped from the other end. 'What's been going on over there? I hear that you took Sergeant Golspie out in choppy conditions and that your constable, McFunny, or whatever his name is, tried to decapitate her with a hammer.'

Torquil took a deep breath. 'It is true I took Sergeant Golspie on a tour of the waters round West Uist, sir. No better way to get an idea of the island's geography than by seeing it from the sea. Apart from that if she is going

113

to be with us for long, then — '

'She will be with you until she has completed her secondment,' the superintendent interrupted.

'I was going to say that she needs to be familiar with all of the surrounding islets. I had not realized that she was subject to sea-sickness. That could be a handicap working out here.'

'What about that constable, McFunny. He's dangerous.'

'Ewan *McPhee* is a very able constable, sir. And he is the Western Isles champion wrestler and hammer-thrower. I believe that Sergeant Golspie was out running and she ran into his throwing area. He is not dangerous.'

'She tells me that you fill the place up with strange smells, and that you boil your bagpipes on police property in police time.'

'I think I would need clarification on that, Superintendent.'

'Well, I have her initial report in front of me. It is all down here and it does not make good reading, McKinnon. Too many tea breaks, piles of things all over the place and a distinct lack of organization in the station. That sergeant of yours might need a bit of overseeing.'

'I think not, Superintendent.'

There was a thumping noise from the other

end of the phone, as if a meaty fist had pounded on a desk. 'What did you say?' Superintendent Lumsden shouted down the phone.

'I said that Sergeant Driscoll needs no supervision, sir. I am happy with the way she runs this office.'

There was an indistinct noise from the other end, then, 'Have you given Sergeant Golspie an area of responsibility yet?'

'Not yet, sir,' Torquil replied. 'I am considering what would be the most appropriate area for her to look after.'

'Well, get on with it.'

The line went dead without any additional pleasantries. Torquil replaced the receiver with a smile then went over to the door and pulled it open. Lorna Golspie was standing there, her hand raised as if about to knock on the door.

'I wondered if I could have a word, Inspector?' she asked.

Torquil stood aside and gestured for her to enter. 'Of course, Sergeant.' Over her shoulder he saw Morag look at Ewan and raise her eyes towards the ceiling. 'I was just thinking it's about time we had a little chat about the way that we work as a team here on West Uist.'

VIII

The Padre had spent the morning doing pastoral visits. In the main they were visits to elderly folk and those with various chronic illnesses that precluded them getting to church. Not surprisingly, he often arrived at a visit only to meet Dr Ralph McLelland, the local GP, making a house call on one of his patients.

'Did you see the news last night, Padre?' he asked, as they came down the path from Agnes Mulholland's cottage, where they had both taken a cup of tea laced with a teaspoon of Glen Corlin malt whisky with her. 'A right state Finlay MacNeil was in. It doesn't reflect well on the island.'

Lachlan scratched his chin. 'I was talking about it over breakfast with Torquil. I am guessing he will be feeling pretty sheepish by now.'

'I doubt if he will have a hangover, Padre. He has a rare tolerance to the whisky.' He opened the door of his old and much loved Bentley, which had done faithful service since the days his father had run the practice, and swung his battered Gladstone bag into the passenger seat. 'Still, we are fine ones to talk, eh? Tea and whisky before noon.' He grinned. 'We'd better both keep out of Torquil's sight.'

'Aye, Ralph,' the Padre replied with a wink. 'And I think I will pay a visit on Finlay before lunch.'

Lachlan watched the GP head off before straddling his classic 1954 Ariel Red Hunter and spurring it into action. Then he zoomed off himself. It was a pleasant fifteen-minute ride along the coastal road, past Loch Hynish with its crannog and ancient ruined tower, to the Black House Museum and Finlay's log cabin. He dismounted and tapped at the door before letting himself in the ever-unlocked front door of the cabin. He called out the museum curator's name with a jocular mention about getting up and having some nice fatty bacon and eggs. He knew that if Finlay was truly hungover, then he would have little stomach for a fat-laden brunch.

But there was no answer. The curtains were still drawn, an empty bottle of whisky stood next to an empty glass on his desk, and his bedroom was empty, the bed unslept in. He retraced his steps and crossed the road to try the door of the Black House, but it was locked.

'Where are you, Finlay, my man?' he mused, as he pulled his battered old briar pipe from his breast pocket and charged it with tobacco. He struck a light and puffed it into life, then went to explore the garage.

Right enough, Finlay's car was there.

Then he saw scuff marks on the gravel path. He imagined Finlay going for a walk, staggering about after too much whisky. 'Where were you heading? Surely not to the stones?'

He looked in the direction of the Hoolish stones, just making out the tops of them out above the undulating terrain. But the marks seemed to be going the other way. More towards the cliff tops. Then he started to feel a little anxious, for if he had gone out during the night, why wasn't he back yet? He tapped his pipe out against his heel and started walking across the heather in the direction of the cliff tops, some 300 yards distant.

'Oh, Finlay, my man, I am hoping that you've just fallen asleep in the heather.'

But as he approached the cliff tops he saw the Drummond brothers' fishing boat approaching the island. He began waving, but as he took a step nearer the edge he looked down and almost immediately felt his heart miss a beat.

There was a body lying on the rocks just above the fringe of seaweed-strewn beach that had been exposed as the waves began to recede.

5

I

'Do you seriously mean you think that he was trying to kill you?' Torquil asked, incredulously.

'You weren't there. He missed me by inches,' Lorna returned, her eyes opened wide in alarm.

'And you think I tried to make you ill?'

'I never said that,' she replied, folding her arms defensively.

'Lumsden did.'

'Oh!'

Torquil tapped the end of his pencil on the pad in front of him as he faced Lorna across his desk. 'Morag would be upset if she knew that you criticized the way she runs the station.'

Lorna shrugged helplessly. 'It all needs tightening up in my opinion. There is not enough discipline. Take the special constables, for instance. They come and go as they please and Ewan is forever running around making tea for everyone.'

'We may lack formality, but we work well together.'

Lorna had been sitting upright on her chair, but now with a pout she slumped back. 'You think I was too harsh in my preliminary report, don't you, Inspector?'

'I do. And you were,' Torquil replied laconically.

Suddenly, Lorna clapped her hands to her face and gave a long pained sigh. 'Damn! Which means that I have blown it with you all, haven't I?' She removed her hands to reveal a deep frown. 'I could kick myself sometimes. I often get too . . . officious. Does this mean that you won't give me an area of responsibility, something to get my teeth into?'

Torquil shrugged and sucked air between his teeth. 'That depends on your answer to my next question.'

Lorna sat forward again and waited expectantly, as if her future on West Uist depended on her superior officer's next utterance.

'Did you really tell the superintendent that I fill the place up with disgusting smells and that I boil my bagpipes?'

Lorna opened her mouth to retort, then she saw Torquil's mask begin to drop as a grin suddenly gave him a boyish look. Then he laughed infectiously and before she knew it they were both laughing their heads off. It was enough to bring a tap of enquiry to the office door and Morag popped her head round. Torquil waved her in.

'Come in, Morag. And bring Ewan. I think it's time we cleared the air, the lot of us.'

'Tea would be good,' Lorna suggested, hopefully.

Morag grinned, realizing that somehow Superintendent Lumsden's phone call had strangely resulted in a dove of peace flying in with an olive branch. 'Two ticks and we'll have a fresh brew. Will you take a biscuit, Sergeant Golspie?'

'Please, call me Lorna!' the sergeant corrected. 'I would love one.'

Five minutes later when Ewan came in with a tray laden with teapot, mugs and the biscuit barrel, Torquil and Lorna were still laughing away, as if they had been best of pals for years.

'I really am sorry, Sergeant Golspie,' Ewan said, his cheeks flushed. 'Do you think you can forgive me?'

Lorna waved her hand in dismissal. 'I think we should forget about the whole thing. I have just been so wound up. I think it was because of the picture Superintendent Lumsden painted of the set-up here. And please, Ewan, call me Lorna.'

The big constable grinned sheepishly. 'OK

121

Serg — I mean, Lorna.'

And moments later, with mugs of tea and biscuits at hand they were sharing anecdotes and building bridges. Then Torquil's mobile went off barely seconds before the office telephone. With an apology, Torquil answered his mobile while Morag went through to pick up the office phone.

'My God! That's unexpected,' Torquil informed Ewan and Lorna a few moments later. 'That was the Padre. He's just been out to see Finlay MacNeil and he thinks he's fallen off the cliffs.'

'Is he hurt?' Ewan gasped.

'He thinks so. He says that the Drummonds are on the scene.'

Morag came in, an obviously pained expression on her face. 'He's dead, I am afraid, Torquil. That was Wallace on the phone. Douglas just checked him. He's fallen on to the rocks and must have smashed himself to pieces. It is not a pretty sight, apparently.'

Torquil sighed and heaved himself to his feet. 'Well we'd better get out there and take a look. Can you get hold of Ralph McLelland, Morag?' He turned to Lorna and gave her a wan smile. 'How are you with motorbikes, Lorna? Have you ever ridden pillion?'

Lorna was already on her feet. 'My brother

122

used to have a Yamaha. I think I can say I won't get travel sick.'

'Don't speak too soon,' Torquil replied, tossing her his spare helmet as he gathered his own Cromwell helmet and goggles. 'We're going on a *real* motorbike.'

II

Torquil left Kyleshiffin and then opened up the throttle on the chicane-like coastal road. As he put the machine through its paces, cornering at speed, he was aware of the ease with which Lorna rode pillion. He was also conscious of her arms about his waist and her body close to his. It had been a long time since he had allowed anyone to ride with him[1] and he was vaguely pleased that it did not upset him, as he had expected it might.

They passed Loch Hynish and then took the road up past the Black House Museum and Finlay MacNeil's log cabin, outside which the Padre's Ariel Red Hunter was parked on its stand.

'Hold on, we're going cross country for a bit,' Torquil said, turning his head and grinning as his tartan scarf blew over Lorna's

---

[1] See *The Gathering Murders*

face. She tapped his waist in confirmation and he turned off the road on to a sheep track leading across the heather and the cliff tops in the distance, where his uncle's unmistakable figure could be seen, pipe in mouth and white mane of hair blowing in the wind.

'Ah Torquil,' he cried upon hearing the Bullet's familiar approach. 'Glad I am to be seeing you. And who — ?'

Torquil cut the engine and waited for Lorna to dismount before doing so himself. 'Uncle Lachlan, meet Sergeant Lorna Golspie.' Then, turning to her as he pulled off his gauntlets, 'Lorna, this is my uncle, Lachlan McKinnon, known to virtually everyone as the Padre.'

They shook hands fleetingly, then the Padre turned again to the cliff edge.

'The Drummonds are down there. I saw them coming in from their fishing just before I spotted Finlay. They landed and checked to see if he was still alive.' He shook his head sadly. 'Poor devil, he had no chance after falling that far. But you'll still need a medical opinion, I am thinking.'

'Aye, Morag sent out a call for Ralph McLelland,' Torquil returned. 'Although how he can get down there will be another matter.'

'Well, we'll see soon enough,' said the Padre, pointing the stem of his pipe in the direction of the Black House Museum and Finlay MacNeil's cabin. 'Here he comes.'

And as they all looked round, the ringing bell of the Kylshiffin Cottage Hospital ambulance sounded out above the wind and they saw the old vehicle leave the road and come buffeting along the coarse track through the heather towards them. It was not a purpose built ambulance, but a fairly old camper van that been donated by a former laird and adapted at public cost. The door opened and the GP-cum-police surgeon jogged across the heather with his Gladstone bag swinging from his hand.

Ralph McLelland was one of Torquil's oldest friends. He was the third generation of his family to minister to the local people of West Uist. He had trained at Glasgow University then embarked upon a career in forensic medicine, having gained a diploma in medical jurisprudence as well as the first part of his membership of the Royal College of Pathologists. His father's terminal illness had drawn him back to the island to take over the practice, which he had then run single-handedly for seven years.

Torquil introduced him to Lorna, then said, 'Lachlan and the twins found him almost simultaneously. He's dead, they say, but you'll need to certify him. Do you need us to get you there? I am thinking it will be a case of taking you out in the *Seaspray*.'

Ralph scratched his chin as they looked over the edge to where the Drummond twins were standing beside the body of Finlay MacNeil. Their fishing boat *The Unicorn*, was anchored and their small rowing boat was moored in the shallows. Wallace was gesticulating up at them and trying to shout above the wind. Ralph shook his head. 'I cannot see that it would be necessary to see him there. It looks clear enough. He's had a fall, possibly when' — he looked at the Padre and shook his head — 'when he had taken a few drinks too many. We were talking about that earlier weren't we, Padre?'

The Padre nodded with a frown. 'The whisky! I think everyone thought it would be the death of him one day.'

Torquil's phone went off and he answered it. 'Aye, Wallace, we were just talking about what to do. Dr McLelland is here and he agrees. If you could take him back to Kyleshiffin harbour we'll meet you with the ambulance and take him to the Cottage Hospital.'

'Is there much of a drink and drug problem on the island?' Lorna Golspie asked, once he had put his mobile phone away.

Torquil opened his mouth to reply, but

Ralph McLelland beat him to it. 'People drink here, just the same as other places, Sergeant. Sometimes they might drink too much, but I wouldn't have said there was a big problem.'

The Padre struck a light to his pipe. 'It is big enough though. Especially if it causes a man's death.'

III

Calum Steele had ridden out past Dunshiffin Castle and taken the narrow track up to the Hoolish Stones. Cutting the engine of the Lambretta he parked behind one of the great gateway stones and then flattening himself on the ground he edged into a position in the bracken to get a view of the Hoolish Farm. From his vantage point he could see the large sign boasting MCQUEEN'S REGAL EGGS — STRAIGHT FROM MCQUEEN'S CHICKEN FARM.

He glanced at his watch and waited expectantly. Five minutes ticked by, then he saw movement and a battered Mini-van came down the drive. As it passed him he saw that it was full of about six men, including young Gregory Todd, the insider who had given him the rundown on the conditions that he and his fellows worked under, and the state that the hens were kept in at the battery farm.

'That's the staff off for a good liquid lunch,' he grinned to himself.

He waited until it was out of view then he pushed himself to his feet, zipped up his yellow anorak and patted his pockets to check that he had the three precious accoutrements of a twenty-first-century journalist — a digital camera, mobile phone and spiral-bound notebook. Then boyed up with his mutton pies and the half bottle of cola he had consumed, he felt in the mood for some honest to goodness investigative journalism.

'OK, Mr high and mighty McQueen, so you think that you can give me orders, do you? Well let's see how you like it when I expose you to the world.'

By the 'world' he of course meant the good folk of West Uist, although on several occasions in the past some of his news stories had been picked up by Scottish TV and broadcast nationally.

'Bugger Finbar Donleavy and that half-witted, white-headed camera-jockey! Ebony and blooming Ivory, they are all right,' he mused, as he ducked down and began creeping towards McQueen's battery farm. 'I don't know what Kirstie Macroon could be thinking of. The man is a boor. She could have had me if she had played her cards right!'

And the thought of Finbar Donleavy canoodling with the full-breasted television anchorwoman had a galvanizing effect on him. Seeing himself as a journalistic commando he quickly covered the ground to the end of the dyke that ran up the length of the drive. He stopped and looked around, squinting slightly, not because it helped him to see any better, but because it suited the mental image he had of himself as a commando spying on enemy territory.

The old farmhouse had been tidied up and renovations were clearly underway. Similarly, the old dog kennels had been demolished and two large functional barns had been erected. Taking up half of one was another huge sign proclaiming that this was MCQUEEN'S CHICKEN FARM. Beside that was a huge rustic picture of Tavish McQueen, grinning as if he had himself laid the proverbial golden egg.

'I bet the bugger has never seen a proper farm,' Calum sneered to himself. He pulled out his digital camera, looked to right and left then crept along the wall and over the yard to the sliding doors of the first barn. He noted with glee that there was no lock.

'A doddle this will be. Quickly in, snap a

few shots, and then I am out of here.'

And that was exactly what he did. He slid the door open, popped his head round to see if there was anyone there, then crept in.

'Bloody hell!' he exclaimed to himself, as he slid the door behind him and turned to inspect the interior. The stench was indescribable and he was forced to cover his nose with his cupped hand as he gagged despite himself. Almost as bad was the plaintiff clucking of innumerable hens.

And yet the sight that greeted him was even worse than he had imagined it would be. The barn was suffused with bright glaring overhead strip-lights. From floor to roof were rows of stacked battery cages, each containing four or five hens in cramped wire-mesh-bottomed cages, with tiny feeding areas in front of them and plastic chutes running along the rows to collect the eggs. Calum estimated that there had to be something over 5,000 hens cramped in this barn alone. Straw was strewn over the dirt floor and trenches under the rows of cages reeked with accumulated chicken manure.

Calum felt anger rise like a palpable force within him. It was accompanied by revulsion and a strange sense of impotence. Part of him wanted to run along the barn unlocking the cages to release the birds, to orchestrate a great avine escape. Yet he realized how futile that would be. It was one thing for animal rights campaigners to behave like that, to take the law into their own hands, but not for him, the responsible face of journalism. No, the best help he could give these beleaguered creatures was to expose the practice.

He began taking pictures of the cages; shots of the wire-mesh bottoms that deprived the birds the comfort of sitting on a sold base, the faecal-covered feathers, and the sores on their bottoms. Even the four or five carcasses that had not been noticed and which other poor birds were forced to live with.

He had moved along and was bending over photographing the pallets full of egg trays, testimony to the vast output of the farm. He did not hear the footsteps behind him, so had no warning of anything amiss until he felt something snake round his neck and suddenly squeeze, causing him to drop his camera and claw at his throat as he fought for air.

IV

It was a sombre group that collected at the harbour in the heat of the afternoon, with

131

holidaymakers thronging the harbour markets, all completely oblivious to the transfer from *The Unicorn* to the Kyleshiffin Cottage ambulance of the bundle wrapped in an old tarpaulin cover.

'He'll smell a bit of herrings, I am sorry to be telling you, Dr McLelland,' said Douglas Drummond.

'Don't worry, Douglas,' Ralph McLelland returned, as he snapped the door closed. 'The smell of fish has never worried me yet. I have to deal with other odours more noxious than that in my work.'

Lorna Golspie visibly shivered. 'Will you be able to tell us the cause of his death, Doctor?'

Wallace Drummond stared at her in amazement. 'I think even dumb fishing folk like my brother and I can tell what killed the poor man.'

Torquil put a hand on Wallace's shoulder. 'We cannot assume anything, Wallace. Finlay MacNeil might have fallen to his death, but we have to go through the motions.'

The Padre knitted his brows and shook his head emphatically. 'I do not think that suicide is at all likely. Not Finlay.'

'You will be wanting a post-mortem as soon as possible, I imagine?' Ralph asked.

'I would be grateful, Ralph.'

Lorna leaned towards Torquil. 'Would you

like me to liaise with the doctor, Inspector? Remember, you said you would give me a job.'

Torquil clicked his teeth pensively. 'Ah yes, Lorna. A job. I am still thinking about that.'

V

Calum's hand came in contact with a bare muscular forearm that held him in a vice-like neck-lock. He patted it frantically as the pressure on his trachea increased and the only noise he could make was a plaintive gurgling.

'Bloody snooper!' a voice at his ear rasped. 'You need a lesson. A final lesson!'

Panic bells began to ring in Calum's mind. A final lesson! He nipped the skin of the forearm, only to feel the grip about his throat strengthen. He felt a wave of dizziness and nausea sweep over him.

Then vaguely he had a picture of a series of articles on self-defence he had published a couple of years before in the *West Uist Chronicle*. Line drawings that he had copied from a series of bubble gum cards he used to collect as a boy. He saw them now, each with the title Bazooka Bob's School of Judo. Each card had three drawings of a judo throw.

Dizziness increased as he almost fell into a trance-like state, and he became the character in the line drawings.

He stiffened, tensed his neck muscles, before suddenly letting all his muscles go floppy as if falling. At the same time he grabbed the arm and jack-knifed forward, tugging as he did so.

To his amazement, never having actually done anything like it before, except in the rich fantasy world in which he saw himself as the hero of a thousand situations, he felt a large body hurtle over his head to land on his back on top of a large pallet of eggs. There was an almighty cracking of several dozen eggs and a deep grunt of pain.

Calum looked down at the sprawling figure of Angus McQueen, the battery farm-owner's son. Tempted though he was to bring his foot down on his attacker's face as he wiped egg yolk from his eyes, he desisted, choosing instead to scoop dirt and chicken dung from the barn floor and throwing a handful into the man's face.

It seemed the right thing to do, for it made him cough and splutter and gurgle with rage. More importantly, it gave Calum the time he needed to gulp air into his lungs and act. He picked up his camera, took a picture of his aggressor before beating a hasty retreat.

'Mission accomplished, Calum, my man,' he grinned to himself as he sprinted down the drive.

It was not until he reached his hidden Lambretta that he realized the enormity of what had just happened. Then a surge of nausea doubled him up.

Regretfully, he lost his breakfast of mutton pies.

VI

After a late lunch for which no one had much of an appetite, Torquil called his staff into his office. 'OK, Morag, let's see what jobs we've got and let's divvy them up.' He smiled at Lorna. 'Sergeant Golspie is keen to get her teeth into something.'

'Let's be hoping it is not one of us then,' said Wallace Drummond with a grin. 'Or then again — ' he added, with a roguish wink at the new sergeant.

He was immediately rewarded with a jab in the ribs from his brother, who addressed Lorna with an even deeper grin. 'Ignore my boorish brother, Sergeant. He got the bad genes.'

Torquil eyed the twins with mock severity. 'That's enough lads. OK, Morag, what have we got?'

Morag shook her head and began hesitantly. 'Calum tops the list, I am afraid. This morning we had a complaint from that TV reporter Finbar Donleavy and the cameraman' — she referred to the duty log book to refresh her memory — 'Danny Wade, about him deliberately breaking their camera. Apparently, it might mean they will not be able to broadcast on the news tonight.'

'Doesn't sound like Calum,' Torquil said defensively.

'I am not so sure, Torquil,' said Douglas Drummond. 'Our Calum is a clumsy wee man.'

'And he doesn't think much of Finbar,' agreed his brother. 'He thinks more about Finbar's girlfriend though.'

Torquil said nothing. Calum's feelings for Kirstie Macroon were well known by them all.

'Also a complaint against him for trespass, criminal damage and assault.'

Torquil slapped his hand on the desk. 'That's rubbish. They're going too far.'

'It is a different complaint, Torquil,' Morag interjected. 'It just came in while you were at lunch. It is from the McQueens. They say he's broken into their *farm*, taken unauthorized pictures and beaten up the son.'

The Drummonds and Ewan looked at one

another for a moment, then all three burst out laughing. 'Calum Steele beating up that big McQueen fellow! That is ridiculous, Inspector,' said Ewan. 'He couldn't knock his way out of a paper bag.'

Lorna snapped her fingers and looked at Torquil. 'Wasn't that fracas in the Bonnie Prince Charlie to do with the McQueens?'

'It was. Maybe they have a vendetta against him. Calum sees himself as an investigative journalist, you see.'

'There is more,' Morag went on. 'And it is to do with Calum again. Logan Burns, the man from The Daisy Institute phoned while you were out. He was complaining about Calum's piece in the paper. He said that he wanted him charging with defamation of character and that he would be taking legal action.'

'That is nothing to do with the police,' said Torquil with a trace of irritation. 'He needs to see his solicitor, not be bothering us.' He gave a long-suffering sigh. 'Calum really knows how to stir people up against him, doesn't he? What else, Morag?'

'Curiously, there is a complaint about Logan Burns himself and The Daisy Institute. Annie McConville and Bella Melville were in. It is like a menagerie when Annie brings her dogs. Anyway, they say that they represent some of the families.' Once again she consulted the log book and read out the names. 'Agnes Doyle, Nancy MacRurie, Alan Brodie and Eileen Lamont.'

'They are all over eighteen, though, aren't they?' Torquil interjected.

'They are, but Miss Melville says that their families are concerned that they cannot get access to them. They say that the institute is just a cult and they demand that we investigate it.'

Torquil looked ceilingwards and groaned. 'Investigate what, exactly?'

'They are claiming that they may be keeping people there against their will.'

'That is an unpleasant thought,' said Wallace.

'A serious accusation,' Douglas agreed.

'So we had best check it out,' Torquil acquiesced. 'Anything else, Morag?'

Morag sighed. 'Annie McConville was also complaining about the Goat's Head Farm people. She was out walking her dogs this morning and she was stopped from going up to the actual headland by some boorish chap in a big green Ford van. He had a Rottweiler or some big dog with him. She says he was needlessly rude to her.'

'Hardly a police matter though, is it?' Torquil queried.

Morag eyed him askance. 'It is Annie McConville though, boss. You know what she's like. If we don't do something she'll be living on the doorstep with her pack of dogs.'

Torquil put his hands over his face in exasperation. Then, turning to Lorna, he said, 'Do you see the sort of things we have to put up with here? This is our bread and butter. Sorting out bickering between folk. If you want crime you've come to the wrong place!' He tapped his fingers on the desk. 'OK, so let's get cracking. I'll go and see Calum. Morag, how about you and Lorna going over to Dunshiffin Castle and doing a bit of digging around. We could do with knowing a bit more about The Daisy Institute and I think the female touch is required.'

He looked up and grinned at Ewan. 'How's about a trip out to the Goat's Head and having a wee word with these folk about being nice to one of our celebrity senior citizens?'

'Sure thing, Torquil,' the big constable said enthusiastically.

'Then you can liaise with Annie McConville.'

Ewan's face dropped. 'If you insist, Torquil.'

Wallace Drummond put an arm around his brother's shoulder. 'Looks like there are no jobs for the handsome specials? I guess we could go — '

'I didn't say that, Wallace,' Torquil cut in. 'It would help if you two followed up on that last task.'

'What was that, Torquil?' Douglas asked warily.

'The post-mortem on Finlay MacNeil. It would be good to know what Ralph McLelland thinks. Why don't you two pop along and see him?'

Wallace shrugged. 'No bother, Inspector McKinnon. But would it be OK if we just popped along to the Bonnie Prince Charlie for a snifter to give us a bit Dutch courage?'

Ewan McPhee answered on behalf of his superior. 'Drinking on duty! Away with the pair of you before I get my hammer to you!'

VII

The Padre pushed open the doors of the Bonnie Prince Charlie and strode purposefully to the half-empty bar. Mollie McFadden was rearranging beer mats and looked up upon hearing his familiar tread. She beamed at him from behind her thick-lensed spectacles, her look of warm greeting immediately transforming into one of concern.

'What's the matter, Padre? You look as if you have seen a ghost.'

'Worse than that, Mollie. A tragedy, so it is. I found Finlay MacNeil at the bottom of the cliffs beyond his cabin.' He shook his head sadly. 'He is dead.'

Mollie gasped. 'Do you think he was — ' She hesitated, then went on in a half-whisper, 'Drunk? I saw him on the TV last night.'

Lachlan shrugged. 'It is not for me to say, Mollie. I believe Dr McLelland will be doing a post-mortem examination.' He pointed at one of the optics. 'A single Glen Corlin, if you please. And will you join me, Mollie?'

'A real shock for you,' Mollie said, reaching for a couple of glasses. 'These are on the house, Padre.' And reaching above her head she tapped the bell then raised her voice to announce to the rest of the clientele, 'We have a tragedy here. Finlay MacNeil has died in an accident. If anyone would care to join us we are having a drink on the house in his memory.'

Amid gasps of astonishment and much murmuring of sorrow the bar came to life. The words of sympathy came thick and fast, and before long the subdued mood was gradually replaced by a lightening of spirits as people fell into anecdotage.

'Do you remember the time Finlay caught

141

a fish in his trousers?'

'He was the most erudite of writers.'

The Padre raised his second glass to Mollie and winked at her as she bustled about with her bar staff raising glasses to optics and pulling a veritable spate of Heather Ale into fresh glasses. Her offer of drinks on the house was a sure-fire way of generating extra custom, as she well knew. A show of generosity by the landlady was inevitably reciprocated by two or three rounds of magnanimity from her loyal customers.

Lachlan was just filling his pipe preparatory to taking his leave when he felt a hand on his shoulder. Turning, he found himself confronted by Finbar Donleavy and Danny Wade, each with a pint of Heather Ale in their hands.

'A sad business this is,' said Finbar with a sympathetic shake of his head. 'To think that we were — er — talking to the man just last night.'

The Padre frowned. 'Not exactly talking to him though, were you? More like filming his outburst.'

'He was pretty vitriolic about Logan Burns. We felt we had to halt the interview.'

'I know. I saw the news,' the Padre nodded affably. 'And I read Calum Steele's piece in the papers.'

Finbar's face darkened. 'That newshound is chancing his arm. He made some defamatory remarks about me in that local rag.'

'That local rag is highly respected in West Uist,' the Padre countered.

'He broke our camera you know,' Danny Wade said. 'We reported him to the police.'

The Padre bit his lip. 'That doesn't sound like Calum.'

Danny Wade snorted. 'It was an expensive piece of Scottish TV property. We expect action from the police for criminal damage. We're just waiting for the next ferry to bring in a replacement camera so we can film for the news tonight.'

'You will be continuing the pieces about the institute then?'

'The solstice won't stop for Finlay MacNeil's death,' Finbar replied unemotionally. 'It is just two days away. I will say a few words about the tragedy, of course.' He sipped his beer, and then asked casually, 'What do you as a man of the church think about The Daisy Institute? They seem to be getting a lot of attention. Have you seen the number of people that are coming into the island?'

The Padre had been half-expecting the question. 'Aye, the island is pretty busy right now, but it is the height of the summer and it is a beautiful island. But I am afraid that I have no comments to make about The Daisy Institute. I am eagerly awaiting whatever revelation Logan Burns is promising us.' He clenched his pipe between his teeth, nodded, then left.

The two newsmen stared after him. 'Nothing there then, eh, Finbar?' Danny Wade commented.

Finbar shrugged his shoulders non-committally. 'Who knows? If the Padre does know anything he isn't saying. That was just a brush-off.' He took a hefty swig of beer. 'Looks like we will still have to do some spade-work ourselves.'

Danny Wade laughed. 'And get it all on camera.'

They both grinned and clinked glasses, neither having noticed the hoodie-clad figure sipping a cola a few feet along the bar from them.

6

Calum had recovered by the time he got back to the *West Uist Chronicle* offices. At least, he had recovered from the shock of the fracas with the younger McQueen, but not from the emotional trauma of being up at the Hoolish Farm again. It had only really hit him when he reached his scooter and hurled up his late breakfast. From that moment, as he rode his Lambretta back along the coastal road, he could not free his mind of the image of Esther Noble hanging from the banister in the hall of the farmhouse.

Resisting the urge to pull out the bottle of Glen Corlin that he kept in the R — S drawer of his filing cabinet — 'R' being for 'restorative' — he went through to the kitchenette, filled the kettle and brewed himself a strong pot of tea. He was just stirring the pot when the bell went and the outer door opened and closed.

'If that is tea I hear being made, I'll have a cup,' Torquil's voice called up the stairwell.

Calum grinned as he heard his friend

mounting the stairs two at a time.

'Aye, you have come for a decent cup of tea then, instead of that ditch water that Ewan McPhee dishes up,' Calum replied with a grin. 'What brings you to the fourth estate, Piper?'

Torquil gave a mock scowl. 'Semi-official business, I am afraid, Calum. Complaints about you.'

The newspaper editor produced an extra mug from the cupboard and poured tea.

'About me? Havers, man. I am a model of respectability. Who is complaining?'

'Just about everyone, Calum man,' Torquil replied, dropping on to the battered settee and accepting the mug. He poured milk into it from the half-empty bottle and stirred it to an agreeable cream colour. He winked to indicate that he was teasing.

'Three complaints actually. In order, Criminal damage, trespass and bodily harm, and defamation of character. The complainants respectively being, Finbar Donleavy and his cameraman Danny Wade, Tavish McQueen and Logan Burns.'

Calum took a sip of tea and wiped his lips with the back of his hand. 'You are joking me, are you not?'

Torquil shook his head. 'I am investigating, Calum. I am here for your version on each count.'

Calum sighed and sat down on the edge of his camp bed. 'Criminal damage, so they are talking about their camera, right? Well, that is simple, it was an accident. They weren't looking where they were going and barged into me. Clumsy buggers. They were peeved because of my review of their news slot.' He sneered. 'What sort of a journalist is he? The simple fact is that he can't take criticism and he's tried to get back at me with this trumpery.'

'Sounds reasonable. Your word against theirs then.'

'Aye, and what's this nonsense from McQueen?'

'They say you broke into their egg farm and assaulted Angus McQueen, the owner's son.'

Calum thumped his knee with his fist. 'He says I assaulted him?'

Torquil could barely keep the grin from his face, as he recalled the all too recent banter between Ewan and the Drummond twins about Calum's fighting ability. 'Aye, he says that you broke into the farm, beat up Angus McQueen and took a lot of unauthorized photographs.'

'Ha! I took photographs all right. That is what we investigative journalists do. But I didn't break in, the door was open and I popped in

147

to — er — make an appointment. When I was there I was shocked at the state of the poor birds there and I did take a few pictures. I will be writing up the article later and it will appear with the photographs in the next edition of the *Chronicle*. It is a scandal, so it is. The place is a health hazard and I am thinking of reporting them for cruelty.'

'Do you want to make that formal, Calum?'

The newsman pursed his lips for a moment then shook his head decisively. 'No. The power of the press will bring other powers to bear. A bit of good old-fashioned exposure should set the wheels in motion.'

'And what about this assault claim?'

'Pah! The bugger attacked me.' Calum sat upright, his chest expanding with ruffled pride. 'He should have thought better than to tangle with a martial artist.' And with a sudden guffaw, he told Torquil about the attack from behind, and of his recollection of the Bazooka Bob bubble-gum cards and the drawings of the judo throw. He chuckled as he put down his mug, stood up and demonstrated the throw with a cushion.

'And here is the picture I took of him after I threw him,' Calum went on, showing his friend the picture on his digital camera. 'That will be going into the paper as well.'

Torquil grinned. 'Spiky wee gink, aren't you?'

'You said it, Piper. Now what about this defamation rubbish?'

Torquil shrugged and swallowed the remains of his tea. 'I think you said it. Sounds like rubbish to me. Logan Burns claims that you have defamed him and his institute. It is nothing to do with us, of course. I just thought I'd warn you in case he decides to take legal action.'

'The *Chronicle* will not be suppressed, Piper. Let him do his worst.' He finished his own tea and stood staring at the mug for a moment. 'But going back to the Hoolish Farm, I have to say that it brought back bad memories.' He bit his lip and swallowed hard. 'I keep seeing Esther's body hanging there. I don't sleep well these days because of it.'

Torquil nodded in agreement. 'An unpleasant business, but you have to put it out of your head, Calum. There was nothing you or anyone could do. Remember what the Fatal Accident Inquiry said.'

'But maybe if I had got there sooner. He passed me on the road, remember. Almost knocked me down.'

Torquil put his hand on his friend's shoulder and squeezed.

'Anyway, I'd better be off,' he said. 'I have

to write up my reports on these three 'cases'. Thanks for your co-operation, Calum.'

Calum grinned sheepishly. 'Always a pleasure, Piper.' He sighed and cracked his knuckles. 'And now I had better get the wheels of the press rolling. I have articles to write.'

Torquil grinned and descended the stairs. But, by the time he reached the door, the grin had disappeared. He had to admit to himself that he had never felt easy himself about the tragedy at Hoolish Farm back in the winter. There was something about it that didn't seem right, but he just couldn't put his finger on it.

II

Morag drew the station's tired old Ford Escort into the Dunshiffin Castle courtyard and pulled to a halt beside a parked Rolls Royce, a Porsche Boxter and one of the latest XK Jaguars.

Lorna got out and looked up admiringly at the great Scottish baronial castle, with its original structure dating back to the four-teenth century when the first of the McLeod lairds had built it. An impressive flight of stone steps led up to the huge main doors, beside which was a seemingly incongruous sign with the logo of a daisy on it. Underneath it, large italicized yellow letters proclaimed it to be '*The West Uist HQ of the DSY Institute*' with small letters underneath explaining that it was: 'Centre for the Study of Divinity and Spirituality.'

'Looks as if there is money to be made in daisies,' she joked, as Morag came round the car to join her.

'The cars are all owned by The Daisy Institute, not by individuals,' came a voice from the top of the steps.

The two sergeants looked up and saw Drew Kelso standing at the open doors, his hands folded inside the voluminous sleeves of his yellow hoodie, like a modern day monk.

'Very nice,' said Lorna, feeling rather caught on the hop.

Drew smiled down at them, his smile reminding Morag of the fixed smile on a ventriloquist's dummy. 'I am Drew Kelso, the Financial Director of The Daisy Institute. Won't you come in? You are police, are you not? We were expecting you.'

'You were expecting us?' Morag repeated, as she mounted the steps, where they introduced themselves and both produced warrant cards.

'Yes, Logan Burns is waiting in his office

with Saki Yasuda. We want to co-operate as much as possible.'

The two sergeants looked at each other as they passed him into the great hall, which Lorna noticed was bedecked with deer heads, antlers and innumerable crossed claymores, shields, and pikestaffs. A large portrait of a kilted laird looked down at them from the top of a magnificent oak staircase.

'Hideous, aren't they?' Drew Kelso said, as he caught her look of wonder. 'Hardly the right message for an institute like ours, but Logan insisted that the castle should still retain its identity. He has very clear views about maintaining character. This way, please.'

A door opened and a stream of young people teemed out, the majority dressed in pink hoodies, but with several dressed in similarly cut white garments.

'Why exactly were you expecting us, Mr — ?' Lorna asked.

'Drew, just call me Drew.' His smile faded and he looked bemused. 'It is about the tragedy, is it not? About MacNeil's death?'

Morag stopped. 'How did you hear about Mr MacNeil's death?'

Drew shrugged. 'Someone heard about it when they were in Kyleshiffin. Everyone at the institute knows. So sad, so very sad.'

'Actually, we were here to have a chat about some complaints,' said Morag.

'Complaints? From whom?'

'Perhaps we could explain in the office as you suggested,' Morag went on.

'Of course,' Drew replied. He turned to lead the way again.

Another door opened and more young people came into the corridor. Morag caught sight of two young women and waved to them.

'Actually, do you mind if Sergeant Golspie has a chat with you all? I've just seen a couple of my neighbours. I'll just have a word with them.'

And before either Lorna or Drew could say anything Morag had linked arms with Agnes Doyle and Eileen Lamont and loudly and assertively proposed that they take her for a cup of tea.

III

Pug Cruikshank was in good spirits, almost literally, as he showed his latest customers around the cages of the barn, while Tyler and Wilf put a couple of the dogs through their paces on the treadmills. There were four customers, two from Ireland, one from

Birmingham and the last from Norway. As was usual, Clem O'Hanlan and his uncle had brought hip flasks of poteen with them, and Lars Sorensen had produced a bottle of vodka. Between them, apart from the teetotal Brummie, known always as Mr Borawski, they had drunk half of each, as well as half a bottle of Glen Corlin before leaving the farmhouse.

'Hey, Mr Borawski, why won't you drink with us? You worried we'll poison you, eh?' Clem OHanlan queried cheerily.

Mr Borawski was a stocky little fellow, widely known throughout the international dog-fighting fraternity as not being someone to trifle with. He had many brothers and uncles and there were rumours of many business interests that would have made the Kray brothers interested at the very least. He said nothing as he lit up a Marlborough and eyed Pug meaningfully.

'Mr Borawski is a religious man,' Pug said quickly. 'The booze is against his religion.'

Clem's Uncle Sean guffawed. 'Sure, I understand that all right. You have to follow your religion and do what your priests tell you. My auld dad he was a priest and he taught by example. Drinking is everything to a good Catholic.' With which he produced a hip flask of poteen and took a hefty swig.

Lars Sorensen scowled, screwing his beetle brows so that they became a corrugated series of lines across his forehead. 'Catholic priests don't have children!'

'Not in Norway, maybe,' interjected Clem. 'But in our country, well, let's say things are a lot more liberal.'

Wilf turned and beamed. He began a lewd anecdote, but was quickly halted by Pug who had no wish to allow alcohol to get in the way of business.

'All right, lads!' he said firmly. 'Let's get down to brass tacks. You've seen our stock and you can see that we've got more on the way soon. Who wants to make me an offer?'

Mr Borawski blew a cloud of smoke from between thin lips. 'I am slightly impressed, Pug. Maybe if — '

'Slightly impressed!' Tyler Brady exclaimed stiffly. 'Why you don't — '

Suddenly, a red light on a wall began flashing and a buzzer started to emit a pulsed warning.

Pug darted to a window and pulled back a shutter slightly. He picked up a pair of binoculars that were perched on the sill and focused them through the gap on the long sweeping track that led from the cattle grid 400 yards away, just beyond which they had strung the pressure wire that alerted them to anyone approaching.

'Shit! This could be trouble.' He let the shutter slip back and turned to the others. 'Looks like the police. Everyone stay here. Wilf, you keep the dogs quiet. Tyler, you and me will go walkies with these two.' He snapped his fingers irritably. 'Quickly, for fuck's sake!'

PC Ewan McPhee felt that he had drawn the short straw, both in terms of the investigation that had been allocated to him by Torquil, and by the mode of transport that he had been forced to take. Ordinarily he would have chosen to use his mountain bike, but twisted front forks had forced him to plead with his mother to borrow Nippy, as everyone in Kyleshiffin lovingly referred to her forty-year-old *Norman Nippy* moped. It wasn't that he minded using it, for it had belonged to his late fisherman father, but rather the fact that a six foot four red-headed police constable looked ridiculous riding it. When it was new its 50 cc engine had a maximum speed of thirty-five miles an hour, but time had considerably slowed Nippy down. Ewan's eighteen-stone frame reduced that figure to an almost pedestrian speed.

Having first of all checked that there was no one at home in the Goat's Head farmhouse he had set off towards the Goat's

Head itself, where Annie McConville had said that she had been turned away by one of the farm staff.

He steered Nippy along the track past the pig fields towards the large distant barn. As he approached, he saw a door open and two men emerged, each with a large dog on a lead. Despite himself, Ewan cringed.

He was not overly fond of dogs.

IV

Morag sat back in one of the refectory chairs and smiled at the four pink hoodie-clad Daisy Institute inceptors sitting around the table. Within minutes of sitting down with Eileen Lamont and Agnes Doyle they had been joined by the two other locals who had recently enrolled. Morag knew them all, at least by sight, but she suspected that their period of seclusion from the other islanders may have somehow stimulated a feeling of homesickness and heightened a need to talk to one of their own. She had no doubt that news of the arrival of two woman police sergeants would have spread instantly round the castle.

'So, how are you all enjoying yourselves?' she asked, picking up her tea and sipping.

'It's fantastic!' enthused Agnes Doyle, a tall, twenty-year-old with long braided hair and prominent, uneven teeth.

'The best thing I've ever done in my life,' agreed Alan Brodie.

Morag nodded, partly because Alan, a nineteen-year-old, had a local reputation as a misfit.

Nancy MacRurie, an attractive brunette like Eileen, sat forward with her arms crossed on the table in front of her. 'We're just fine, Sergeant Driscoll. Why do you ask? What is it to the police?'

Morag shrugged the question aside with a wave of her hand. 'Actually, my colleague is here seeing your director. She has just joined us so I was showing her around. And seeing Eileen and Agnes here I just grabbed the opportunity to buy you a cup of tea.'

Eileen Lamont sniggered girlishly, almost a little hysterically, Morag thought. 'It is brilliant, Sergeant Driscoll, really it is. Even though I didn't think so in the first couple of weeks. I almost left, you know.'

'Why was that?' Morag asked casually.

'I was lonely. I missed my folk. I missed Mrs McConville and her dogs.'

'Of course, you used to help her with the dog sanctuary, didn't you?'

'I did. In between my work at the vet's, but

I suppose I just felt I needed a change from all the animals for a while, and that was why I joined the institute. And I am glad I did. Logan Burns is a . . . a . . . genius.'

'What stopped you leaving?'

Eileen smiled and pointed to a group of three white-hoodied individuals who had just come in and sat down at a nearby table. 'Those three acolytes stopped me. Especially Johanna Waltari. She is fabulous.'

Morag pretended not to notice the meaningful looks that the other three inceptors about the table exchanged between themselves. Her suspicions seemed to be confirmed by the wave from Eileen that was reciprocated with a little smile by the one called Johanna.

'Well, well,' called out Peter, upon spotting Morag and the inceptors. 'Look, Henry, it's the lovely sergeant we met the other day.' And as Henrietta beamed and waved he gave Morag a wink.

Morag acknowledged them with a wave. 'That is Peter, isn't it?' she whispered softly to the others. 'I met him in Kyleshiffin the other day. He seemed — '

'Totally up himself,' Alan volunteered.

'He and Henrietta are practically an item,' said Nancy. 'More's the pity. I think he's hot!'

And before long the floodgates opened and

159

they were filling Morag in on all the gossip, far more freely and eloquently than they would if she had been formally interviewing them. And that was just what Morag wanted. She made mental notes that she would transcribe on to paper later on.

V

If there was one thing Lorna prided herself on it was her ability to think on her feet and to assess situations quickly. That had been part of the attraction of the Force in the first place, being presented with a situation and having to come up with an action plan in one's mind immediately. As she sat down in the chair proffered to her by Drew Kelso her eyes took in the décor of the office with its large thick Persian rug, the plush leather armchairs, the murals hanging on two of the walls and the old bookcases full of a mixture of original leather-bound books and numerous brightly coloured works that she assumed were more recent additions to the old castle library.

'We have added substantially to the old library,' Logan Burns said from the other side of the old oak desk, as if divining her thoughts. 'And you are Sergeant — ?'

'Golspie. Sergeant Lorna Golspie.'

'May we call you Lorna?' Drew asked, as he took a seat on the settee beside Saki Yasuda, the impression of a twinkle in his eye. 'And would you like tea, coffee?'

Ordinarily Lorna would have preferred to maintain a strictly professional manner, especially as she felt somewhat outnumbered by the three directors of the institute, but instead she smiled and shrugged her shoulders. 'Lorna is my name,' she said, with as much casualness as she could muster. 'Nothing to drink, thank you.'

'People do not show enough of themselves,' Saki Yasuda said with an encouraging nod of her head. 'There is a tendency to hide behind titles and job descriptions.'

'Do you think so?' Lorna returned. She noted the way that Saki Yasuda sat, gracefully like a cat. Her voice almost purred.

'I do. That is what we go to such great lengths to instil into our inceptors. They have to let go of the strict uniforms that society makes us wear.'

Lorna raised an eyebrow and added jokingly, 'Really? Aren't we all still wearing uniforms? I've got on my police pullover and you are all wearing these hoodies. Aren't they uniforms?'

Saki Yasuda's brows wrinkled slightly and

for a moment Lorna thought she was going to lose her feline-like composure. Logan Burns came to her rescue.

'Well said, Lorna. It is true, no one can truly escape the confines of their position in society. But these hoodies of ours are designed to be loose, casual.'

'But they show a hierarchy, do they not?' Lorna asked. 'You three are all in yellow, some of your staff are in white and the newer members are in pink.'

Logan clapped his hands. 'You have us there. But it is a hierarchy of attainment, not of supremacy.'

'Isn't it? It looks a bit like teachers, prefects and pupils to me. In fact, that is one of the reasons I and my colleague Sergeant Driscoll have come to see you. There have been complaints.'

Logan Burns leaned on his desk, his hands interlocked. 'Against the institute? Tell me more, Lorna.'

'The families of four of your — what do you call them — inceptors, have complained that they have been denied access to their relatives. They claim that the institute is too regimented and that it is, well, that it is a cult.'

The three directors looked at each other in amazement then burst into synchronized,

162

disbelieving laughter.

'That is utterly ridiculous,' Logan Burns said at last. 'The Daisy Institute is a serious study organization. Our purpose is to waken people up to the divinity and spirituality that is all around us, in every religion and philosophical system that there is. Our inceptors and acolytes — and we have centres in five countries — all come to us of their own free will for instruction on how to get in contact with their own inner selves and inner spirituality. We don't stop anyone from communicating with their families. If they don't communicate it is their choice not to, and not because they have been prevented in any way.'

'We teach them how to communicate with themselves,' Saki volunteered.

Lorna frowned. 'I don't quite understand.'

'We teach them to meditate, to get in touch with their energy systems and through that with their higher selves.'

Drew sat forward. 'It is through one's higher self that one can communicate with the divine.'

Lorna felt that the conversation was getting too metaphysical. She decided to bring it back to her purpose. 'So the inceptors can call out and they can receive phone calls here?'

163

'Not exactly,' Logan Burns replied, with a shake of his head. 'We do not allow mobile telephones in the institute. They can, if they wish, use one of the directors' lines.'

'How do you explain the complaints about not being able to speak to their relatives?'

Drew Kelso shook his head. 'It can't have happened often. Perhaps the inceptors have been in different parts of the castle, meditating, or doing personal study. Or doing one or other of the vigils that we ask them to do. For example, we use the old dungeon as a room of contemplation for focusing on fear and eradicating it. And one night an inceptor keeps a vigil over the Hoolish Stones from the top of the north tower.'

Logan Burns unlocked his hands. 'We really can assure you that if anyone would like to speak to their relatives they may do so.' He laughed. 'And as you can see, we have no locks on the doors, no chains. Everything that you have mentioned can be put down to free will.'

'So they can visit them whenever they wish?'

'Preferably not in the first three months. We do like that time to acclimatize them to meditational practices. After that, they may come and go as they please. Just ask any of our senior inceptors, or any of the acolytes.'

Lorna nodded. 'That is good to get that cleared up. Which brings me to the other matter. I believe it is a complaint that you made, Dr Burns, against the editor of the *West Uist Chronicle*.'

'Call me Logan, please,' he returned with a smile. 'And let us just say that I would like to withdraw my complaint. I was a little piqued by something the good editor wrote in his paper. I have calmed down now and really have no wish to pursue it.'

Lorna smiled. 'Nice to make short work of that then. I won't keep you any longer.'

They all stood and Drew opened the door for her.

'Oh yes, there was just one thing,' Lorna said at the threshold, as she stood looking Drew straight in the eye. 'Why did you think we would be coming to ask you about Finlay MacNeil? You did say that you all wanted to co-operate with us. Why was that?'

Drew looked at the others before replying. 'We heard about his sudden, tragic death. After his drunken rampage at the Hoolish Stones last night we thought that you might — '

'Might what?' Lorna prompted, as he hesitated.

'That people might think that we had put a spell on him,' said Saki Yasuda, with the suggestion of a sarcastic smile on her lips. 'That's what people think cults do isn't it, Sergeant?'

Logan Burns guffawed. 'But we are no cult, are we, Saki?' He held out his hand to Lorna. 'Feel free to call anytime you like, Lorna.'

Drew Kelso shook her hand. 'Absolutely anytime,' he added, holding her regard for a moment and making her feel conscious of that odd twinkle she had noticed before. Somehow it gave her a tingle down the spine. It was at variance from the feeling of antipathy that she had picked up from Saki Yasuda.

She gave a professional smile. 'Thank you all for your cooperation,' she said, as she heard Morag's voice outside in the corridor. 'Meeting you all has been very . . . enlightening.'

VI

Ewan rode up the track towards the two men, each with a muscular dog on a chain.

'You are on private property!' Tyler Brady said, waving his hand as if to indicate that Ewan should stop and go back.

Ewan thought he saw the other man grunt something and the gesticulating one dropped his hand to his side.

He rode up to them and drew Nippy to a halt.

'*Latha math*, good morning,' Ewan greeted, as he sat on the moped saddle planting his long legs firmly on the ground. 'I am PC Ewan McPhee of the local police force. I have come to see you about — '

Immediately the two dogs started to strain at their leashes and growl menacingly.

' — I have come to see you about a complaint,' Ewan went on, his mouth suddenly going very dry.

Pug Cruikshank's face registered astonishment. 'A complaint, Officer? About what?'

'Your attitude for one thing. One of our respected citizens was told in no uncertain manner that this was private property and that she should not walk here.'

'That will be that mad old dog woman I told you about, Pug,' said Tyler Brady. 'I saw her off this morning because she and her dogs were disturbing the pigs.'

'Mrs Annie McConville would not have allowed her dogs to disturb your pigs, I am sure,' Ewan returned. 'She is an expert in dog-handling.'

One of the dogs growled and bared its teeth.

'I hope you keep those dogs under good

control,' he added. 'What breed are they?'

'This is an American Staff and Tyler there has got a boxer-terrier mix,' Pug explained quickly. 'Both perfectly legal. And both expertly trained and controlled.'

'And this is still private land,' Tyler Brady said belligerently.

Ewan did not like the man's tone. Sitting astride the moped he felt slightly disadvantaged, since both were tall men. He dismounted and kicked the moped's stand down and drew himself up to his full height, which was a couple of inches taller than either of them.

'As you should know,' he said. 'Mrs McConville was free to walk over your land as long as she did no harm to your crops.'

'Or livestock,' Pug interjected. Then, with a smile, 'But look Officer, we have no objection to anyone walking over our farm, just as long as they stay away from the pigs. The saddleback sows are highly strung animals and soon get upset. If they get upset, their milk dries up and the poor wee piglets are at real risk.' He patted Tyler Brady on the shoulder. 'Tyler here is mad about our pigs and can be a wee bit territorial, that's all.'

Tyler Brady eyed Ewan fiercely. 'Aye, territorial, that's me. And I don't take any crap from anyone. Not even the police.'

'Tyler, calm down,' Pug soothed. He turned to Ewan. 'We lost three piglets recently. He's chewed up, so he is. Will that be all then, Officer?'

Ewan stood a moment pensively chewing his lip. 'I think so. Just as long as there are no more complaints about rudeness, or about your dogs.'

'There will be no complaints about our dogs, don't you worry,' Pug returned, bending down to pat his brown-headed American Staff firmly, which began furiously wagging its stumpy tail. 'And tell your Mrs McConville she is welcome to walk our farm as long as she keeps well clear of the pigs.'

Ewan nodded to them, remounted Nippy and set off, vigorously pedalling until the Norton motor kicked in.

Once he was well out of earshot Tyler Brady spat then sneered, 'We could have kicked that big oaf's arse!'

He was rewarded by Pug Cruikshank grabbing a handful of his shirt and yanking him almost off his feet. 'You bloody idiot! You could have had him on to us. If you ever make a bollocks like that with the police again, I'll knock your bloody head off! Understand?'

Tyler Brady, stared in horror at the unbridled anger written across Pug's face. He swallowed hard and nodded eagerly. He was all too well aware of the damage that temper of Pug's could inflict.

VII

Wallace and Douglas Drummond had taken Ewan's advice and gone straight to the Kyleshiffin Cottage Hospital rather than make a detour to the Bonnie Prince Charlie. Ralph McLelland was pulling into the car park just as they were entering the main door. He jumped out of his old Bentley, hauling his Gladstone bag along with him.

'Are you here to watch me, lads?' he asked. 'I had to dash out on a house call to the south of the island first so I haven't had time to start.'

He saw their simultaneous looks of disappointment. 'Why don't you pop along to the Bonnie Prince Charlie for a half-pint while I get changed and get the body ready?'

Wallace shook his head and made a sad clacking noise with his tongue. 'We are not allowed. Duty, you see.'

'Ewan McPhee said he'd get his hammer to us, the big lummox,' Douglas added with mock fear.

Ralph stroked his chin. 'But post-mortems

are not for the faint-hearted. You need a good stomach.'

The twins gave each other a swift appraisal. 'I think we can safely say that neither of us is faint-hearted,' said Wallace.

'And gutting fish the amount of time we have to probably means that we have good enough stomachs, thank you, Dr McLelland.'

'That's a pity,' Ralph McLelland said, eyeing the two of them good-humouredly. 'I was going to offer you both a dram from my special medicinal bottle before we begin.'

Their eyes lit up.

'Well, if it is for medicinal purposes, Dr McLelland, then who are we to refuse?'

'Aye, you wouldn't want us getting light-headed while you are working, would you?'

'No,' Ralph replied. 'To the mortuary it is then.'

7

I

The skirl of the bagpipes greeted Morag and Lorna when they arrived back at the police station just as Ewan chugged up Kirk Wynd on Nippy.

'Don't mind me asking, will you, Morag,' Lorna said as she got out of the station Ford Escort, her expression a study in concealed disdain, 'but is Torquil good?'

Morag looked bemused for a moment, then beamed. 'Good? He's the best, Lorna. Torquil is a Silver Quaich champion. We are proud of him on the island. That's why so many folk just call him *Piper*.'

'That's what I thought,' Lorna replied, as she followed Morag in. 'He sounds — great.' She suppressed a smile at the unconscious phonetic connection. In truth, she had never been a fan of the great Highland bagpipe.

Ewan fell into step behind them. 'Great, isn't he?' he said with a grin.

'Just what I was thinking,' Lorna replied, with a blush.

'Ah! Just in time,' Torquil said, dropping

the blowpipe from his lips and instantly silencing the pipes with a swift chop to the bag. 'I have the kettle on and was just having a quick practice before you all came back.'

He grinned at Lorna. 'You will not have heard the pipes properly, I am betting. You will need to hear them outside. I'll give you a recital when we get some time.' And at her smile he winked. 'Maybe even let you have a go.'

'You are honoured,' Morag said, with a look of surprise as Torquil disappeared into his office. 'He doesn't usually let anyone within fifty yards of his pipes. Maybe he is — ?'

But the blush that appeared on Lorna's cheeks stopped her from speculating further. Instead, she turned to Ewan and patted him on the shoulder. 'How about you making the tea, eh, my precious? You know how the boss makes it too weak.'

Five minutes later they were all gathered in Torquil's office ready to report on their individual investigations.

Morag was the first to report on her interview with the four local inceptors of The Daisy Institute. 'They really couldn't have been more content. Every one of them seems on a high and they seem to regard the three directors as sort of demi-gods. They are all looking forward to the solstice.'

'And why is that?' Torquil asked. 'Just what is so special about this summer solstice? They have been coming and going for thousands of years, so why all the big interest now?'

'Logan Burns is going to reveal something mind-shattering,' Morag replied blankly. 'They say it has something to do with revealing ancient knowledge and bringing enlightenment, but that seems to be as much as any of them knows.'

'So there is no problem as far as they are concerned with access to their families?' Ewan asked over the top of his tea.

'None at all,' Morag replied. Then turning to Lorna, she asked, 'Did Logan Burns say anything interesting?'

Lorna consulted her small black notebook. 'He just refuted any problem. I didn't really explore about the solstice, but all three of the directors, that is Logan Burns, Drew Kelso and Saki Yasuda, all seemed pretty spiritual. A bit hippy-ish, actually. Logan Burns is clearly in charge, but I get the impression that there is something between them.'

'Woman's intuition?' Torquil asked with a mischievous grin.

'Don't knock it, Inspector,' Lorna returned with a raised eyebrow. 'But yes, I would say there is some sort of relationship going on there. At least between Drew Kelso and Saki Yasuda.'

'And why do you think that?' Torquil queried.

'Because he was giving me the eye and she saw it and didn't like it. She became icy towards me as if she was trying to show that he belonged to her.'

'Interesting,' Morag remarked, tapping her lips with her silver pen. 'Because Eileen Lamont told me that all the students think she has the hots for Logan Burns.' She looked at her notebook and absently drew a circle round one of her entries. 'And then again, they all think that Logan Burns has an eye for anyone female.'

Torquil dunked a ginger biscuit in his tea and then held it up and watched as it went floppy before popping it in his mouth. Then he nodded. 'So we can really put that complaint to bed, can't we? There is no restriction. The young folk are not being held against their will and it isn't a cult.'

Lorna shook her head. 'I would just say it was a slightly off the wall New Age organization. Harmless.'

'And what about the complaint against Calum Steele?' Torquil asked.

'Logan Burns says he wants to drop it,' Lorna replied.

Torquil nodded with relief. 'That's good. It seemed a waste of time anyway.' He nodded at Ewan, who was also in the middle of watching a dunked ginger biscuit bend. 'What happened up at the Goat's Head Farm?'

Distracted momentarily, Ewan flinched as the biscuit dropped into his tea, splashing his jumper. He laid the mug down, wiped his jumper and blushed to the roots of his red hair.

'Nothing really, boss. I met two of the chaps. The owner, Pug Cruikshank and a bloke called Tyler Brady. I think he is the pig man.' He shivered. 'And two great hulking dogs. Ugly buggers, I thought.'

Morag gave him a mock scowl. 'Ewan, you don't talk about members of the public like that.'

'No, not ... not them,' he stammered, before realizing that his sergeant was teasing him. 'At least, although I didn't mean it, they were fairly big lads. Handy in a fight, I expect. In fact, the Tyler guy was a bit pushy. I think he was trying to intimidate me. But anyway, I meant the dogs, not the men.'

'You do know that Cruikshank was a boxer? A former contender for the British light-heavyweight title?' Torquil informed him.

Ewan accepted the information without enthusiasm. As the wrestling champion of the

Outer Isles for three years in a row he had always believed that if it came to a scrap, a wrestler would have the edge over a boxer. 'Actually, Torquil, that's funny, because I asked him what breed the dogs were and he said one was an American Staff and the other was a boxer-something cross.'

'And what did they say about intimidating Annie McConville?'

'That was the Tyler chap. He was a bit belligerent and was going on about it being private land, so I told him about the law. I think he would have argued it out with me, but his boss shushed him up. He said that in future Annie can walk her dogs as long as they don't go up there near the pigs.'

Torquil nodded. 'Which sounds pretty reasonable, I suppose. Thanks, Ewan.' He grinned. 'How was Nippy, by the way? He got you there and back.'

Ewan coloured again. 'As a matter of fact, Torquil I was going to ask you about that. Now that there are so — er — many of us, what with Sergeant Golspie and all, do you think we could do something about police transport?'

Lorna sat forward. 'Actually, Inspector, I have taken action on that. I have hired a car from the local garage and should have it in action tomorrow.'

Ewan persisted. 'I was thinking about something for me, actually. My mum doesn't mind me using Nippy, but I wondered if the division funds would stretch to buying me a bicycle. I know where I can get a good one.'

'Tell us then,' Torquil said, humouring the big constable.

'Dairsie, the ironmonger, has a mountain bike for sale in his window. I popped in and asked him on my way back from the Goat's Head. It used to belong to Rab Noble.'

Morag shivered despite herself. 'Och, are you sure you would want to be riding that, after the tragedy and everything? Was it not up at the milking parlour when he . . . died?'

Ewan raised his hands innocently. 'It wouldn't bother me. I could just do with some wheels. And it would be good for my exercise regime.'

Torquil grinned. 'Have a look at the finances will you, Morag? Now, about Calum.' And he told them about his own interview with the *West Uist Chronicle* editor.

Ewan shook his head. 'I still cannot believe that he pulled off that judo stunt.'

Torquil grinned back. 'I assure you, he must have. I saw the photograph that he took. And I must say that I don't really like the idea of this battery farm. It doesn't reflect well on West Uist.'

'Should we investigate it, Torquil?' Morag asked.

'I don't see how we can,' Torquil replied pensively. 'It is not illegal, is it?' He scratched his chin. 'Although I think that I had better interview the McQueens and get the whole picture. It would probably be as well to establish a baseline before Calum writes his next piece in the paper, and really stirs things up.'

'Aye, he's a wee firecracker when he gets going,' Ewan agreed.

The bell in the outer office rang out, followed by the sound of heavy boots and the raising of the counter flap.

'It is only us,' called out Wallace Drummond.

'Two drip-white characters from the local mortuary, in need of a resuscitating cup of Ewan McPhee's tea,' Douglas called.

And a moment later they entered, looking anything but drip-white.

'What news, lads?' Torquil asked. 'Did Ralph finish the postmortem?'

Wallace held up a large manila envelope. 'We have the report, Piper. He says that he has a lot of other tests to finish it off, but in a nutshell he was full of whisky and every bone in his body was broken.'

'Entirely consistent with a fall from the top of the cliffs while under the influence of alcohol,' added Douglas. 'Doctor McLelland said that his inner organs just about exploded on impact.'

Torquil noticed that Ewan's face had suddenly drained of colour. 'Are you OK, Ewan?' he asked concernedly.

In answer, the big constable clapped a hand to his mouth and rushed from the office. They heard him race through to the toilet and a moment or two later came the sound of violent retching.

'Always a bit queasy is our Ewan,' Wallace explained to Lorna.

'How about a tune on the pipes, Piper?' Douglas asked, pointing to Torquil's pipes on the top of the filing cabinet and then nodding in the direction of the toilet and Ewan's retching. 'We could do with drowning out the lad's tummy frolics.'

II

The Padre had felt pretty miserable after finding Finlay MacNeil's body and had gone back to the church to say a prayer for him before having a few holes on the golf course to calm his nerves. He was kneeling before the altar when he heard the door open and footsteps as if someone had entered and was letting their eyes adjust to the dimly lit church interior.

He turned in time to see a white hoodie-clad figure retreat through the door and pull it after them. He felt sure that it was the girl Johanna, whom he had met the other day. He smiled and returned to his prayers, content to think that she found his church worthy of a second visit.

And yet as he finished and thanked the Lord for listening to him, his eye fell on *Eilthireach*, the Pilgrim Stone, and as he surveyed the ancient carvings upon it, his mind turned again to Finlay.

'You knew as much about these strange markings as anyone, didn't you, old friend?' he mused, feeling strangely close to his old golfing partner as he did so. 'I wonder if you ever actually translated their meaning.' He sighed as he broke free from the spell of the stone and turned to leave. 'Perhaps you never did. And maybe that is why Logan Burns at The Daisy Institute bothered you so much. Perhaps he actually has.'

Collecting his waiting clubs from the porch he headed off to the course and played the ninth, then the short fifth before cutting across to play the eighth, his intention being to finish off with the ninth then pop back to the manse. He was one over par as he stood on the tee, debating whether to go for his usual two-wood or go for the big one with a driver. With a click of the tongue he decided on the driver and teed the ball appropriately high. After a couple of practice swings he set up and drove, trying for extra length. But, as so often happened when he tried to force a few extra yards, he pulled the shot. It started travelling to the right of the fairway then curved back to roll some 270 yards from the tee in the light rough. Unfortunately, it was almost directly behind the ancient standing stone that they called *Carragh*, the Pillar.

'Oh man, that is just where Finlay was when we last played,' he mumbled morosely to himself as he struck a light to his pipe and ambled up the fairway.

By the time he reached it he had quite lost the taste for his pipe and tapped it out on the side of the stone as he absently inspected the lie of his ball. There was no way that he could clear the Pillar so he pulled out his seven iron with the intention of chipping out sideways. His eye fell again on the wavy lines and whorls of the ancient carving on the stone and he felt his spirits sink.

'I am going to miss you, Finlay my friend.

You and your ever-ready hip flask.' And he felt the desire for a dram come over him, coupled with the desire for some company, for, as often happened, he was the only player on the course. He sighed and lay his seven-iron against the ancient monolith while he reached into his jacket pocket for his mobile phone. He rang Torquil's number as he traced the pattern on the stone.

'Is that you, laddie?' he said into the instrument. 'I don't know about you, but I am feeling the need of company this evening. I am making finnan haddie tonight and there's a problem.' He smiled as he waited for Torquil to respond. 'No, not a big problem. Just a question of quantity. Aye, there is too much for the two of us. I thought it was probably about time we invited that new sergeant of yours.' He grinned to himself as he heard his nephew speaking at the other end. 'She'll come! Excellent! We'll have a dram while we watch the news then we can show her some West Uist hospitality.'

He deposited the phone in his pocket then reached for his seven-iron. He felt confident that he could still make the green in three and with luck sneak a birdie to get back to par.

III

Eileen Lamont and Nancy MacRurie were sitting studying in their shared room in the west wing of the castle when they saw Johanna cycle into the courtyard. Nancy smiled to herself as she saw Eileen's eyes light up.

'I wonder where she's been?' Nancy asked. 'Must be nice to be able to ride off to Kyleshiffin, or wherever you want, without having to get permission from the Gestapo.'

Eileen shook her head as she shut her study folder and stood up. 'Och it isn't that bad, as we told the sergeant. Anyway, I need to catch Johanna. It's the last chance I will have today, what with it being my turn to do the Hoolish Stones vigil tonight.'

'You like her, don't you?'

Eileen blushed and nodded.

'And she likes you?' Nancy probed, ever one to enjoy confidences. She giggled as Eileen nodded again.

'OK, so how about if I do your vigil tonight, then you can — do what you want.'

Eileen let out a little gasp of delight, threw her arms about her friend's neck and planted a kiss on her cheek. Then she knocked on the window to catch Johanna's attention. As Johanna looked up a smile of recognition lit up face. Eileen gesticulated to say that she was coming down.

'Good luck!' Nancy said to Eileen's fast retreating back.

IV

Saki Yasuda peered out of Logan Burns's office window and watched the two young women talking animatedly together in the courtyard below.

'Eileen and Johanna are getting very friendly,' she announced.

Drew Kelso looked over her shoulder and frowned. 'Yes, but we can hardly discourage it, can we? I mean, people often pair up.'

Logan Burns took two quick steps across the room, his brow furrowed. 'Well, I think we ought to discourage these liaisons. This is a serious study enterprise, not some kind of dating agency.'

Eileen and Johanna crossed the courtyard hand in hand and were met by Peter and Henrietta coming down the great steps. They seemed to enjoy a few words of banter then they all retreated back up the steps into the castle.

'See what I mean?' Logan said warmly. 'These sexual tensions are bad for them. They muddy the waters.'

Drew and Saki looked at each other in concern.

'It is just youthful attraction, Logan,' Saki ventured, placatingly.

'It isn't actually causing any harm, is it?' Drew asked.

Logan spun round. 'I don't like it. It is too near the solstice. It is all too important to be screwed up by — by — '

His phone rang and he crossed the room and snatched up the receiver. 'Burns!'

His expression altered almost immediately. 'All fixed and ready? Excellent. I will be there.'

Replacing the phone he ran a hand through his hair, his ire all dissipated. 'That was Finbar Donleavy. They have managed to get a replacement camera so they are going to run a piece as planned.' He frowned. 'I suppose I had better make appropriate noises about our late unlamented friend, Finlay MacNeil.'

V

Peter and Henrietta had made the most of the afternoon and gone to bed with a bottle of Niersteiner. When they finally rolled apart after their passionate love-making, each bathed in perspiration, they lay in post-coital bliss staring breathlessly at the ceiling.

'You are a horny devil, aren't you?' Henrietta said at last. 'I know what set you off. It was seeing Johanna and Eileen getting it together.'

Peter turned on to his side and leaned on his elbow. He grinned. 'I just like to think about sex. It turns me on.'

'Thinking about other people having sex makes you horny? So am I just here to gratify your needs?' she said, tongue very much in cheek.

He gently stroked her breast. 'You are a pleasure in your own right, dearest Henry — as you well know. But what is wrong if thinking about your friends having it off stimulates one?'

'As long as it is only thinking about them.'

'Hey, come on. You were the one making lewd jokes to Johanna about having a three-some.'

'She is an attractive girl.'

Peter laughed. 'Ha! So you fancy her as well!' He pouted. 'But at least now you know that she is into other girls.'

'I suspected it already. She never mentioned it, but I have seen her look at a photograph in her room. It is of another girl. A good-looking girl. I suspect she was in love.'

'It all makes sense now then,' Peter said, the feel of Henrietta's breast under his hand arousing him again. 'And talking of thinking about other people having sex,' he said, lasciviously, 'what do you think of Miss Saki?'

She playfully elbowed him in the ribs, and then turned to him with a coquettish smile. 'Come here,' she purred. 'Let me show you what I think.'

VI

The mouth-watering aroma of slowly poached finnan haddie greeted Lorna as Torquil opened the front door of the manse and ushered her in.

'Ignore the motorcycle bits and pieces,' he said, indicating the line of carburettors, chains and shards of gears and brakes that lay on oil-soaked newspapers along the length of the hall. 'My uncle is not the neatest of men.'

'I heard that!' boomed out Lachlan McKinnon, emerging from the kitchen, wiping his hands on an apron. 'At least twenty-five per cent of this debris belongs to my scatterbrained nephew here, another twenty-five per cent is mine, and the rest are spares for the Excelsior Talisman that we have both been rebuilding over the past decade.'

Torquil stood wrinkling his nose apologetically. 'It is slow work.'

Lorna gave him the slightest of winks. 'Like seasoning bagpipes?'

Lachlan tossed his head back and laughed. 'Don't get started on that, lassie. I am forever moving chanters and drone reeds. But come on through, we'll have a dram before dinner.'

Lorna followed him through and began by refusing a drink on the grounds that she would somehow have to get back to her hotel in Kyleshiffin. 'I'll probably get a taxi,' she said with a questioning look at Torquil. 'That way you can have a drink without worrying about taking your bike out.'

'No need to go back,' Lachlan stated. 'Stay the night, Lorna. We have rooms galore, a well-stocked bathroom with all conveniences, spare toothbrush and all.'

'Yes but — '

'And where could you be safer than with a minister and a police inspector?'

'But — ?'

'But nothing, my dear.' The Padre's face creased into one of those smiles that few could resist. 'Just say that it is about time you got to know the locals and this old local could do with a bit of company tonight.' He poured three Glen Corlin malt whiskies and handed her a glass. 'Now sit you down, it's time for the news.'

Torquil switched on the television and then dropped on to the settee beside Lorna.

The credits were rolling at the end of one of the imported Australian soaps and then the theme music for the Scottish TV *Six O'Clock News* rang out. And then Kirstie Macroon was reading out the headlines:

'SCOTTISH MINISTER RESIGNS AMID CAN-NABIS CLAIMS.'
'TRAGEDY OF THE WEST UIST ARCHAE-OLOGIST.'

The familiar inter-slot jingle sounded then:

'First we go across to West Uist where Finbar Donleavy is joined at the Hoolish Stones by Logan Burns, the Director of The Daisy Institute. Good evening, Finbar.'

The scene moved to the periphery of the Hoolish Stones where Finbar Donleavy was standing with a microphone beside Logan Burns.

'Thank you, Kirstie. I am here with Dr Logan Burns at the famous stone circle where last night we were joined by local historian and

190

archaeologist Finlay MacNeil. It is with great sadness that I have to report that early this morning Mr MacNeil's body was found at the foot of nearby cliffs.'

He slanted the microphone in Logan Burns's direction and The Daisy Institute Director began talking.

'Thank you, Finbar. Yes, it is a great tragedy. Finlay MacNeil was one of the great local historians and he will be sorely missed on the island.'

'You did not always see eye to eye with him, though, did you?'

'No, we had different opinions about the stones' carvings on the island, and the purpose of these great stones. I am afraid that often happens. A local amateur feels that he has a monopoly on knowledge, even greater than that of an acknowledged scholar.'

'And you are a scholar, Dr Burns, are you not?'

Logan Burns made a self-deprecating gesture.

'I don't really want to expand on that now. Not in the light of this tragedy. This evening I would just like to symbolically pay my respects and the respects of my institute to the late Finlay MacNeil.'

He held up his hands and produced a long daisy chain.

'I made this today and would like to just drape it across this stone in memory of a great local historian.'

He skilfully tossed it upwards, like a lasso, to drop over the top of the great stone. He then bowed.

'In memory of Finlay MacNeil. We will be thinking of you in two days when we celebrate the summer solstice.'

The shot moved to Finbar Donleavy who also bobbed his head and gave a wan smile.

'And on that sombre note, it is good night from us at the Hoolish Stones.'

Kirstie Macroon took over and moved smoothly into the other stories.

The Padre raised his glass. 'To Finlay! Although I am not sure what he would have made of that daisy-chain stunt.'

'Was it a stunt, Padre?' Lorna asked. 'He

192

seemed genuine to me. An ageing, but genuine, hippy.'

'Lorna interviewed Logan Burns today,' Torquil explained.

'He is a smooth operator,' Lorna volunteered. 'And so were the other two.'

'Except Saki Yasuda didn't care for you, did she?' Torquil pointed out.

Lorna smiled at him. 'There is no accounting for who we like and dislike, is there?'

The two pinpoints of colour that instantly developed on Torquil's cheeks did not go unnoticed by the Padre.

VII

By nine o'clock, Calum Steele had finished production of the morrow's edition of the *West Uist Chronicle* and was debating whether to settle for a fish supper and a pint or shove a ready meal into the microwave and wash it down with a can or two of lager. He had just opted for a trip out to The Frying Scotsman for a supper before dropping in for a nightcap at the Bonnie Prince Charlie, and was zipping up his anorak when the window exploded and a brick caught him on the side of the head. He slumped unconscious on to

193

the floor, a pool of blood trickling down his face to form a pool about his head.

VIII

Nancy MacRurie looked over the battlemented wall of the north tower at the silhouette of the Hoolish Stones in the moonlight. Although she had lived on the island all her life yet she had never until recently taken the slightest notice of the Stones. Now she thought they were both beautiful and incredibly meaningful.

'Thank you, Logan, and The Daisy Institute,' she mused to herself, as she leaned against the wall, enjoying her vigil. 'You have put some purpose into my life.' And reaching into her pocket she pulled out her tobacco pouch and rolled a spliff.

'No harm in a little comfort, is there, girl?' she said, lighting up and taking a deep inhalation to hold the smoke in her lungs for a few seconds. And within moments everything seemed to become more relevant, even the purpose of the Stones and her own presence in the institute. 'I wish I could fly,' she mused to herself.

She did not hear the muffled footsteps behind her. She felt something drop over her head and tighten about her throat. She clutched at it but rapidly felt her grip on consciousness start to slip away. Then a hand landed on her shoulder and spun her round. Momentarily she felt her senses return and she saw the face suddenly looming towards her.

'What the — ?' she gasped in horror, then, 'You!'

She opened her mouth to scream, but the ligature tightened again and a blow to the side of her head made her reel so that she was only dimly aware of arms sweeping behind her knees, lifting her upwards to somersault over the parapet.

Then she was airborne. Thrashing wildly with arms and legs in some vain attempt to fly or catch something solid. The spliff fell from her fingers and landed on the ground a fraction of a second after her. Blood trickled from her mouth on to the ground and her sightless eyes stared out at the distant Hoolish Stones, as if in death she was maintaining her vigil until the morning.

8

I

Torquil was woken at six in the morning by Morag's call. He shot up in his bed as he received the news that Calum had been admitted to the Cottage Hospital at four in the morning.

'He woke up in a pool of his own blood,' she explained over the phone. 'Someone had thrown a brick through the *Chronicle* office window and unluckily he must have been standing in the wrong place. Anyway, he managed to call Ralph McLelland on his mobile and Ralph dashed round and admitted him.'

'Is he badly injured?' Torquil asked concernedly.

'He is concussed and needed half-a-dozen stitches, but there is no fracture.'

'Thank the Lord for that. Any idea who did it?'

'You know Calum, he has a way of putting folk's backs up. His main concern apparently was about getting the morning edition of the *Chronicle* out in time. He hasn't been

196

interviewed yet; I just thought I'd let you know as soon as possible. Do you want one of us to pop round and see him?'

'No, that's all right. Lorna and I will go and see him after we have had breakfast.'

There was a moment's pause on the other end of the phone.

'Did Lorna stay the night then?'

Torquil felt a strange feeling deep inside him at the question. Somewhat nonplussed, he replied simply, 'Aye.'

'Oh!'

'See you later then,' he said, replacing the receiver with a grin.

II

After a frugal breakfast, despite Lachlan's offer to send them off with a decent fry-up, Torquil and Lorna sped off to Kyleshiffin. As they hurtled along the chicane-like bends of the coastal road Torquil fancied that Lorna's arms were holding on to him just a tad tighter than before. He grinned to himself, for he had to admit that they had enjoyed a pleasant evening, and had talked about all sorts of things, apart from work, after the Padre had retired and left them to their own devices.

Calum was in one of the side rooms of the

Cottage Hospital, lying with a cold compress on his forehead and the room in shadows.

'Torquil, do me a favour and talk sense into Ralph McLelland. He will not discharge me and I have a newspaper to run.'

'I saw him on the way in, Calum,' Torquil replied. 'He wants to observe you for a while. He says you were lucky and that it's a good thing you have such a thick skull.'

'I'll give him a thick skull! And I'll give the bugger who did this to me a — '

'A piece of your mind?' Lorna interjected with a smile. 'You don't want to get in trouble with the police yourself, do you?'

Calum shoved himself up on his pillows and sighed. 'Aye, you are right. I meant I was going to give them a proper telling off. An erudite piece of purple prose in the *Chronicle*. Remember the pen is mightier than the sword.' He rubbed his hands together. 'Torquil, pull up the blinds, will you? Lying here like an invalid is getting on my nerves.'

Torquil complied and the early morning sun made Calum blink. Torquil grinned. 'You are concussed, Calum. You are bound to have a sore head for a while.'

Calum removed the compress to reveal a waterproof dressing over the stitches on his temple. 'Ach! It's a bit sore, but no worse than a half-decent hangover.'

'Any idea who did it, Calum?' Lorna asked.

'No. We crusading journalists make the odd enemy along the way. It could have been any of half-a-dozen folk.' He nodded his head with satisfaction. 'At least that many.'

He recounted all that he could remember of the previous couple of days, right up until the moment the brick came through the window and knocked him out.

'When I came round the bloody thing was lying next to me. Whoever threw it had the cheek to wrap it in a copy of the *Chronicle*.'

'Which issue?' Torquil asked.

'Don't know. I didn't look. I felt so wretched all I could do was phone Ralph, and then I must have passed out again. The next thing I knew I was waking up in this bed while they got me ready to X-ray my head.'

Torquil pulled out his phone. 'I'll get Morag to send Ewan round to get the brick. And let's see what you were writing about on the day of the paper your assailant used to wrap the brick.'

'You think he'd taken issue with something I wrote?' Calum asked with a grin.

'Glad I am to see that you haven't lost your sense of humour,' Torquil replied as he called Morag.

Calum laughed. 'It's the only way, Piper.

When someone tries to kill you I say laugh as you spit in their face.'

III

Alan Brodie had risen at 6.30, breakfasted on toast and black coffee, smoked half a spliff then made his way to the north tower to relieve Eileen from her vigil at seven. His own vigil was the shortest of the day, only lasting until ten o'clock when it was time for a group meditation. When he found the top of the tower deserted he assumed that she had sloped off early, so he went to check the room that she shared with Nancy. Finding their room unoccupied and their beds obviously unslept in, he began to panic.

Saki Yasuda was the director on duty and after she and Alan did a swift check throughout the main communal rooms of the castle she rapidly put the wheels in motion. By 7.30 a more formal search was underway and all of the inceptors and acolytes were roused from their beds.

Johanna and Eileen emerged from Johanna's room, both bleary-eyed from lack of sleep. They were immediately surrounded by friends and fellows all uttering sighs of relief.

'But where is Nancy?' she asked Saki

Yasuda, after she had heard that everyone had been looking for her. 'Nancy kindly did my vigil for me.'

'Why did she do this?' Saki returned sharply. 'It was your vigil and your duty.'

'She off . . . offered to do it while I . . . I — '

'While you what?' Saki demanded, her arms folded in front of her.

Johanna answered for her. 'While Eileen stayed with me. We had long conversations in the night.'

Saki Yasuda's lips tightened and she was about to remonstrate, when from somewhere at the other side of the castle, someone shouted. Then there was a clangour of people calling to one another and before many moments the castle was bubbling with activity and noise as people moved quickly out into the corridor to congregate at the steps leading up to the north tower.

'Outside!' someone called. 'She's outside. She looks — !'

Logan Burns and Drew Kelso came bounding down the steps from the main hall and sprinted through the main gate. 'We'll take if from here, Saki,' Logan called over his shoulder. 'Keep everyone inside the castle.'

'And better call an ambulance,' Drew said, as he went past. 'We need a doctor.'

Nancy was lying in the shadows at the foot of the tower, barely visible from the top. She was lying on her front, with limbs splayed outwards and her right cheek resting on the ground in a pool of blood.

It was clear to both men as they knelt down beside her that she was long past the care of any doctor.

IV

Morag had sent Ewan straight round to the *West Uist Chronicle* offices. Ralph had left the door open when he and Alex Lamb, the cottage hospital nursing sister's husband and cottage hospital multi-purpose porter-cum-handyman, had taken Calum off to hospital. There was glass all over the main upstairs office and a pool of blood had soaked into the already multistained carpet. Ewan photographed the room from several positions, as Morag had instructed him, then he took further pictures of the broken window and the newspaper-covered brick that still lay on the floor. Then he gingerly put it in a polythene bag ready to take back for Torquil to examine.

He was bending over to tie it when he fancied he heard a floorboard creak behind him. He was just in the process of looking round when he heard a definite noise as of a heavy step, then something thudded into the back of his head and he started to dive into a deep pool of unconsciousness. As he drifted down he had two fleeting impressions, one auditory and one olfactory.

He heard the familiar ring of the West Uist Cottage Hospital ambulance dashing off somewhere.

And he seemed to register a faint agricultural smell.

V

Doctor Ralph McLelland had arrived at Dunshiffin Castle minutes before Torquil roared up the road on his Royal Enfield Bullet. Torquil found him kneeling beside the body of a young woman, with the two male directors of The Daisy Institute looking on a few feet away.

'What happened?' Torquil asked, as he approached, pulling off his goggles and stripping off his gauntlets. 'Morag told me that there had been an accident. I came straight away.'

Logan Burns held out his hand and introduced himself and Drew Kelso. 'We had

203

already called for the doctor here, but when we found her and saw that she was dead we thought we had better alert the police.'

'A tragedy,' Drew Kelso said, shaking his head and almost seeming to shiver with emotion.

Ralph McLelland removed his stethoscope from his ears and stood up. 'Poor girl! She's been dead a number of hours, I would say. She's had a tumble from the tower.'

Torquil grimaced at the sight of her lying there, her body obviously smashed. 'It is young Nancy MacRurie, is it not?'

'It is,' Logan Burns confirmed. 'She is — or rather — was one of our inceptors.'

Torquil was looking about and spotted the spliff. He picked it up and sniffed it, then knelt down and gingerly sniffed the dead girl's mouth. 'Cannabis,' he said. He reached inside his jacket and drew out a small polythene bag into which he dropped the spliff. 'Will you be able to detect it at the post-mortem, Ralph.'

'If it is in her system, then yes. Will you be informing the next of kin?'

Torquil sighed. 'Aye, we will get straight on to it. She will have to be formally identified. Can you take her back to the hospital, Ralph? Make her look . . . respectable?'

And as the local GP-cum-police surgeon

went over to the ambulance, Torquil pulled out his notebook and pen and started to make notes. 'What would she have been doing up there in the night?'

'It was a vigil,' Logan Burns returned. 'All of the inceptors have to do an overnight vigil on the Stones.'

Torquil was about to ask more when a scream rang out from the top of the tower. Looking up they saw two females leaning over the top of the battlement. Screwing up his eyes Torquil recognized one as Eileen Lamont. The other was a blonde-haired young woman that he did not know. Like Nancy, Eileen was wearing a pink hoodie, while the blonde girl was wearing a white one. The blonde girl had her arm about Eileen and seemed to be comforting her.

'No! Not Nancy!' Eileen Lamont cried. 'It shouldn't be you. It should have been me!'

Torquil stared at the faces of the two directors. He was not sure what emotions they were going through, except they both looked extremely worried.

VI

Wallace and Douglas Drummond had been called in by Morag when Ewan failed to return from the *West Uist Chronicle* offices and failed to answer his mobile phone. She explained about the attack on Calum Steele and the accident at the castle.

'What do you want us to do, Morag?' Wallace asked.

'Go and check that he's all right,' she replied worriedly. 'It isn't like Ewan to dawdle.'

'We are on our way,' said Douglas, heading for the door, only for it to be pushed open as he reached for it.

'Ewan!' Morag exclaimed, at the sight of the big red-haired constable as he staggered in clutching a blood-soaked handkerchief to the back of his head. 'Whatever happened, my wee darling?'

The twins grabbed an arm each and helped him through the counter and sat him down while Morag prised his improvised dressing away from his head and inspected the wound.

'I've got it,' he said, with a wan smile, holding up the polythene bag containing the brick. 'But some devil was hiding and biffed me from behind.' He reached into a pocket and drew out a smashed camera. 'And while I was out he smashed this up.' He held it out apologetically. 'I'm sorry, Morag. I know it is police property.'

'Never mind about all that,' Morag said,

replacing the handkerchief while she went to get a damp flannel and the first-aid kit. 'It is you that I am more worried about. Who could have done such a thing?'

'The same bugger who threw the brick, I am guessing,' said Douglas, through gritted teeth.

'We'll get the swine, whoever it is,' Wallace announced, meaningfully smashing a fist into the palm of his other hand. 'And when we do we'll show that you don't push West Uist men around like this.'

'You'll do nothing hasty at all,' Morag said firmly as she cleaned dried blood from Ewan's hair to get a good sight of the wound. She winced as the big constable yowled with pain. 'Och, I think we are going to need to get Ralph McLelland to put stitches in.'

'Shall we go and have a look at the *Chronicle* offices, Sergeant?' Douglas asked.

'No,' Morag returned. 'It is an even more serious crime scene now. Before it could just have been hooliganism, but now it is the scene of the serious assault on a police officer.' She dabbed antiseptic around the edges of the wound. 'It could even be attempted murder.'

'Aye, you will be wanting a proper police person then,' said Wallace. 'What about the lovely Sergeant Golspie. Could she not go?'

Morag was silent for a moment. 'I am not sure where she is at the moment. She went for tea last night with the boss and this morning when I called him about Calum he said they'd go straight round to see him. She hasn't answered her mobile.'

The twins and Ewan all looked round at her at once.

'She stayed the night at the manse then?' Douglas asked.

'Then she'll be with him now,' Wallace mused. 'At the castle.'

'I expect so,' Morag replied.

'Oh,' said Ewan.

VII

Lorna Golspie was at that moment concluding a deal.

Torquil had dropped her off on Harbour Street as he made his way to Dunshiffin Castle. She had gone straight to Drysdale's Garage and managed to haggle the price down on a second-hand Golf GTI. It was only as Padraig Drysdale went to the office for the paperwork that she switched on her telephone to receive three messages. The first two were from Morag, both asking her to call her immediately. The third was from

Superintendent Lumsden abruptly demanding she phone him, in his terms, 'yesterday!'

She phoned the superintendent first, before rapidly signing her hard-earned money away on the Golf GTI. She was feeling anxious and her mouth was dry even before she phoned Morag. She had not realized how much Superintendent Lumsden clearly hated Inspector Torquil McKinnon.

VIII

As soon as Torquil received Morag's phone message about Ewan he excused himself with the assurance that they would be back in touch very soon. He left Ralph to organize the removal of Nancy's body to the Cottage Hospital mortuary, then he almost flew back on the Bullet to Kyleshiffin. He felt desperately sorry for young Nancy and her family who had yet to be informed, and he always felt responsible for his staff, regarding Ewan more as a younger brother and friend than a junior officer. And then there was Calum. Just thinking about his two friends, both victims of violence, made him feel even angrier and he opened the Bullet's throttle right up.

Lorna Golspie was waiting behind the counter for him as soon as he entered the station. 'Inspector McKinnon, I need to tell you something — '

'Just give me a minute, Lorna. I need to see Ewan. Is he through the back?'

She nodded with a pained expression on her face. 'He's with Morag and the Drummond twins. I think they're debating about taking him to see the doctor.'

'The doctor will be a while. He's busy taking Nancy MacRurie's body back to the mortuary.' And he told her of the discovery of her body.

Lorna sighed. 'That is an awful shame. A young girl like that.' 'It was a horrible sight, Lorna. It was all the worse since she was one of us.' He bit his lip. 'But as I said, I need to see Ewan.'

Lorna nodded, all too aware that he did. Another native of West Uist, or 'one of us', as he had just said. Not for the first time she felt an outsider.

They were all in the rest room, drinking tea. Ewan made to stand up as soon as Torquil came through the door, but he was immediately pushed back into the settee by the strong hands of the two Drummond brothers. Torquil listened to a joint summary on the events from Morag and Ewan.

'We'll get whoever did this to you, Ewan,' Torquil promised, his face grim.

'I should have been more on guard,' Ewan replied. 'I just wasn't expecting anyone to be there.'

'Did you notice if whoever it was did anything, moved anything while you were unconscious?' Ewan shifted uncomfortably on the settee. 'I . . . I didn't notice, Torquil. Sorry.'

Torquil waved his hand. 'No problem. We'll get it checked out soon enough. The most pressing matter though is to inform the MacRurie family and have one of the family identify poor Nancy's body.'

Morag nodded. 'I know them pretty well, boss. Shall I do that?'

'You are a star, Morag,' he replied giving her a wink. Then he turned back to Ewan.

'As for you, it is a trip to the hospital to see Ralph, then home and off to bed.' He looked at the twins. 'Will one of you take him over to the hospital?'

'I'll take him, Inspector,' came Lorna's voice from behind him. 'I have wheels now.'

'That would be a big help, thank you,' he said, turning and seeing her grimace uncomfortably.

'I am afraid that I have something else to tell you,' she said, apologetically. 'I had a call from Superintendent Lumsden. He wants to talk to you — like straight away.' She shrugged her shoulders apologetically. 'I'm sorry, but he didn't seem in a very happy mood.'

Torquil smiled at her. 'It would be a first if he was.'

IX

To say that Superintendent Lumsden was not in a happy mood was something of an understatement, as Torquil found out a few moments later when he called his superior officer on Bara.

'About time, McKinnon,' the gruff, low-land voice snapped over the telephone. 'Just when were you planning to let me know your progress on the MacNeil case?'

'The MacNeil case, sir? Are you talking about Finlay MacNeil?'

There was the noise of a sharp intake of breath from the telephone on Bara. 'Of course I mean Finlay MacNeil. He's the local historian whose body was smashed on the rocks yesterday, in case you had forgotten.'

'But there is no MacNeil case, Superintendent Lumsden.'

'What! You mean to say that the outburst

he had on national television the day before didn't ring some kind of an alarm with you? He insults that hippy man and his odd-ball outfit and then he is found at the bottom of cliffs. You don't think that is suspicious?'

Torquil himself took a deep breath and forced himself to speak slowly, politely. 'There was a post-mortem, of course. And there will be a Fatal Accident Inquiry. All the documentation is already on its way.'

'Except for your report that should have been faxed through to me straight away! I want you to investigate this and report to me pretty damned quick. And why has Sergeant Golspie not been given an area of responsibility yet?'

'That isn't how we work on West Uist, Superintendent.'

'That is how I want you to work, Inspector McKinnon. I gave you an order and it hasn't been carried out.'

'With respect, Superintendent, we have been rather busy. And Sergeant Golspie has been investigating things together with Sergeant Driscoll. And then of course with the events of today everything has got — '

'What do you mean events of today?'

Torquil made a face at the phone. 'The attack on the *West Uist Chronicle* offices last night and the assault on Calum Steele, the editor. He is in hospital with a head injury. And then the death of the young girl, Nancy MacRurie, at Dunshiffin Castle. And the attack on my constable, Ewan McPhee.'

'You are kidding me?'

Torquil replied icily. 'There is nothing there to joke about, Superintendent, I assure you.'

'Why didn't Sergeant Golspie tell me about any of this?'

'I presume because she did not know about it, sir.' Then he added with a touch of mischief, 'Perhaps you didn't give her a chance to talk, Superintendent.'

'Don't be impertinent, Inspector.'

'No impertinence intended, Superintendent. It is just that you don't seem to listen very often.'

There was a spluttering noise from the Bara end. 'You have me worried, McKinnon. You seem to be infecting a potentially good sergeant with your own brand of lethargy and indolence.'

'Thank you, sir,' Torquil replied glibly.

'It wasn't a compliment, McKinnon. Now get on with it. And let me have a faxed report by the end of the day. It would be nice, just once, to get a report from you before I see and hear about some disaster on national television news.'

'Of course, Superintendent. Shall I — ?'

He heard the click of the line being disconnected and he looked down with a hint of amusement at the dead receiver.

X

Together with the Drummonds, Torquil cursorily examined the *West Uist Chronicle* offices, making sure not to handle anything before Morag returned later to dust the place for fingerprints.

As he expected, there was some damage. Calum's computer had been trashed, and five bundles of the latest edition of the *Chronicle* had been tossed out of the back window, where they had scattered all over the back lane. Already there were a few people who had picked up copies and started reading them as they went about their business.

'Looks like whoever did this didn't want Calum's latest edition to be read,' said Wallace.

'Aye,' his brother agreed, 'but the damned fool doesn't know some of the good folk of West Uist. There are free papers here just for the taking. Everyone will have heard about this and will want one. They'll soon do the rounds.'

'I doubt that The Frying Scotsman will be getting a consignment of the residue of this edition to wrap fish suppers up in.'

Torquil gave a short laugh and slapped them both on the shoulder. 'Come on then, boys. Let's get a copy or two and see just what our local investigative reporter had been up to. There should be a clue or two to get us started.'

But although he didn't say it, he wondered whether instead of clues and fish suppers there might just be a red herring or two in the latest edition.

XI

After playing four holes of golf, the Padre had set off on his Ariel Red Hunter to do a few outlying pastoral visits before heading into Kyleshiffin to chair a meeting of the St Ninian's Benevolent Fund for Fishermen and Lighthousekeepers. It was his plan after that to call in to the Cottage Hospital to see Calum and two of his other parishioners.

He was not sure exactly why he took the turn up towards Loch Hynish, except that he felt somehow compelled. It was one of the island's beauty spots, with its crannog and ruined tower in the middle of its still waters.

He drew to a stop as the road reached a slight crest above the loch. Down below was a small jetty and moored to it was a small rowing boat, known locally as the 'wee free ferry,' for it was there for anyone who cared to row out to the *crannog*, the artificial Iron Age islet, to explore the old ruin that rose from a swathe of bracken and dwarf rowan tees. It was a place of bittersweet memories, for he had often rowed his nephew there when he was a boy, left in his care when Lachlan's brother and his wife, Torquil's parents, had drowned in a boating accident. Happy were those days. Yet unhappy was the memory of the tragedy that had befallen a friend of Torquil's a little more than a year before.[1] He sighed, as memories of happier times came flooding back. And then he realized just why he had taken this road today. He wanted to see the Black House Museum, and probably pop along to the cliff top from whence he had spotted Finlay's body lying on the rocks below. He tapped the Bible in his pocket and nodded.

'A prayer over the spot is the least I can do for you, old friend,' he mused as he set off again.

He rode on and passed the sign for the

---

[1] See *The Gathering Murders*

Black House Museum, which had the CLOSED UNTIL FURTHER NOTICE board hanging below it. He smiled, for although Finlay rarely closed the museum, whenever he did he would do so without forewarning and without information as to when it would reopen. It was his way of broadcasting his freedom to pursue other work and interests, like his writing or his golf.

The road snaked round and the Black House Museum and the nearby log cabin came into view. Parked outside it was a maroon four by four. The Padre slowed down as he approached the Black House Museum and saw that the door was standing open. He stopped and switched off his engine, kicked down the stand and dismounted.

'Hello there,' he called out, as he went over to the open door. He looked in fully expecting to find the driver of the four by four, but the old house was empty. He came out and pulled the door after him, feeling a momentary surge of irritation that whoever had come to look at the place had wondered off and left the door open. He shook his head in despair, thinking of how that would have angered Finlay.

Mechanically, he had pulled his briar pipe from his top pocket and was contemplating filling it when he heard voices from nearby.

To his surprise they seemed to be coming from Finlay MacNeil's log cabin. That really fanned the smouldering embers of his ire and he crunched across the road and tried the door handle, which opened at his touch.

'And just what on earth do you think you are doing here?' he demanded upon seeing Finbar Donleavy standing by Finlay's desk, moving papers about while he talked into a microphone in his free hand. A few feet away from him Danny Wade, the blond-haired cameraman was busily filming.

Finbar Donleavy stopped talking and signalled Danny Wade to stop filming.

'You are trespassing on a dead man's property!' the Padre said accusingly. 'I think you had better explain yourselves.'

'No harm, Vicar,' said Danny Wade. 'We're just doing a — '

'I am a minister, not a vicar,' Lachlan said curtly. 'And I think that you may be doing a good deal of harm.'

Finbar Donleavy came forward, a placatory smile on his lips. 'We were just doing a piece on Finlay MacNeil for this evening's news, Padre. We didn't think we'd be doing any harm.'

'I don't think that going through his personal papers is justified,' Lachlan returned. 'Finlay MacNeil was my friend and I do not

219

think that intruding like this is either a seeming way for the media to behave, nor a respectful act to someone who has just passed away so tragically.'

'The piece we were doing was quite respectful,' Finbar returned. 'I was just demonstrating that he seemed to be in the middle of some research.'

'He was writing a book,' Lachlan conceded.

'About the Hoolish Stones?'

'That is correct.'

'And you saw the way he interrupted the live broadcast the other night?'

Lachlan had seen out of the corner of his eye that Danny Wade had started filming again, just as he was aware that the broadcast journalist was attempting to extract information from him, presumably to be included in the broadcast. He had no intention of being drawn into saying anything contentious.

'Yes, I saw the programme. I told you that yesterday, as I am sure you remember. Finlay MacNeil was upset, right enough.'

Finbar's mouth almost registered a smile as he pressed on. 'He did not approve of Dr Logan Burns and The Daisy Institute, did he? Would you think it was fair to say that he vehemently disagreed with Dr Burns's theories about the Hoolish Stones?'

Lachlan reached into his side pocket and drew out a box of matches. He casually shook it and drew out a match. Then he struck it and reached past Finbar to light a small candle that stood in a Toby jug candleholder. Straightening up he smiled benignly. 'It would not be right for me to speculate on that.' And before Finbar could formulate another question, he produced his Bible. 'Now since you are here, would you care to join me in saying a few prayers in Finlay MacNeil's memory?'

Then turning directly to the camera he began, 'Finlay MacNeil was a local historian, a respected member of the West Uist — '

'Actually Padre, before you get started,' Finbar said hurriedly, 'I think we will be going.'

'Yes, we have other places to visit,' agreed Danny Wade, dropping his camera from his shoulder.

'Of course,' Lachlan replied affably. 'But about this little piece of footage, I would suggest that you do not show it on the television. You don't want to alienate the West Uist viewers, do you? I am sure that they would regard this invasion of Finlay Mac-Neil's home in a poor light, what with him not even buried.'

The two men took their leave.

'And pull the door closed after you, will you?' Lachlan called after them. 'We don't want anyone coming in here uninvited, do we now?'

A few moments later the four by four was started up and shot off. Only then did Lachlan permit himself a smile. 'Almost a case of bell, book and candle, eh, Finlay?' he said to the ether. 'Exorcising unwanted spirits.'

His eye fell on the whisky bottle and the tobacco pouch lying on top of the desk, and the piles of papers that the journalist had been rifling through. He straightened the piles and cast an eye over some of the notes his friend had been making. Then he noticed the old diary in one of the recesses of the desk. Finlay had always been a keen diarist, he knew.

He held up his Bible and said a prayer before blowing out the candle and preparing to leave himself. Then he clicked his tongue thoughtfully and turned back to the desk to pull out the diary. 'It wouldn't do to leave your personal thoughts here, would it, Finlay?' He popped his Bible in one pocket and the diary in the other. 'I will look after them for you.'

9

Annie McConville was just returning from the outhouses where she had fed all of the dogs under the care of the Kyleshiffin Dog Sanctuary. Zimba, her own German shepherd, and Sheila, her small West Highland, padded along beside her, like a sergeant major and corporal in her personal canine army. The amazing thing was that Annie did indeed seem to have a magic connection with most animals, but dogs in particular. She was passionate to the nth degree and was rewarded by the affection of all those waifs and strays under her care. Now well into her seventies, she was still remarkably fit for her years. Although she missed the help that Eileen Lamont used to give her in walking the dogs, yet she was still able to fit in a walk for all thirteen of them throughout the day. Everyone on the island knew her well, so raising money to keep her charges in food and medicine was never a problem. On the other hand, finding new homes for them was always difficult.

She was humming and swinging the large basket back and forth against her wellingtons as she made her way back up to the house. Then first Zimba stopped, his hackles rising as he emitted a low-pitched growl. Then Sheila started jumping up and down making an altogether less restrained barking noise. Immediately, the kennels erupted in an assortment of sympathetic barking and yowling.

'Wheesht! Wheesht, the lot of you,' Annie cried, putting a whistle to her lips and receiving instantaneous quiet in response.

And looking up the path she saw two men waiting for her. Father and son, almost certainly. Tavish McQueen was standing feet apart and hands clenched by his sides, while his son Angus leaned against the wall of her house, arms folded in front of him.

'Ah, it is Annie, isn't it?' the elder McQueen said, coming down the path towards her, his leather-soled brogues clacking assertively on the concrete. 'I am Tavish. That is Tavish McQueen of McQueen's Regal Eggs.'

Annie shook his hand. 'I know who you are, Mr McQueen. I have seen your face on the billboard by your farm and on your egg vans.'

'The face will soon be on TV, too, Mrs McConville. We are a growing business. It will

224

be good for West Uist.'

'That I am not so sure of,' Annie replied dispassionately. 'You are still a newcomer, you know.'

Tavish McQueen's brow tightened somewhat, but he did not allow his smile to fade. 'Well anyway, let me get down to business. You may have heard that we were broken into?'

'I heard rumours, but I saw an article in the *Chronicle* today.'

'Oh, I heard there was no *Chronicle* today,' McQueen returned.

'There was indeed, no thanks to whoever attacked poor Calum Steele and tried to sabotage his paper. The folk of West Uist are not so easily hoodwinked. The galoot who attacked him threw the papers away, but Calum's distribution lads salvaged some and got them out to those who are loyal to the *Chronicle*.' She tilted her head and eyed both McQueens askance.

'That just about means all of the islanders,' she added meaningfully.

'Aye, and that is good. Folk should stick together. But what I meant to say, Annie, was that — '

'*Mrs McConville*,' Annie interrupted.

'Pardon me?' McQueen asked, taken aback.

'My name is Mrs McConville. I have been a widow for twenty-three years and you have not been invited to use my Christian name.'

'Aye — right — sorry. Mrs McConville, I would like to buy a couple of your dogs. A couple of the collies that used to live on our farm.'

'No. I am sorry, you cannot buy two of them.'

Angus McQueen pushed himself off the wall with his elbows. 'What about if we bought all three, Mrs McConville? We could do with them as guard dogs at the farm.'

'You cannot buy any of them,' Annie replied firmly.

'But — but this is a dog sanctuary isn't it?' Tavish McQueen spluttered. 'I am offering to take the dogs off your hands.'

'They are no trouble,' Annie replied. 'Which is more than I can say about a battery farm on West Uist. I saw the article in the *Chronicle*. And I saw the pictures of the good hiding this young hooligan got from Calum Steele when he attacked him from behind.'

'Now just a minute, woman!' Angus McQueen began, taking a pace forward.

Immediately Zimba's hackles went up and he bared his teeth menacingly. Sheila did a respectable imitation of the same and the younger McQueen retreated a pace.

'I love my doggies,' Annie went on. 'And I have respect for all of God's creatures. You battery farm people clearly do not. You don't look after your chickens and so I will not let you look after these poor doggies.'

Tavish McQueen had been chewing the ends of his moustache as his face grew redder and redder.

'Come on, Angus. We'll see if we can have a word with Pug Cruikshank. He'll maybe sell us a real dog.'

'And I won't be buying any eggs from you!' Annie called after them, as they stomped away.

II

The great hall of Dunshiffin Castle was full of hoodie-clad inceptors and acolytes. They sat cross-legged on the floor watching the three directors walk to the front to stand before them. There had been much muttering and chatter, but it was silenced as Logan Burns raised his hands.

He pushed his wire-frame spectacles back on his nose and stood surveying them with a sad expression.

'My friends, you all know the tragedy that has befallen us today. We are one less in number after Nancy's terrible accident.'

Eileen Lamont was sitting in the second row and immediately she began to sob. By her side, Johanna Waltari put a comforting arm about her shoulder and drew her close. Other people in the hall began to weep freely.

'That is it, my friends, let the emotion out. Show the universe that we are sad to have lost one of our number. Do not be afraid of your emotions.'

'Let them free,' Saki Yasuda echoed.

'Show her spirit it is not forgotten,' Drew Kelso added.

'That is right,' Logan Burns went on. 'Our emotions give us a chance to connect with the divine, with the spirit. And so in a curious way Nancy has taught us something. By her passing — and note that she passed from this world when she was doing her vigil over the Hoolish Stones — she has given us a link with our greater purpose. The summer solstice is almost upon us and we must not allow anything to lessen the experience of it for us. It is going to show us the link. The real link between the ancients and ourselves. Nancy has shown herself to be a messenger. She is the first to light up the way, to show us that Atlantis is with us here.'

His voice had been gradually gaining in

fervour, just as his eyes had almost seemed to glow in intensity.

'Nancy hasn't gone!' someone cried.

'Her light lives,' yelled someone else.

'She sacrificed herself to show us.'

Logan Burns raised his hands again. 'The solstice is symbolic of the link. We must celebrate it, just as many people are coming to the island to celebrate it with us. The television coverage has brought them here, to the last great temple, the last great link with Atlantis. And this evening, on Scottish television, I shall reveal the secret of the Hoolish Stones. For it was here that great messengers carried their wisdom to the top of the world.' He raised his hands higher, looking ceilingwards, yet through the ceiling almost as if he could see to the stars and through time to the infinite beyond.

And the mood of the hall rose with him. Instead of the tears and the sobbing, people started to laugh, to chant, to lift their arms in imitation of Logan Burns.

'Yet there will be no more accidents,' Logan Burns went on. 'I myself shall do the vigil tonight and tomorrow we shall all go and gather round the Hoolish Stones through the whole night to watch the sunrise. To communicate with the divine. And we shall be full of love. We shall all love one another

— just like they did in ancient Atlantis.'

The whole hall erupted into rapture and people embraced one another.

Drew Kelso caught Saki Yasuda's eye and gestured out of the window, where Finbar Donleavy and Danny Wade could be seen getting out of their four by four. They smiled at one another and began clapping Logan Burns. Amazingly, their founder appeared to have averted the disaster that had seemed inevitable after the death of Nancy MacRurie.

They both felt there would be need for celebration.

III

Torquil sat back in his chair and listened as Morag briefed Lorna, the two Drummond brothers and himself about her meeting with Nancy's family.

'Her mother is distraught, of course, but Hamish, her father, is worryingly calm. Even when I took him to identify her body at the Cottage Hospital, he seemed like a man in control of his emotions. It was afterwards that he had me most worried.' She sighed. 'I can't say that I blame him, but he said that it was all the fault of The Daisy Institute. He said

230

that he would not rest until he finds out just what happened.'

'Understandable,' Torquil remarked.

'I would probably want to tear Dunshiffin Castle apart, stone by stone,' said Wallace Drummond.

'But he said it without raising his voice or anything,' Morag went on. 'That is what worried me.'

'We had better keep an eye on him, don't you think, Inspector?' Lorna asked.

Torquil sniffed and sat forward. 'Absolutely. We don't want him doing anything rash. Now this afternoon, we have some things that we need to follow up on. I need to have a word with the McQueens.' He tapped the newspaper that had been wrapped around the brick and smoothed out on his desk. 'The main article is no surprise. Calum went to town on the article about the battery farm. He might have just shot himself in the foot this time though. He admits that he entered the farm without permission.'

'But he was attacked,' Douglas Drummond said, pointing at the picture of Angus McQueen sprawled on a pallet of smashed eggs. 'The wee man did well!'

'That is why I need to interview this Angus McQueen,' Torquil went on. 'It looks as if he could have had a score to settle with Calum.'

231

'Morag and Lorna, will you go back to the castle? Interview Logan Burns and Eileen Lamont.'

'Why Eileen?' Morag queried.

'She cried out that it should have been her, not Nancy,' Torquil replied. And he recounted the events when he had arrived.

'What about us, boss?' Wallace asked.

Torquil clicked his tongue. 'Despite everything we still have this event tomorrow that we have to police. Go up to the Hoolish stones with the ropes and cordon off the main site, then start sorting out car-parking.'

The Drummonds scowled at one another. 'A pair of traffic wardens, that's what we are, Brother,' said Wallace.

'Aye, but it might be fun giving out tickets.'

IV

'Tickets! You've got to be joking!' Tyler Brady exclaimed, slapping the table in front of him so hard that several of the pints on it wobbled precariously and beer slopped on to the tabletop.

The public bar of The Bell was busier than usual, and several people looked round at the group drinking in the corner.

'Keep it down, Tyler,' Pug Cruikshank said

through gritted teeth. 'Of course we'll have tickets. We don't want any busy-bodies straying into the meeting tomorrow night. They won't exactly be tickets; nothing to say what they are for, but they'll be identifiable to us all right.'

'I'll be collecting them at the cattle grid when they come in,' explained Wilf in a hushed voice, producing a small green piece of paper with the print of a stone circle on it and showing it to Tyler. 'No one would have any idea what this was about.'

'How many have you got rid of so far?' Tyler asked.

'Fifty odd,' replied Pug. 'I've mailed out thirty-five, and Wilf has distributed the rest to the usual punters.'

Clem O'Hanlan grinned and lifted his half empty pint to his mouth. 'And we have ours. It will be a good do, so it will. I am looking forward to taking some money off you all.' He winked at his uncle, Sean O'Hanlan, and then addressed his neighbour.

'Do you not fancy putting your new purchase up to the test Mr Borawski?'

Mr Borawski shook his head and contemplated his glass of lemonade. 'I will have a few bets, but I am taking my dog back home in one piece. We will try him out there, once he is used to his new home.'

Lars Sorensen nodded in agreement. 'I am with you there. I am not going to cripple my own investment before I have personally done some training.'

'Ach, you boys should live a bit more dangerously,' said Sean O'Hanlan, cheerfully. 'Me and the young fellow there have bought a good piece of action and we plan to clean up.' He downed the rest of his pint and tapped the glass on the table.

'Another one, boys?' Pug asked, standing and picking up the Irishman's empty glass. 'Just one thing though. We've taken all precautions for the meeting. Make sure you hold on to your tickets and don't gab to anyone you don't know. I for one don't plan to live in the least bit dangerously.'

'We'll get these,' came a voice from behind him. Pug turned to see Tavish McQueen and his son Angus.

'Get a round in, Angus,' McQueen ordered, as he took a seat beside Pug. 'Did you hear about that Steele idiot?'

Wilf Cruikshank guffawed. 'Someone cracked him one and he's in the hospital. Couldn't have happened to a nicer chap.'

'Just what my Angus thinks,' Tavish McQueen replied. Then, leaning forward and lowering his voice, 'Tomorrow night is still on, I take it?'

'Of course,' said Pug.

'Good. But I need to do a bit of personal business, Pug. Since that bloody little reporter broke into our place I feel we need a couple of guard dogs. I went to that old mad woman's dog sanctuary this morning and tried to buy the Noble collies, but she sent me away with a flea in my ear.'

Tyler Brady snorted. 'She's another one who could do with a crack! She had the police up at the farm after I told her to keep off our land.'

Pug eyed him coldly. 'There will be no more of that talk, Tyler. Remember what I told you.' He turned back to Tavish McQueen. 'So what business do you want to do, Tavish?'

'I want to buy a couple of dogs.'

Pug pressed his lips together. 'They're not exactly guard dogs. They are all *special*.'

Angus McQueen came back from the bar with a tray of fresh pints. He distributed them then drew up a seat beside his father.

'Did you hear — ?' he began enthusiastically.

'They know all about Steele,' Tavish McQueen cut in without looking round. 'I know that, Pug. I need special animals to deter nosy parkers from prying into my affairs.'

Pug considered for a moment. 'In that case I think we can accommodate you, Tavish.' He grinned. 'For the right price.'

Tavish McQueen picked up his pint and took a hefty swig. Then, putting the glass down, he wiped froth from his moustache. 'You know me, Pug; I always pay my debts.'

V

Calum Steele was getting bored, as a result of which he was starting to lead the cottage hospital staff a merry dance. Having read all of the magazines that visitors had brought him and counted all the cracks on the wall of his room, he had developed a passion for his buzzer. Three times he had Sister Lizzie Lamb come to check his stitches, reassure him that the headache would go and that he would be seeing Dr McLelland when he did his round later on. Twice he had called Maggie Crouch, the ward clerk, and got her to bring him a notepad and pen, then pop out to bring him back a mutton pie and a bottle of Irn Bru. Four times Nurse Giselle Anderson had answered his buzz, each time for increasingly frivolous tasks.

'Calum Steele, if you press that buzzer one more time,' Giselle snapped, eying him threateningly, 'then it will not be your head that will be hurting.' And she brought her hands from behind her back and let a long plastic tube dangle from her fingertips. 'Sister Lamb thinks that all this attention may be due to constipation. Maybe it is a soapy water enema that you need.'

Calum pulled his sheets up slightly and slipped down on the pillows. 'I . . . er . . . think maybe I'll take a nap,' he said, his face draining of colour.

Giselle hung the tubing over the bottom rail of the bed and left with a malicious smile on her face.

Ten minutes or so later Calum was wakened from a doze by a firm hand on his shoulder. His mind immediately flashed a picture of the enema tube advancing before him and he shot up in bed with a start.

'Easy, Calum, easy does it,' said the Padre. 'You must have been dreaming, I am thinking. I have brought you some grapes — and a copy of the *Chronicle*.' He pointed to the bedside cabinet where he had deposited the grapes and the slightly soiled newspaper. 'I am sure that you heard about how they got delivered. Whoever did this to you dumped them out of the window, but they have been gathered up and have just about sold out. It is a good edition.'

'Thanks, Padre. It is the first one that really has cost me blood.'

'Have you any idea who did it?'

'As I told Torquil, there could be a queue of folk.'

Lachlan shook his head. 'You know that is not true. But this is not what we expect on the island. Violent crime should have no home here.' Then he raised an eyebrow and added, 'Mind you, that picture of the younger McQueen lying on his back covered in eggs has made many folk giggle. That was you throwing your weight around,' he said jokingly. 'You'll need to stop that.'

Calum eyed the enema tube and shuddered. 'Nurse Anderson said something similar just a wee while ago.' He pumped up his pillows and sat back against them. 'But I need to be out there, not lying in bed like this, Padre. I have news to cover.'

'Aye, it is sad about Nancy MacRurie. A terrible accident.'

Calum's eyes widened. 'What's that?'

The Padre raised his eyebrows questioningly. 'You didn't know? Ah well, I only heard about it myself. I thought you might have heard, what with her parents having to identify her body in the mortuary.' And he told Calum as much as he knew.

'I didn't know anything about it, Padre. I

guess they deliberately kept it from me on Ralph McLelland's orders. I am to be kept in bed apparently.' He folded his arms petulantly. 'It is hard though. I am a newsman and I should be reporting. I expect that Irish TV bletherer has been on to it.'

'Finbar Donleavy? Actually, I don't know if he has. At any rate he seemed very interested in Finlay MacNeil's house.' And he described his earlier encounter with the broadcast journalist and his cameraman, Danny Wade.

'I am thinking that it wasn't showing suitable respect to go rooting in his cabin without permission.'

'Ebony and Ivory strike again! That is scandalous!' exclaimed Calum. 'Highly unprofessional!' Although he knew that was exactly what he would have done himself if he had been following a story.

After the Padre left, Calum was still rankled about being cooped up in hospital. It bothered him that he was missing all the news, his very *raison d'être*.

'So Finbar Donleavy has been breaking and entering, has he?' he mused to himself. 'I wonder what Kirstie Macroon would think of that?'

And with that thought he risked Nurse Anderson's threat of the enema tube and pressed the buzzer. He needed to make a phone call.

VI

Finbar Donleavy pulled his four by four into the side of the drive leading up to Dunshiffin Castle to allow the Golf GTI to pass. Lorna raised her hand in thanks and drove into the courtyard, braking hard as she did so to skid slightly on the gravel surface. Once she switched off the engine Morag let herself out and nodded approvingly.

'It is certainly smoother than the station's old Ford Escort. Ewan will be envious when he sees it. I think he's getting fair embarrassed about having to use his mother's old moped.'

They mounted the stairs to the hall and were met at the door by Peter and Henrietta. To both sergeants' surprise they seemed quite upbeat. A stream of pink-hoodie-clad inceptors passed them, giggling among themselves.

'You will have come about the accident,' Peter asked with a smile.

'We are all so upset,' Henrietta agreed, with an equally unruffled manner. 'I expect you will want to talk with Logan. He's expecting you.'

Morag nodded as the duo started to lead the way to Logan Burns's office. 'Well actually, Sergeant Golspie is going to see him, while I have a chat with Eileen Lamont and her friend.'

Peter pointed to the great staircase, at the top of which hung the portrait of a tartan-clad eighteenth-century laird. 'They are both up in Johanna's room. Eileen has moved in there after the accident. I'll take you up, shall I?'

Morag followed him while Lorna went off with Henrietta. He led the way upstairs then along the long east wing and knocked on a door. Floorboards creaked and a moment later it was pulled open by Johanna Waltari. Inside, sitting on the edge of one of the two beds Eileen was sobbing with her head in her hands.

'I am Sergeant Driscoll,' Morag introduced herself. 'May I come in and talk with Eileen?'

'Of course,' Johanna replied. 'I will go with Peter and let you have some peace.'

'No need for that,' Morag said, raising a restraining hand. 'In fact, it would be as well if I could have a word with both of you.' She turned her head and smiled at Peter. 'Perhaps I can have a chat with you afterwards, Peter.'

Peter beamed at her, then gave her a wink that disconcerted her and worried her that he might have misconstrued her meaning. 'Later it is, Sergeant,' he said and left.

When the door closed Eileen looked up. Her eyes were red-rimmed and swollen. 'Sergeant Driscoll,' she said, trying to force a smile. 'Fancy meeting you here. You've come about Nancy, I suppose.'

'Awful news.'

'It should have been me, Sergeant!'

Johanna had sat back beside her and put an arm about her shoulders. Morag sat on the other side and did the same.

'That is nonsense, Eileen,' she said.

'But she took over my vigil so that . . . so that — '

'So that what?'

Johanna took over. 'So that she could come and see me. We had a long talk into the night. Almost all night.'

Morag noticed the framed photograph beside the other bed. It was of a young woman of Eileen's age. Scandinavian, by the appearance.

'And what were you talking about?'

'The Daisy Institute and the reason we are all here. About the solstice and everything.'

'You said before that you had thought of leaving?'

'I had but Johanna, Peter and Henrietta persuaded me to stay.'

'And what did Nancy feel? Did she ever have any doubts?'

'No, she was brilliant. She loved it here. She liked the way everyone gets on. And she liked — well, she liked having sex. I think that was one of the things she liked about the place.'

Morag was used to receiving all sorts of information in interviews. She maintained an interested, but unshocked visage. 'Do a lot of people have sex here then?'

Johanna answered for her. 'Everyone here is an adult. Free love is not exactly encouraged, but . . . ' Her voice trailed away meaningfully.

'What do you think happened to Nancy?' Morag asked.

Eileen took a deep breath and leaned closer to Johanna. 'I think she smoked too much weed, got high and leaned too far over the edge of the tower.'

'Did she smoke a lot?' Morag asked, knowing full well that she did.

'Yes. All the time. Both she and Alan were always sharing spliffs. I tried to tell her it was no good for her.' Tears welled up in her eyes and she began to weep again.

'How . . . how right I was,' she said between sobs.

Lorna thought that Logan Burns seemed to be in a strange mood. He was more relaxed than he had been at their previous interview, and yet he was also more animated. In part, she thought that it was due to the fact that he had clearly taken some sort of stimulant very recently. She had seen enough of drug taking in her time in the Force to recognize the signs. She suspected that it was simply cannabis.

'Forgive me for mentioning it, but no one seems desperately upset by the death of Nancy MacRurie,' she stated in her opening gambit.

The corners of his mouth cured up slightly. 'It is a terrible accident, of course, and awful that she was so young, yet we all know that she has gone to a better place. To a higher realm.'

'And that is what? Heaven?'

Logan leaned back in his chair behind his desk and shrugged. 'The name is immaterial. It is a higher state beyond the physical. That is what all religions teach, and they are all correct. How can one be sad about someone going further on their spiritual journey.'

'But she is dead!'

'She has left the ties of her physical body.'

Lorna decided not to get tied down in a

spiritual discussion. 'That is as may be, but we, the police, have to investigate all fatal accidents. There will, you realize be a Fatal Accident Inquiry.'

Logan Burns nodded. 'Ask whatever you like, Lorna.'

'OK. Why was Nancy up the tower in the middle of the night on her own?'

'She was doing the night-time vigil. We expect the inceptors to do that, to look out over the Hoolish Stones as the solstice approaches. It gives them a sense of the importance of the place. We do the same thing in our other centres across the world. They are always based near to an ancient religious structure.'

'Why?'

'To communicate with the divine and tap into the spirituality of the place. These sites allow us to link up with the ancients and their great knowledge.'

'And I understand that you believe that the Hoolish Stones have some connection with Atlantis?' Lorna knew enough to keep the disbelief from her question.

'I do. There is absolutely no doubt in my mind. In fact, you'll get a good idea about it on this evening's news. The news team left just before you arrived.'

At the mention of the news team Lorna felt

a shiver run up her spine. Superintendent
Lumsden had castigated her because he had
heard about Finlay MacNeil's death from the
news instead of directly from them.

VIII

Peter was leaning against a wall when Morag
emerged from Johanna's room. He smiled as
he ambled towards her.

Morag returned the smile, aware now that
he was a young man who was very sure of his
charms. She recalled how her first impression
of him had been so favourable when she saw
him at his stall at the harbour market in
Kyleshiffin. Clearly he was close to Henrietta.
Indeed, she remembered Nancy herself
saying that they were practically an item, and
that she herself thought he was 'hot.' Seeing
him move towards her made her suspect that
fidelity was not high on his list of virtues.

'So, lovely Sergeant Driscoll, what do you
want to talk to me about? Would you like to
go somewhere more comfortable?'

Morag felt herself bristle. Outrageous, she
thought. The young pup actually thinks he
could bed me, a mother of three young ones!
And this morning one of his fellows died
when she fell from a tower. Whereas she had

246

previously thought him an attractive young man, now he made her flesh crawl. Yet she could not allow that to show.

'Here will be fine, Peter. I just wanted to ask you why everyone — Eileen and Johanna apart — seem singularly unaffected by what happened today?'

Peter stared at her intensely for a moment and then he smiled. 'Everyone has to die some time, Sergeant. Nancy was here to learn about the divine, about spirituality. Now she knows.'

Morag could scarcely believe her ears. 'Thank you, Peter. That was all.' She walked past him. She badly needed to get to fresh air.

IX

The great hall was packed as usual for the Scottish TV Six O'Clock News. Kirstie Macroon ran through the headlines with her usual aplomb.

'PARLIAMENT ROCKS OVER ALLEGATIONS OF CORRUPTION IN THE CIVIL SERVICE 'TRAGEDY ON WEST UIST.'

There was much shuffling about as the assembly waited to hear about Nancy

MacRurie's sudden death.

And sure enough, the screen showed a picture of Dunshiffin Castle and homed in to reveal the north tower. Then a picture of Nancy appeared in the bottom left quarter of the screen.

'Tragedy occurred on West Uist early this morning at The Daisy Institute, which as viewers may be aware, is now based at historic Dunshiffin Castle. The body of Nancy MacRurie was found at the foot of the tower. It is speculated that she fell from the tower during an overnight vigil that she was keeping, overlooking the famous Hoolish Stones.'

Eileen Lamont was sitting with Johanna, Agnes Doyle and Alan Brodie. She immediately burst into tears and had to be comforted by her friends.

Kirstie Macroon gave some background to the accident.

'Earlier today Finbar Donleavy met with Dr Logan Burns, the Director of The Daisy Institute as part of our regular series about the Hoolish Stones in the run-up to the summer solstice tomorrow night. Dr Burns told us about how well Nancy MacRurie was doing at the institute and of the plans that she had been making.'

Eileen continued to sob, but all around her people were chatting and murmuring happily as they heard Logan Burns talk about Nancy.

'And then Finbar talked to Dr Burns about the solstice, and he finally revealed his theories about the Hoolish Stones.'

At the back of the hall Drew Kelso and Saki Yasuda exchanged worried glances.

X

Calum watched the news from his bed in the cottage hospital. He had his spiral notebook on his lap and had been making copious notes as was his custom.

Logan Burns and Finbar Donleavy were standing beside a screen in a room of the castle that Calum recognized as the old gun room, where successive lairds had kept their shotguns, pistols and fishing tackle. With practised ease he had been giving a power point demonstration to Finbar.

'So you see, these carvings are undoubtedly Atlantean in origin. The significance of this is that the knowledge of the Atlanteans directly spawned the Ogham script and runes of the

Scandinavian countries. I have studied early language and epigraphy for years and this discovery effectively turns history on its head.'

Finbar nodded his head non-committally. 'But does this really matter, Dr Burns?'

'It is of vital importance, Finbar. Because the writings reveal much more about the knowledge of the Atlanteans. And tomorrow, at the solstice, all will become clearer.' He tapped a button on his laptop and an aerial view of the Hoolish Stones appeared on the screen. 'As you can see, the Hoolish Stones are formed by three perfect concentric circles, with the great chambered cairn in the centre and the aisle leading all the way through.'

He waited expectantly, as if this revelation alone would produce a reaction in the journalist.

'The significance of this is that this is a direct ground-plan of the city of Atlantis. It is exactly as Plato described it. The writings on the stones, which I have deciphered, confirm not only this fact, but that this ground-plan was used for all of the temples of Atlantis that were built after the great cataclysm that destroyed the continent.'

Calum had been watching with ever increasing amusement as he jotted down notes. 'So that is your great revelation, is it?

The Hoolish Stones are what is left of a temple built by survivors of Atlantis. Good one, Logan!'

The usual Scottish TV jingle sounded out and the shot returned to the studio. Kirstie Macroon was studying a sheaf of documents. She looked up and smiled.

'We are extremely sorry to hear of more news from West Uist today. Apparently our old friend and sometime special correspondent, Calum Steele, was attacked last night and sustained a head injury. He is now recovering in the Kyleshiffin Cottage Hospital. We all wish him well for a speedy recovery. Get well, Calum.'

The *Chronicle* editor had watched entranced. Although he had talked to her by telephone that afternoon, basically to protest about the way that Finbar Donleavy had breached one of the first rules of responsible journalism by breaking into Finlay MacNeil's cabin, he had not expected a personal message from her on TV. He felt that the smile had been deliberately aimed at him and he felt his heart miss a beat.

And then she was talking again.

'The solstice is due tomorrow and our series of meetings with The Daisy Institute is just

251

about over. Yet our reporter, Finbar Donleavy, feels that there are some important questions to be posed. We go back to Finbar.'

Finbar Donleavy appeared in front of Dunshiffin Castle, in front of the large sign with the daisy logo.

'The Daisy Institute has been based on the island of West Uist for eight months now. Their purported aim is to further the study of divinity and spirituality, and as you can see their logo is that of the humble daisy. This is reflected in the uniforms that they wear. The directors, of which there are three, including Dr Logan Burns, the founder, wear yellow hoodies. As you will note from our past features these bear more than a passing resemblance to monks' gowns. The acolytes, that is those members who have reached a certain state of awareness and understanding, wear white hoodies, while the newest members, the ones they call inceptors, wear pink ones.' He pointed to the logo of the pink-tipped daisy. 'Truly this looks like a harmless throwback to the days of flower power and the hippy movement.'

Calum watched, his jaw dropping as he did so. He was beginning to see Finbar Donleavy in a new light. This was brilliant! True investigative journalism.

'Yet there may be a darker side to The Daisy Institute. Enough to be alarming. The first question we ask is, why choose a castle as your base? Is it to keep people out? Or to keep people in? There have been allegations that inceptors have been prevented from talking with their families for three months. After that time they show no desire to make contact. The question is, could there be a form of brainwashing going on? And then we have the sudden death of Finlay MacNeil, a critic of Dr Burns, as shown on Scottish TV News just the other night. And now this tragic death of one of the inceptors. A lot of questions are cropping up, the main one being, are we witnessing the emergence of a powerful cult right here on West Uist?'

The jingle sounded again and Kirstie Macroon did a link to the next news item.

'Well what do you know!' Calum exclaimed to himself. 'That's a story, Donleavy. A damned good story. And while you are working on that, I reckon I had better get started on a bit of investigation of my own.' He pressed his buzzer and threw back his covers. When Sister Lamb came in he was

253

pulling his clothes out of his bedside cabinet. He cut her remonstrations short. 'Have you got one of your dockets, Sister. No offence, but I need to discharge myself.'

XI

After clearing his desk at the station, Torquil had typed out his report of the day and faxed it through to Superintendent Lumsden. He phoned his uncle to say that he would not be returning for dinner that evening, because he had other plans. It had been more of an impulse than a plan if the truth be told.

He asked Lorna to have dinner with him and she, to his surprise and pleasure, accepted. A quick call to Jenny McVicar at the Peat Inn resulted in a candlelit dinner for two upstairs in the special annexe to the inn's restaurant, where they shared a meal of roast grouse and a half carafe of claret. Over the meal they chatted superficially about work, the Force in general and Superintendent Lumsden in particular, both agreeing that as a line manager he was as supportive as a sponge yet as prickly and poisonous as a jelly-fish. Then they talked about their interests; Torquil's piping, his passion for motor bikes; and about Lorna's love of cars, horses and racing. It was not so much that they had interests in common, as that they were aware of a chemistry that had been working between them. By the end of the meal their hands inadvertently touched as he poured her wine, and the touch lingered.

By moonlight they rode out on the Bullet to St Ninian's Cave and crunched down the shingle beach to watch the crabs frolicking in the shallow waters. There seemed an inevitability about their first kiss. And about all that followed.

XII

The Padre had taken a relaxing bath before heading to his study in his dressing-gown with a whisky nightcap and Finlay's diary. He flicked on the green-shaded desk lamp and charged his pipe before settling down in the old armchair to read. The grandfather clock ticked sonorously away as he strained to read Finlay's handwriting. It was not an easy task, for the handwriting varied, depending upon the museum curator's state of sobriety. The best written pieces were neat, scholarly entries, compared to the spidery segments that were scrawled in marked states of inebriation. And the frequency of the latter had been increasing as he went through the diary.

The whisky by his side stayed mostly untouched and his pipe grew cold as the import of the writings became clearer — apart from the entry about 'the dogs'. Finally, he reached for his phone and left a message on Torquil's mobile. 'Oh Finlay, Finlay!' he said, shaking his head as he thought of his old friend. 'If only you had said something I think you might still have been with us.'

10

I

Saki Yasuda enjoyed making love in the moonlight. Particularly, she enjoyed sex with a modicum of pain on both sides. The rubber clothes, chokers and flails set the mood as their perspiration-covered bodies gleamed in the moonlight that flooded through the slats of her window shutters and enhanced the build-up of passion. Then with a gradual disrobing and tearing away of remaining clothes, so that there was only naked flesh, she scratched, bit and slapped, and enjoyed having the same given back. The release was simultaneous and they lay gasping side by side for some moments.

Drew began to laugh.

'Not quite the reaction I expected,' she said coyly.

He rolled his head to face her. 'I'm sorry Saki, that was as fantastic as usual. It is just that I was thinking about Logan.'

'Because you know I do the same with him?'

'No. That doesn't bother me. Why should

it? Jealousy is a waste of time. I was just thinking of him up there in the tower on his vigil, while we — pleasured and destressed each other.'

'And do you feel less stressed, Drew? That Finbar Donleavy has been treacherous. He called us a cult.'

'Well, we are, aren't we? Let's be fair, Saki, that is just what we are.'

Her brows beetled. 'No, we are not. We are a serious scholarly institute. We study spirituality and we teach love.'

'Love like this?' He gave another deep throaty giggle.

'That is not funny, Drew. Logan Burns is a genius. He has made earth-shattering discoveries. And he is feeling stressed right now, just like you and I. Just think what he must be feeling up in the tower on his own right now.'

'Then I suppose you would rather that he had been here for you to thrash and make love with instead of me,' he returned sarcastically.

She jumped up and stared down at him, her chest heaving. 'I would like you to go, Drew. Now!'

He rolled off the bed and gathered his things into a pile. 'It is all falling apart Saki, you know that, don't you? We can't survive another Geneva. That is what could happen when they have the Fatal Accident Inquiry over Nancy. We should all be worried. Especially Logan.'

She shook her head. 'I think you are worried about something else, aren't you? You are worried that Logan will find out about the finances?'

His eyes narrowed. 'What do you mean?'

She stared back at him, arms akimbo. 'I have seen the books, Drew. You should be worried.'

He squeezed the riding crop in his hand. Then he smiled and swished it gently too and fro before dropping it on his pile of things. 'You be careful too, Saki,' he said, as he pulled on his hoodie.

II

Logan Burns had many times proudly, yet modestly, announced that he could meditate anytime, anywhere. Indeed, in some of his lectures he showed photographs of him taken in trance perched on top of a flagpole during a world congress on transcendental meditation held some years previously in Simla. It had been a technique that he had developed to a fine art and which had been his personal salvation over the years, during bad patches when he had faced adversity about his beliefs and his teachings.

When things were really bad, he found that a spliff of cannabis helped to get him in a susceptible mood. He had smoked two since taking up his vigil, overlooking the Hoolish Stones and, as he flicked the butt of the last one over the battlement wall, he made a mental note to commend Pug Cruikshank on the quality of the latest batch that his brother had grown.

He was sitting in the lotus position atop the north tower of Dunshiffin Castle, his hands resting palm-upwards on his knees, to open his palmar chakras and allow him to free his mind from the shackles of consciousness. He had emptied his mind of all extraneous thoughts and sensations, thinking of nothing except the Hoolish Stones and the key that they gave to the wisdom of the Atlanteans. He was unaware of the breeze that played over him, brushing wisps of his abundant hair about his face. He was unaware of the gradually dropping temperature. And he was unaware of the figure in black with a black balaclava that had emerged from the stairs leading on to the top of the tower where he sat.

He didn't see the metal flask being produced, or hear the movement of metal on metal as the top was screwed off and the sulphurous smell arose from the liquid inside.

Johanna crept slowly nearer, raising the flask in both hands, ready to pour the contents of the flask over his head.

He was also unaware of Eileen Lamont moving swiftly behind Johanna and putting a hand across her mouth and grabbing her wrist with the other.

Johanna twisted her head round and saw Eileen vigorously shaking her head. And then, as if a spell had been broken, she felt her resolve suddenly disappear and she allowed Eileen to draw her back towards the stairs.

Logan Burns was unaware of the footsteps retreating back down the stairs. And he was unaware of how close he had been to having a flask of concentrated sulphuric acid poured over his head.

III

Torquil left the Commercial Hotel rather sheepishly at six in the morning and rode back to the manse in high spirits. It was only when he dismounted outside and pulled off his goggles and gauntlets that he switched on his mobile and received his uncle's message of the night before. He did not imagine that it would be a matter of real urgency so he tiptoed along the hall to the foot of the stairs, planning to have a quick shower then a spot of breakfast before leaving for a quick practice at St Ninian's Cave on his way in to the station. He thought that if he was careful his uncle might just imagine that he had come back late in the night.

'Morning, laddie,' came the Padre's voice from the kitchen. He appeared a moment later, already dressed with his dog collar on and his dressing-gown on top of his clothes, a saucer in one hand and a steaming cup of tea in the other. 'Busted, is the term they use nowadays, I am thinking. I popped my head round your door and saw that your bed had not been slept in.'

'Ah!' Torquil said, turning to face him with a guilty grin.

'And you have either been running, or the colour in your cheeks indicates some secret that you have been keeping.'

Torquil averted his eyes for a moment, then nodded and looked his uncle straight in the eye. 'Uncle Lachlan, would you think I was mad if I told you I think I am in love?'

'With Lorna?'

'Aye. We seem to have a certain . . . er — '

'Chemistry? I had noticed. And you look like a man in love.' He deposited his tea on the side table and advanced towards his nephew with his hand outstretched. The Padre pumped Torquil's hand, then said, 'You have needed some luck, Torquil. Especially after all that you have been through. And she seems a nice, bonnie lassie. I am pleased for you. But — '

Torquil's eyes widened slightly. 'But what?'

The Padre sighed. 'But, I have something important to show you. Something that I think you need to see. About Finlay MacNeil. Come through to my study.' He led the way and pointed to the diary laid open on the desk. Beside it was a sheet of paper with notes written in Lachlan McKinnon's neat handwriting.

Torquil sat down and read the notes. Then he scowled before picking up the diary and flicking through the entries.

'I see what you mean, Uncle. It is all quite worrying.'

'I was planning to say a few words at the clifftop where he fell,' the Padre explained. 'But on the way I saw this four by four outside the Black House Museum. It was empty, so I tried Finlay's cabin and found that broadcaster Finbar Donleavy and his cameraman filming inside. He tried to bamboozle me and do a bit of sneaky filming while I was there, but I rather saw them off.'

Torquil looked up with a thin smile. He was all too aware of his uncle's abilities and almost felt sorry for Donleavy.

'I didn't like the fact that they had just sneaked into his place without permission, so I locked it up.' He nodded at the diary. 'And I took that away with me. It was only when I saw Donleavy's piece on the news last night that I thought I had better have a look at it.' Then, when Torquil made no comment, 'You did see the news, didn't you?'

When Torquil shook his head Lachlan told him about Finbar Donleavy's little diatribe and his questions about The Daisy Institute being a cult.

Torquil blew air through his lips. 'I think I had better have a shower and we should have breakfast, Uncle. Then I had better go in and go over everything with the team.' He pulled out his mobile phone. 'I'll get Morag to tee everything up for nine o'clock.'

A few minutes later after speaking to his sergeant he sat back and looked hopefully at his uncle. 'Would you mind coming and sitting in on the meeting? Finlay's handwriting is not easy and you may be able to help us.'

'For Finlay, anything,' the Padre replied, picking up his empty cup and saucer. 'You go and shower while I knock something up to eat, then I'll race you to Kyleshiffin.'

Torquil grinned at his uncle's retreating back. Then he phoned Lorna's mobile. His face creased into a smile when she answered. 'Hi, it's me,' he said. 'I need you in early, Lorna.'

He felt a tingle run up his spine when she replied softly, 'And I need you too, Torquil.'

IV

The Macbeth ferry, *Laird o' the Isles*, from Lochboisdale in South Uist slowly manoeuvred into the crescent-shaped harbour of Kyleshiffin. Eventually, the great landing doors slowly and noisily descended to allow the walking passengers to disembark before the inevitable cascade of traffic. Sitting as unobtrusively as he could on the harbour wall, finishing off a mutton pie, Calum Steele picked up his old polaroid camera and took photo after photo of various passengers and an assortment of cars.

It seemed a very mixed population. The usual bands of holidaymakers; young families come to visit the island's famous harbour town, groups of nature-watchers with cameras, binoculars and folded up tripods, and many with the same bright-eyed enthusiasm that he had noted on the faces of The Daisy Institute people. Yet with his eagle eye Calum was also aware of another sub-section of people, mainly men, without any particular outstanding features that would differentiate then from the average traveller, except that they had the look of gambling folk. No one seemed to notice him, yet some journalistic sixth sense suddenly made him aware of goose-pimpling at the nape of his neck. Gathering up his pile of photos from the spot on the wall where he had been depositing them, he slid off the wall and merged into the crowds that were milling around the ever-busy market stalls. He ducked down and circled a couple of stalls, finally hovering at Alice Farquarson's second-hand book stall.

He raised a finger to his lips and tapped the side of his nose when she began to hail him. Alice grinned, all too aware that Calum was in the middle of his 'newspaper snooping', as all the locals who knew him referred to the activities that he preferred to think of as investigative journalism.

Picking up a coffee-table book he peered over the top and watched the spot he had just vacated. He recognized Wilf Cruikshank and Tyler Brady from the Goat's Head Farm. They were talking to one of the recent disembarkees from the *Laird o' the Isles* ferry. He could not hear what they were saying, but he immediately spotted Wilf Cruikshank's hand disappear into his Barbour jacket and come out a moment later to hand over a green card surreptitiously in exchange for a number of banknotes, equally surreptitiously passed over.

Calum raised his camera above the book and snapped the transaction. He took another six photos of other similar dealings before shoving the camera inside his anorak.

'Thanks, Alice. See you later,' he said at last, winking at the stall-holder, as he made to lay down the book.

'I think that the least you can do is buy that book, Calum Steele,' said Alice with a stern look as he made to leave. 'We all have to make a living, after all. I am not just a bit of camouflage for your snooping.'

'Oh — aye,' Calum returned, checking the price then delving into his pocket for a couple of pounds. He grinned as he looked at the title for the first time. '*The Complete Book of Dog Training and Grooming*,' he read out. 'Couldn't be more apt, Alice. Couldn't be more apt.'

V

Morag had arranged the station rest-room as Torquil had instructed and had phoned the Drummond twins. Fortunately, they had not set off in their boat and they told her they would be there at the back of nine. Ewan had felt fully recovered after a good night's sleep and had already opened the office when she herself had arrived. But Dr Ralph McLelland was out on an emergency home visit and was not answering his mobile phone, so she was unable to invite him to Torquil's emergency meeting. Accordingly, she had sent Ewan off to the Cottage Hospital to see if they could find anything out about where he had gone.

'Good morning, Sergeant Golspie,' Morag greeted Lorna with a knowing smile when she came in. 'Did you have a good evening with the boss?'

Lorna blushed then smiled demurely. 'Only one word, Morag. Fabulous.'

'Do I detect a sea change in the emotions around here?'

Lorna nodded. 'Torquil and I are — getting on really well.'

Morag pointed to the rest-room. 'Tell you what, why don't you get the white board all set for Torquil. He said he wants to make notes on it, and I'll put the kettle on. They should all be along soon enough.'

And indeed, the twins came through the door instants before the noise of a couple of motor bikes heralded the arrival of Torquil and his uncle, the Padre.

'I have asked Lachlan to join us,' Torquil explained shortly afterwards as they sat round the ping-pong table in the rest-room. Morag had laid out paper and pencils in front of each place setting. Torquil picked up the diary in front of him. 'This is Finlay MacNeil's diary, which Lachlan recovered from Finlay's log cabin yesterday.'

He glanced at his uncle and asked him to describe the encounter with the broadcast team while the others took notes.

'I watched the news last night,' the Padre went on, 'and when Finbar Donleavy made that jibe about The Daisy Institute being a cult I thought I would have a peek through Finlay's diary.'

'Thanks, Uncle,' said Torquil. 'Essentially, like all diarists Finlay was pretty obsessional about making a daily entry. They vary in the content and the way they are written. Sometimes they are just single line entries, other times they are observations about life, or recaps about the day's events or about how his work was going. Sometimes he gets angry and his writing reflects that. And again, at times he seems the worse for drink and his handwriting becomes pretty scrappy, and at times it is just a scrawl.'

He looked round the room with raised eyebrows. 'But some of the entries, especially the ones over the last seven or eight months, are quite venomous and vindictive. And they raise some uncomfortable questions.'

'Basically, ever since The Daisy Institute took over Dunshiffin Castle and they started studying the Hoolish Stones,' the Padre added.

'Is this not just Finlay getting territorial?' Morag asked.

Wallace nodded sagely. 'I am thinking that could be right. He almost thought of the Stones as his own.'

Torquil shook his head. 'I doubt it. Listen to this first reference:

'10 October — Met Dr Logan Burns of The Daisy Institute today, up at the Hoolish Stones. He was photographing the inscriptions. Bloody fool! Tried to tell me that he was an expert on epigraphy and that he would decipher them within a week!'

Lorna tapped the end on her pencil on her note pad. 'Not a good start to a relationship.'

'It didn't get any better,' Torquil went on. 'Listen to this:

'17 October Saw Burns at the Pillar Stone on the golf course. The idiot had the audacity to tell me he has deciphered the inscriptions and that he was studying the markings on the Pillar Stone. He thinks it confirms his decipherment and confirms his theory. And his theory is — ATLANTIS! Good grief, what an idiot! The bugger put me off my round.'

The Padre gave a soft chuckle. 'I remember that. And I also remember that just playing his ball near the Pillar would almost send him apoplectic.

'His entries go on like that. Then we come to this alarming one. It is hard to read, almost a scribble that looks as if he was the worse for wear when he wrote it, as if he had a couple of stiff drinks before he sat down:

'21 December I watched the flower fools up at the stones at the winter solstice. They know nothing about the significance of the solstices. And that Burns idiot and his henchfolk — Kelso, a shifty bugger, and the little woman, Japanese, I think — they are telling the benighted folk that come to study with them all sorts of nonsense.

'It was pissing it down up at the stones when I went to take some moon positions late afternoon. Got caught in the thunderstorm. I trudged back by Hoolish Farm and saw the shapes through the curtains. I heard the voices, going hammer and tongs. The dogs were going mad outside. Then I saw him dash out and get in the Jeep. I thought it didn't look like Rab. Shit that I am, I sat down and sheltered against one of the outer stones and had a dram. Then I fell asleep in the rain and woke when I hear Calum Steele on his scooter. Then all hell broke loose.'

Morag gave a soft whistle. 'It didn't look like Rab? Did he say anything else?'

Torquil shook his head. 'No more entries for a week. Maybe it was just because it was Christmas.' He shrugged then continued, 'I couldn't read the next one, so if you wouldn't mind, Lachlan.'

The Padre reached across for the diary and turned it towards him. He pushed his spectacles back on his nose and read:

'30 December I feel bloody awful. Poor Esther and Rab. It wasn't Rab. But how can I say anything? I've left it too late and they would all think I was just drunk again. Or stoned.

272

Damn these addictions of mine. I'll have to give up the drink and the weed.'

The Padre shook his head. 'Then he writes another whisky-sozzled bit the following night:

'31 December Cruikshank wants his money. Bloody weed.'

Lorna frowned. 'Does he mean Cruikshank is a weed, or is he on about smoking cannabis?'

'The latter, I think,' Lachlan replied.

Torquil looked sternly at the Drummond twins. 'Do you know anything about this Cruikshank? Is he a supplier of cannabis?'

Wallace and Douglas sheepishly shook their heads in unison.

'No idea, boss,' Wallace replied.

Torquil frowned. 'Well, anyway, the entries about Logan Burns and the institute get more and more irate, as I said.' He consulted the sheet of notes that his uncle had supplied him with. 'Then he wrote this piece just the other night, after he had been up at the Hoolish Stones and interrupted the television broadcast. Would you read it, Uncle?'

The Padre cleared his throat and squinted to read the diary entry:

'I confronted the bugger on the TV news last night. Rattled him I think. And I made it clear that I know about them. That I know about what really happened at the winter solstice. Maybe I could make some money here. Enough to retire and finish my books in peace. Anyway, just one more drinkie I think, then we'll see.'

The Padre held up the diary and pointed to a discolouration of the paper. 'It looks as if he even spilt his whisky on the diary at that point.'

Lorna chewed the end of her pencil. 'Am I missing something here? Did something happen at the winter solstice?'

'We had a tragedy,' Douglas replied.

'A local farmer hanged his wife and — well, not to put too fine a point on it, blew his brains out,' Wallace explained.

'We don't know any such thing, Wallace,' said Morag. 'Remember that an open verdict was declared at the Fatal Accident Inquiry.'

Wallace and Douglas looked at each other doubtfully. Wallace shrugged and Douglas sat back and folded his arms.

Torquil gave Lorna a brief summary of the events surrounding the deaths. Lorna sat through it all making notes.

'Is this the Hoolish Farm? The one that is

274

now a battery farm?' she asked.

'The very same,' replied Torquil.

'And Calum Steele found the wife, Esther Noble's body?'

'He did and he hasn't been himself since then. You see, he had a thing about Esther Noble going back to our schooldays. I think that is partly why he has had a thing about incomers to the island since then.'

Lorna gave a wan smile. 'Which as one of the most recent incomers must make me *persona non grata* with him.'

Torquil hummed non-committally. He stood up and crossed to the white board. 'OK, so Finlay MacNeil's diary has raised a serious question. Let's see what we have so far. We have the winter solstice tragedy.'

He picked up a marker and wrote the words MURDER SOLSTICE at the top left corner, then underneath it in a box the name ESTHER NOBLE and under it *Found hanged in hall — murdered?* Then under that in another box the name RAB NOBLE and beneath that *Blown brains out — shotgun — suicide?*

'And then we have Finlay MacNeil.' And at the top of the board he wrote FINLAY MACNEIL and surrounded it with another box. Under it he wrote *Diary.* He looked round the others. 'What else? Let's brainstorm.'

Morag raised a hand. 'Fatal Accident Inquiry declared the Nobles an open verdict.'

Torquil nodded and wrote *FAI open verdict* next to the Noble boxes, then he drew a circle round it and added lines to connect the circle with their boxed names.

Wallace bit his lip pensively, then said, 'I am thinking that the Hoolish Farm is awfully close to the Hoolish Stones. Finlay says he was out there the night the Nobles died.'

Torquil nodded and wrote HOOLISH STONES in the middle of the board and surrounded it with a circle. Then he added a line to Finlay MacNeil's box, before writing HOOLISH FARM in another circle under the Noble boxes. He then added dotted lines linking the farm to the stones.

'So I suppose we need to add the new owners of the Hoolish Farm below that,' suggested Lorna. 'And how about the battery farm?'

'I suppose so,' replied Torquil, adding the words BATTERY FARM and the name MCQUEENS beneath it.

The Padre cleared his throat. 'I am thinking that Calum Steele could do with a little circle; he has had a bad time of it, what with discovering the Nobles and then being attacked and having his office trashed.'

'I agree,' said Torquil, adding a circle for

the *West Uist Chronicle* editor. 'And the question about who attacked him is fairly open.'

'What about these television interviews?' Lorna asked. 'Finlay MacNeil died after the drunken episode on the news.'

'Absolutely,' Torquil agreed, writing TV and circling it, then adding the names FINBAR DONLEAVY and DANNY WADE. He added lines connecting this circle to FINLAY MACNEIL, and the HOOLISH STONES, then another to CALUM STEELE. Beside the latter he added a question mark. 'And since we have added this we have to put THE DAISY INSTITUTE into the picture, don't we!' And so saying he drew another circle with DAISY INSTITUTE inside and the names LOGAN BURNS, DREW KELSO AND SAKI YASUDA underneath. 'And it links up to TV and FINLAY MACNEIL.'

Morag sighed. 'And now we have Nancy MacRurie. I think her accidental death has to go up there, since she was one of the inceptors.'

Torquil added her boxed name and added a line to join it to THE DAISY INSTITUTE circle.

'And don't forget that Eileen Lamont said it should have been her, not Nancy,' Morag added.

Torquil frowned as he added another circle with Eileen's name. 'And we have the question about cannabis to add. Remember that Finlay said in his diary entry that he would have to give up weed. And Nancy seemed to have been smoking a joint when she died.' He added CANNABIS, circled it and drew lines to FINLAY MACNEIL and NANCY MACRURIE. 'And he also said something about Cruikshank wanting his money and 'bloody weed!' '

He added another circle with GOAT'S HEAD FARM inside it and underneath it the name CRUIKSHANK.

'And what about dogs?' Lorna asked. 'That old lady, Annie McConville, had complained about one of the farm people's attitude and didn't like the look of his dog. And then Ewan had a run in with them.'

There was a few moments' silence while Torquil wrote on the board. Then the Padre spoke the disquieting thought that was becoming all too apparent to them all. 'The boxes show the people who are now no longer with us, right? I am thinking that there are too many dead people on that board.'

There followed another tense silence, which was broken by the office telephone.

'We could do with that being Ralph

278

McLelland,' said Torquil, as Morag went through to answer it.

She put her head round the door a moment later, a look of pained chagrin upon her face. 'It's Superintendent Lumsden for you, Torquil.' She shrugged her shoulders sympathetically. 'It sounds as if he's on the warpath.'

VI

Ewan was on his way back from the Cottage Hospital when he was side-tracked as he passed Dairsie, the ironmonger's shop. In the window he spied Rab Noble's mountain bike with its price ticket showing a reduction of twenty-five per cent. Ewan decided to buy it straight away before someone else snapped it up.

'You are lucky, Constable McPhee,' said Dan Dairsie as he rang up the old-fashioned till that had been installed by his grandfather before the Great War and which had occupied the same spot on the Dairsie counter ever since. 'I have had no end of enquiries since I reduced the price.'

And, as Ewan happily wheeled it towards the door, he added with a wink, 'Mind you, I am happy to be having it taken away. I am not so sure that I like the thought that it was up at the milking parlour when Rab Noble — you know what.'

'In that case, Dan Dairsie, if you are so pleased to get rid of it, maybe you should be throwing in a little extra.'

The ironmonger shoved his hands deep into the pockets of his brown shop coat and smiled apologetically. 'Business, Constable McPhee. It was never my grandfather's practice to offer free gifts, and it is not the policy of the current proprietor. The reduction has squeezed my profit margin as it is.'

Ewan shook his head with a good-natured smile, for he had expected such an answer. He left the shop and wheeled the machine across the pavement to the road. He was in the act of mounting it when he heard a shrill voice that made him squirm.

'Constable McPhee, just the person I was looking for,' came Annie McConville's voice.

Ewan turned to see the old lady advancing upon him with her dogs on leads, one in each hand. Both dogs recognized Ewan and approached with wagging tails.

'Ah, Mrs McConville,' he said warily, forcing a smile to his lips. 'What can I do for you?'

Annie looked back and forth to ensure that

no one on the crowded street was eavesdropping, before leaning towards him. 'It is more what I can do for you, Ewan McPhee. Information, that is what I am offering you.'

Ewan looked at her hesitantly. 'I am afraid I am not at liberty to offer any money, Mrs McConville.'

Annie looked scandalized. 'Money! Civic pride is all that motivates me. No, I wanted you to know about that awful egg man, McQueen. He tried to buy two of the Nobles' doggies from me.'

'But there is nothing illegal in that,' Ewan pointed out.

'Of course not. I wouldn't sell him one anyway, so guess where he is going to buy one?'

Ewan stared back at her in puzzlement. 'Where?'

'The Goat's Head Farm. From those rude men that you went to see.'

'Ah well, remember that I told you that you can walk your dogs there whenever you want, just as long as you don't upset the pigs.'

Annie snorted derisively. 'I know that. But it is the type of dog he wants to buy. He wants a guard dog. I had a word with Netty Lamont, you know, Eileen Lamont's mother.' Then as Ewan continued to stare at her vacantly, 'Eileen used to help me walk my doggies. You know her well enough; she was one of the veterinary nurses before the flower people got to her. She was a great friend of poor Nancy.'

'Ye-es,' Ewan replied slowly. 'A tragic accident. Tragic.'

'Tragic indeed. The two of them were such friends. Well, I was talking about Eileen. She used to help out at the Cruikshanks' farm when old Watty Cruikshank was still alive. He was her uncle. Then, when the new folk came — they are her cousins you see — she stopped going. Netty says she didn't like what they were doing to the farm. And she didn't like the type of dogs they were breeding.'

Understanding came to Ewan. 'But they are not breeders, are they?'

Annie's eyes sparkled. 'Ewan McPhee, not everything that happens in this world is done by the board. Netty says that was partly why she stopped going. That and the fact that she didn't take to her cousins.'

Ewan ran a hand through his mane of red hair. He recollected the two dogs that he had seen the other day.

'And have you been looking about you?' Annie went on. 'Have you not noticed some of the folk that have been coming to the island today?'

'You mean the folk coming for the solstice, Mrs McConville?'

'You just start looking, Constable McPhee. If you ask me, it is not just the solstice that's attracting people to West Uist at the moment. You just think about what I have said. Tell the inspector about McQueen and the Noble dogs.'

'I will tell him, Mrs McConville,' Ewan replied.

'And you might also tell him that I told Calum Steele the very same thing. He seemed more interested than you,' she added cryptically, as she headed off into the throng of the market.

VII

Torquil was still in his office talking to Superintendent Lumsden when Ewan came in. Morag filled him in on the meeting so far while he poured himself a mug of tea.

'What about Dr McLelland? Did you track him down?' Morag asked.

'No, he's not expected back until his late morning surgery at eleven.'

The door opened and Torquil returned. 'I take it that is Rab Noble's old mountain bike parked behind the counter?'

'Oh, aye,' Ewan replied quickly. 'Is it OK parking it indoors, Torquil?'

'Fine,' Torquil replied diffidently. 'Morag will reimburse you later.'

'What did the superintendent want, Inspector?' Lorna asked somewhat anxiously.

Torquil pursed his lips. 'Basically, my teeth. He said he is furious about learning about what is happening in part of his jurisdiction from watching the news instead of from my reports. He has given me a warning. He said that if he has one more problem with me then I will be suspended.'

'That is outrageous!' exclaimed the Padre, thumping his fist upon the ping-pong table.

Ewan shook his head. 'That man has it in for you, Torquil.' He pointed at the network of names, boxes and circles on the whiteboard. 'But, before I forget, I'd better tell you about my meeting with Annie McConville.'

The group listened, then Torquil added some notes beneath the circled GOAT'S HEAD FARM. He stood tapping the end of the marker on the board. 'There certainly seems to be a lot that needs investigating here. Let's divvy the tasks up.'

Lorna coughed. 'Did you tell him about these lines of enquiry, Inspector?'

Torquil shook his head. 'It didn't seem a good time to mention it.'

Ewan frowned. He was trying to puzzle out what Annie McConville had meant about Calum Steele being so interested in the fact that Tavish McQueen wanted to buy a dog from the Goat's Head Farm folk.

11

I

Tavish McQueen handed over a wad of twenty pound notes to Pug Cruikshank and stood nodding his head admiringly as his son Angus took possession of the boxer.

'You will find he is a good guard dog, Tavish,' Pug said, with the reassuring tone of one who has just sold a commodity for a good price.

'Aye, a good guard dog is what I need. To stop any more shenanigans from that Calum Steele and his like.'

Angus McQueen snorted derisively at the mention of Calum Steele's name. 'He'll maybe be minding his own business now, eh, Dad?'

Tavish McQueen ran a finger across his moustache. 'A good thing too. But I don't want anybody else looking into my affairs. Like that television crew that have been giving the flower folk a bad time.'

'My cousin is one of the flower folk,' Pug said meaningfully, in case Tavish McQueen had it in mind to be too derogatory about them.

Tavish McQueen took the hint. He pointed with his chin at the large fighting arena. 'Is this one vicious?'

Pug shook his head. 'He is no fighting dog. Not like these ones,' he said, pointing to the cages of sleeping animals. 'Oh, he'll make plenty of noise to frighten off any intruders and given half a chance he'll nip the arse off anyone who tries to get into your place, but that's it.'

Tavish gestured to his son to take the dog out to their waiting car.

'About tonight then,' he began, once they were alone. 'Have you had a thought about letting me in on some of the action?'

Pug gave a short laugh and slapped the other on the shoulder. 'There will be plenty of rich pickings, Tavish. And what are friends for, that's what I say. You scratch my back and I'll scratch yours.'

II

Logan Burns looked exhausted. His eyes were red-rimmed and his normally cleanly shaven cheeks were showing a fine dark stubble. Yet there was an unmistakable sparkle in his eyes as he addressed the assembled institute in the great hall at Dunshiffin Castle.

'We are on the verge of the great revelation, my friends. This evening we shall be starting the final vigil — all of us — at the Hoolish Stones. We shall stay through the night and watch the sunrise on the day of the solstice. And you will see how the stones are so perfectly aligned with the sunrise, just as the ancients set them up.'

There was a murmur of wonder and nodding of heads in the audience. Saki Yasuda and Drew Kelso, standing a little back from and on either side of Logan Burns looked at each other and nodded approvingly.

'And on Scottish TV we shall show our critics how wrong they are.'

Alan Brodie and Agnes Doyle were sitting cross-legged on the floor in the front row. Agnes prodded Alan in the ribs. He looked at her then with a nod of assent, raised his hand.

'Excuse me, Logan, but are you sure the television will be coming? What with that outburst by Finbar Donleavy.'

'And after Nancy's death,' Agnes Doyle added.

Logan Burns's lips tightened. 'I have no reason to think otherwise. They want the story just as much as we want the world to receive the message.' He held out his hands, almost beseechingly. 'Are you all still with me on this?'

Peter and Henrietta both cried out assent in unison and turned with raised hands to orchestrate a cheer from the assembly. When the clamour calmed down after a few moments, Saki Yasuda took a pace forward and put a hand on the director's arm.

'And you should get some rest first, Logan.'

Logan Burns patted her hand affectionately. 'You are right, Saki. I will go. Could you do a group meditation now? It would be a good preparation for this evening.'

The sitting inceptors and acolytes began shuffling apart to leave an aisle for Logan Burns to leave by. He pressed his fingertips together in a gesture of thanks and made to leave.

'And while you are resting I shall contact the police,' said Drew Kelso, as he followed the founder. 'Just to make sure that they are on hand this evening in case there are any troublemakers.'

Logan Burns stopped and held his hands out to the assembly. 'Do you see how my fellow directors look after me? How fortunate I am.'

III

Dr Ralph McLelland replaced his ophthalmoscope in its case on his desk then reached across to pull up the window blind and allow the light in again.

Calum Steele blinked and muttered an indistinct curse, which was rewarded with a stern look from the GP.

'You have been a lucky bugger, Calum Steele,' he said, rebukingly, as he sat behind his desk and reached for his prescription pad. He thought for a moment then dashed off a prescription in the classical scrawl shared by all doctors. He tore it from the pad and held it out, but held on to it as Calum went to take it. 'But you were a damned fool to discharge yourself last night. I am not surprised that you have a headache. I wanted you to rest for another day.'

Calum gave him a lopsided grin. 'Och, Ralph, man — I needed to find out what was really happening in the big world. I couldn't wait there and find out from the news.' He pointed his thumb at his own chest. 'I am the news on West Uist and I have a newspaper to run. Besides, I am here, am I not, your first patient?'

Ralph released the prescription and watched as Calum folded it and stowed it in a pocket of his anorak.

'Poor Nancy MacRurie,' Calum remarked casually. 'I heard about her accident. You told the nursing staff to keep it from me, didn't you?'

'I hadn't wanted you to get too agitated, Calum,' Ralph returned. 'I knew you would want to get up and start snooping around.'

Calum shrugged. 'Actually, I ran into Annie McConville and she told me that Nancy was a big friend of Eileen Lamont.'

'Possibly,' Ralph returned slowly.

'Eileen used to help out at Goat's Head Farm, as well as helping at the vet's and at the dog sanctuary.'

'Out with it, Calum,' said Ralph, glancing at his watch. 'I have other patients waiting.'

Calum gave one of his cheesiest smiles and rose to go. 'Oh, I heard that Eileen was gay. I just wondered if you had any idea whether Nancy — '

Ralph's brows almost seemed to join together and his manner turned frosty. 'Calum Steele, we have known each other all our lives, but you never seem to learn.'

Calum smiled nervously. 'Learn what, Ralph.'

'One, that doctors are bound by the Hippocratic Oath. And two — ' He stood up and made to march round the desk, only halting when his telephone started ringing. His hand hovered over it and he wagged a finger of his other hand at the newspaper editor.

'Just you remember that I am considerably bigger than you and I used to play shinty for the Western Isles. Now off with you, Calum Steele!'

Calum retreated swiftly, massaging his ego with the sentiment that investigative journalists were sometimes forced to annoy even their best friends in the pursuit of the truth and a good story.

IV

'Aye, thank you, Ralph,' Torquil said into the receiver. 'I understand. Oh, and did Calum say where he was going? I need to talk to him, but he is not answering his phone, which is unusual.'

He nodded as Ralph replied, then replaced the receiver and stood for a moment tapping the saddle of the mountain bike that Ewan had stashed behind the office counter. Something was niggling him, but he could not put his finger on it. With a scowl of frustration he returned to the rest-room where the others were waiting.

'Ralph doesn't feel able to commit himself. He cannot add anything about his examination of any of the bodies. The clinical findings were consistent with accidents in the case of Finlay MacNeil and Nancy, and the Noble case is closed.'

'But it could be reopened, couldn't it?' Lorna asked.

'It could if we had any reason to reopen it,' he mused, as he strode over to the whiteboard with its network of squares, circles and notes. He tapped it with his fingertips. 'There is something here that isn't right, folks. But I can't see it.' He rubbed his eyes, suddenly feeling very tired. He stifled a yawn and caught sight of Lorna doing likewise. Then he was stifling a grin that had threatened to erupt.

'I think we should break for an early lunch then reconvene this afternoon. Let's all mull things over.'

The others stood up and gathered notes together.

'Well I think I will be off, laddie,' said the Padre, pulling his pipe from his breast pocket in readiness for hitting the open air. 'Will you be home for tea this evening?'

Torquil shook his head, a trifle too readily, he realized. 'I think we'll need to keep an eye on the crowds up at the Hoolish Stones for a

293

while, at any rate. I'll see you later, Uncle.'

The Padre understood only too well. He gave them all one of his practised pastoral smiles, revelling in the blush that ascended to Lorna's cheeks. Then he left.

Morag turned to the Drummonds. 'Why don't we head up to the stones now, and just check on the parking arrangements, so that we are prepared for later?'

'Ach, Sergeant, we have it all in hand. Everything is marked out and cordons are in place,' said Wallace.

'You can trust us,' Douglas affirmed.

'I'll buy lunch afterwards,' Morag persisted.

The twins bumped into each other as they both went to open the door for her.

'I'll get on with a bit of tidying, Torquil,' Ewan volunteered. 'Then I'll get some of my reports written up.'

'Excellent,' Torquil said, beaming at his constable. 'And meanwhile Sergeant Golspie and I shall . . . go for a think.' He picked up his Cromwell helmet, goggles and gauntlets and pointed to the spare passenger helmet on the filing cabinet.

When they had left, the Drummonds and Morag grinned at each other. Wallace began whistling 'Love is in the air,' and Douglas and Morag joined in with him.

V

The Padre rode home, gathered his clubs then played six holes. He had intended playing a full nine, but gave up at the sixth having had by his standards a poor result. His concentration had not been good and his swing had felt out of synch. Accordingly, he left the course and strolled up to the church to say a few prayers before heading back to the manse to prepare a late lunch.

Unusually, the door was standing ajar and he fancied that he heard a mixture of sobbing and plaintiff voices from within. He laid his clubs against the wall in the porch and entered. Sitting in the front pew were two women, one with her arm about the other, clearly trying to offer comfort. They were both members of The Daisy Institute. The one who was sobbing was wearing a white hoodie and the other, offering consolation was wearing pink. As he approached along the aisle they looked round sharply and he recognized both of them.

'Why, Johanna, what is the matter?' he asked concernedly. Then said, with a nod at the girl in the pink hoodie, 'Hello, Eileen. It is a while since I have had the pleasure of your presence in my church.'

'*Latha math*, Padre,' Eileen said. 'I hope

you don't mind us coming here like this, but Johanna has had a bit of a shock.'

'Not another accident at the castle?' the Padre queried.

Johanna looked up at him and wiped tears from her eyes with the back of her hand. 'No, not an accident, Padre. It is something that didn't happen. Something terrible that Eileen stopped me from doing.' She sighed and then her whole body started to tremble. 'I am so ashamed of what I was thinking of doing.' She pointed to the metal thermos flask on the stone floor in front of her. 'I have been mad, I think. I was going to maim someone.'

Eileen held her close and stroked her hair. 'She has been carrying a great secret burden around with her for too long, Padre.'

'What secret is this, Johanna?' the Padre asked, sitting down beside her.

'Guilt, Padre. I feel so guilty.' She turned and squeezed Eileen's hand. 'When Nancy died I felt so worried about Eileen and I felt I had to bring my plan forward.'

The Padre picked up the thermos and was about to unscrew the lid.

'No! Be careful!' Johanna cried, snatching it away from him. 'It is acid and it is dangerous.'

Lachlan pushed his spectacles further back on his nose and whistled softly. 'Acid? This

296

sounds serious, Johanna. Would you like to tell me what has been happening?'

Johanna looked at Eileen for guidance. Eileen nodded encouragingly.

'It is a bad story, Padre,' Johanna said. 'But I would like to tell you, because I am so scared.'

The Padre patted the back of her hand. 'Go ahead, lassie. You are in the right place. Nothing bad can happen to you here.'

VI

Torquil and Lorna had bought sandwiches and a couple of bottles of water and then rode the Bullet along the coastal road for a couple of miles before taking sheep tracks across the moor to reach the sanctuary of the tall bracken. All thought of their picnic disappeared as they fell into each other's arms, before dropping to the ground to carry on where they had left off that morning. They made passionate love, unaware of the passage of time until a few flecks of rain on their bare flesh and a slight breeze brought them back to reality.

'My God, if Superintendent Lumsden could see us now,' Lorna giggled as she kissed his nose.

'He would have a blue fit!' Torquil replied with a laugh. 'As would anyone else. You just make me feel so happy, Lorna. I can hardly believe that this is happening. Here and now, and all so quickly.'

'Yes, we barely know one another. But it feels so perfect. As if it was meant to happen.'

Torquil's brow clouded. 'I didn't think I would ever meet anyone again,' he said. 'After what happened before. I need to tell you — '

She silenced him with another kiss. 'I know all about it,' she said softly. 'Morag told me.'

Rain started to fall and reluctantly they separated and gathered up their clothes and dressed quickly.

'I don't seem able to think when you are about, Lorna,' Torquil said as he ran his fingers through his thick black hair. 'All of these problems, all these unanswered questions back at the station, they just don't seem to bother me.' He bit his lip. 'And that is bad, isn't it?'

Lorna threw her arm about his shoulder. 'Look, Torquil, we know where we are for now, don't we? I feel exactly the same way about you. We'll just have to pinch ourselves and get back to reality.'

'I agree, let's get back to problem-solving. I think I can now that my head has been cleared of all my lustful thoughts.'

'Not all of them, I hope.'

He looked up at the darkening sky then winked at her as the rain began to fall. 'Looks like we are in for one of our classic West Uist squalls. Let's get the Bullet back on the road.'

Lorna tossed her head back and laughed. 'I love all these odd things about you. Your bagpipes, your insubordination to the superintendent, your old motorized bike.'

'Motorized bike! How dare you!' he exclaimed, making to grab her hair. Then his eyes opened wide in amazement. 'Good grief, Lorna. That's it. That's the thing that has been bothering me about the whole thing. The bike! Come on, we have to get back.'

VII

'We were getting worried about you two,' Morag said as Torquil and Lorna came in, their clothes sodden. 'You got caught in the squall, I see. Well, the pair of you had better just get dried off and slip into the interviewee dressing-gowns before you catch a chill.'

'Morag, I am fine really — ' Lorna began.

'I would just do as she says, Sergeant Golspie — I mean, Lorna,' said Ewan. He pointed at the puddles that were accumulating around their feet. 'Morag is a bit house-proud, you see.'

'Aye, comes from looking after her three bairns,' Wallace ventured.

Morag eyed him sternly. 'And the bairns that I have to look after here. And that includes you two, Wallace and Douglas.' Her withering eye caught Torquil. 'And as for the inspector — '

Torquil raised his hands. 'OK, we're going. How about hot tea and we'll be with you in the ops room in a minute. Morag, get out the file on the Hoolish Farm case; I think we have something to chew over.'

And indeed, when Torquil and Lorna reappeared a few minutes later in yellow dressing-gowns, still towelling their hair as if fresh from showers, the tea was ready. As were the other members of the division.

'Ewan's bike is the thing that has been bothering me,' Torquil said immediately. 'Or rather, Rab Noble's bike.'

'I don't understand, Torquil,' Morag replied.

'It was up at the milking parlour, wasn't it?'

Morag flicked the pages over then nodded. 'It was. He often cycled there, apparently. What are you getting at, Torquil?'

'The puzzle. It is a puzzle, because all of the dogs were at the farm. Don't you see, the bike and the dogs were in the wrong places.'

Lorna pulled the file across the ping-pong table and started reading to familiarize herself with the main aspects of the case.

Ewan nodded. 'It was a terrible sight. But the bike was parked at the parlour. It was leaning against the outer wall. I remember that because I ran out after finding the carnage inside and I almost puked over it.'

'But what do you mean about the dogs?' Douglas asked in bemusement.

'Well, you would have expected him to take the dogs to bring the cattle up. Even if he cycled there, you would have expected that, wouldn't you? They would have run alongside of him.'

'But Calum Steele said that he was almost knocked off his scooter by him driving like a maniac.'

'If it was him!' Torquil announced. 'What if the reason the dogs were not with him was because he had cycled directly to the milking parlour from somewhere else? And what if the reason the dogs weren't with him was because he had been somewhere that they would have been a nuisance?'

Morag had raised her tea to her mouth, but quickly replaced it on the table untouched. 'I see what you are getting at. If the bike was there, it couldn't have been Rab Noble in the Jeep. And that means that — '

301

Torquil shook his head. 'It means that there is a possibility that whoever was in the Jeep went to the milking parlour and may have shot him with his own shotgun. Made it look like the suicide of someone who had lost the plot.'

Lorna looked up from the file, her eyes wide in horror. 'And that might mean that the Jeep driver had already murdered Esther Noble.'

Silence fell about the room as the import of it all fell upon them. The storm clouds had darkened the sky and a fork of lightning outside was followed by a peal of thunder.

'Bloody hell! That is spooky!' exclaimed Douglas Drummond.

'It is more than that, Douglas,' said Torquil pointing at the whiteboard. 'It looks as if we are about to open up a can of worms.'

He stood and went over to the whiteboard and picked up the marker. It squeaked on the board as he wrote beside the boxed names of Rab and Esther Noble the word: MURDER?

'It raises questions about where Rab Noble could have been on his bicycle? Who gained by their deaths? And, most importantly, who killed them?'

'There are a lot of links to the Hoolish Farm on that board,' Wallace pointed out.

'And to the Hoolish Stones,' Douglas added.

'And to The Daisy Institute,' offered Ewan.

Torquil made a fist and tapped his forehead. 'Damn! All of which makes it look as if the other deaths, of Finlay MacNeil and Nancy MacRurie should be regarded as suspicious.'

Lorna bit her lip and winced. 'Then maybe it would be an idea to have a word with Superintendent Lumsden, Inspector? Remember what he said.'

Torquil glanced at Lorna and gave her a fleeting smile. Then he turned to the whiteboard. 'There is not anything here that directly links the institute with the Noble deaths, is there? I am just a bit wary of talking to the superintendent until I have this fleshed out a bit more.'

'Is there anyone who would be a suspect in the case?' Lorna asked. 'What do we know about the wife, Esther Noble?'

'That is one of the reasons I wanted to talk to Calum Steele,' Torquil replied. 'If only he would answer his mobile.' He tapped his teeth with his fingernail. 'It makes me think that he's up to something.'

Morag sipped her lukewarm tea. 'But she was in your class at school, wasn't she, Torquil?' she asked, rhetorically. 'What you don't know, Miss Melville almost certainly will.'

'I know that Calum used to have the hots for her, but she left school at sixteen and got married. I totally lost touch with her. I supposed she had just dropped into the farmer's-wife role. Rab Noble had always been a bit of a recluse.'

He pointed at the file. 'What did Calum Steele say in his interview?'

Lorna shoved the file across the table to Morag. 'Perhaps you would like to check, Morag? It is your file, after all,' she said, diplomatically.

Morag graced her with a smile and flicked the pages over. 'Here we are. He said that she telephoned him and said that she told him — and I quote — '*Get here right away, Calum Steele, and I will give you the biggest story you have ever had. The sadistic bastard! I will blow the lid on him and his band of sickos'.*'

Torquil's eyes opened wide. '*The sick bastard?* Was that a reference to Rab Noble, as we originally thought, or was it someone else. Someone who then killed her? And if so, was she killed because she was going to talk to the press about something?'

'Dogs!' Ewan suddenly exclaimed.

'Yes, Ewan?' Torquil asked. 'What about dogs?'

'Sorry, boss, I just had an idea. Rab Noble might have left his dogs at home because he was going to visit somewhere that there were other dogs.' He pointed at the notes Torquil had made earlier, when he had told them about his meeting with Annie McConville. 'He could have cycled easily to the Goat's Head Farm. They have dogs, as we all know.'

'Good thinking, Ewan. We will have to check that out.' He tapped the box containing Finlay MacNeil's name. 'Now what about this? The links are clear between the Hoolish Stones and The Daisy Institute, especially Finlay's animosity to Logan Burns.'

'We have to interview him again, I think, don't we?' Morag said.

'And we have to look at that poor girl, Nancy.'

The sky darkened and another fork of lightning flickered outside.

Torquil pointed to the word TV and the name FINBAR DONLEAVY. 'The Padre told me about the news last night and Finbar Donleavy's little piece.' He wrote the word CULT underneath the circled DAISY INSTI-TUTE and added a question mark. 'This word begins to make me feel very uneasy. It is the eve of the summer solstice tonight, the time that the institute has been harping on about for ages. That they have been getting TV coverage about. If the death of Finlay and Nancy have something to do with the institute, and if it is a cult, then maybe we have reason to be really worried.'

Morag bit her lip anxiously. 'I keep thinking about Eileen Lamont saying that it should have been her that had died, not Nancy. Poor kid.' She shook her head, and then asked, 'You don't think that this solstice has something sinister about it, do you? That Eileen Lamont could still be at risk?'

'Worse than that, Morag,' Torquil said. 'The whole institute could be at risk. If it is a cult, remember some of the atrocities that have happened in other parts of the world. There was that mass suicide in Jonestown in Guyana back in the seventies.'

'And the Waco siege in Texas,' Lorna continued. 'How many people died in that?'

No one answered immediately, for a succession of lightning flashes made them all aware that the atmosphere was full of electricity. But they were all also aware that it was not the static that was making the hairs on the back of their necks seem to stand up.

VIII

Lachlan had let Johanna Waltari pour out her tale, interspersed here and there with comments from Eileen who kept her arm about her through it all.

'So let me get this straight,' he said at last. 'Your real name is not Johanna Waltari, but Jaana Hakinen. You joined the institute the year after your elder sister Aila died in Geneva.'

'That is right, I know I did not explain it well. There was only me and her left when my parents died. But she joined this crazy group and I could not see her. Then she died in an accident. She fell from the top of a building and died instantly. There was an inquiry, but it was declared an accident.'

'But you did not believe this? Could it have been suicide?'

The girl Jaana shook her head vigorously. 'No, Aila was level-headed before she joined the institute and fell under the spell of Logan Burns. She was a graduate of Helsinki University and was going to be physiothera-pist — until they turned her head.'

Eileen nodded emphatically. 'It is true, Padre. They are so persuasive about every-thing. You really believe that they have the answers to all that you could ever ask.'

307

Lachlan smiled thinly but made no comment. Instead, he asked, 'So you think that your sister was murdered?'

Jaana frowned. 'Perhaps not in so many words, but I think she was put in a bad state and may not have known what she was doing.'

'And put in this state by the process that they put you through?'

'That and the jealousy that she had for the other woman. She had kept a diary, although she was not supposed to. They do not allow such things. But one of her friends sent it to me after she died. It told me that she was having an affair. She just wrote 'with the director'. But this other woman, another inceptor, a British woman, she stole her lover.'

'And you planned to get even?' the Padre asked. 'But why with this acid?'

'He deserves it. He is a charlatan. He has fooled everyone and he wants the world to accept his crazy ideas. Tonight he means to reveal everything.' She turned to Eileen and kissed her cheek. 'I bless the day that I met Eileen. She has saved me from much stupidity.'

'Maybe from prison,' the Padre said. 'But tell me again why you were so worried about Eileen?'

Jaana sighed. 'When Nancy died I thought — I thought that she had been killed, like my sister.'

'It was supposed to have been my vigil, you see, Padre,' Eileen explained. 'Only Nancy did it for me so that I could go and see Johanna, I mean Jaana. When Jaana told me some of her story, we sort of thought that it could have been me, because Logan had taken a shine to me.'

'Are you serious though? Do you really think that Logan Burns is a murderer?'

'I think he is a monster.'

'And what about this evening? Are you planning to go and stay up to see this solstice?'

The two girls nodded in unison. 'We feel that we must be there. For Nancy's sake, and also because some of our friends are there.'

The Padre nodded and sucked air in through his teeth as a crack of thunder seemed to rock the rafters of the church. 'Well, let us hope that the weather brightens up a bit or you will all get soaked to the skin.' He stood up and nodded. 'And now I think I had better be off myself. I need to have a word with my nephew, Inspector McKinnon. Especially after this tale. Do you have any objections about me telling him all this? If you are really suspicious about what happened to your sister, then I think he should know.'

'You tell him, Padre. And if he wants to talk to me I will tell him everything.'

12

I

Calum Steele had gone to ground. That was the way he liked to describe his extra special thinking time when he was working on a case and did not wish to be interrupted by anyone, friend or foe. And, at the present time, he believed that he had plenty of the latter. Going to ground sometimes just meant unplugging his phone and retiring to his camp-bed in the *West Uist Chronicle* offices for a nap. On this occasion he did not wish to risk another attack like the last one, when his window and his head had been smashed with the brick. Accordingly, he had gone off to the old but 'n' ben cottage, the traditional two-roomed crofter's cottage, at the end of Loch Hynish that he had inherited from his grandfather and which he had used to develop his photographs before the days of digital cameras. While not exactly liveable, it still had a sound roof, a water supply and a gas stove so that he could knock up a meal and brew tea.

And so, tucked up in the old sleeping-bag

that he left in the cupboard for such occasions he had whiled the rainy afternoon away as he worked out his plan of campaign. Not that it was anything too subtle. He had stowed his Lambretta round the back of the but 'n' ben and planned to set off for the Goat's Head in the early evening.

'This is meant to be, Calum my man,' he cooed to himself. 'Some old-fashioned West Uist weather, a fine sea squall that brings plenty of rain and mist.' He glanced at his watch then unzipped his sleeping-bag. 'Time for some soup, a dram and a mutton pie.'

He struck a light and turned on the gas stove. Then, while the soup heated up, he assembled the equipment he needed. His old polaroid camera, his hand-held tape-recorder and the old two-foot long sawn-off axe-handle that he carried as a cudgel, just in case. Then he turned his attention again to the photographs spread out on the old trestle table and picked up the magnifying glass that lay beside them. He selected the photograph of the green card that he had taken of Wilf Cruikshank exchanging for a wad of notes down at the harbour.

'Eight o'clock,' he mused to himself with a grin. 'Soon be time for me to get into a good position then. Somewhere upwind so that I don't give any of those mutts the chance of sniffing me out.'

Outside the rain had stopped and the mist swirled against the window panes. Calum ate his soup unaware that at that very moment his but 'n' ben was being closely watched.

II

Superintendent Lumsden was in a foul mood when he called the West Uist station to talk to Torquil. He was in an even worse one when Morag answered and told him that Inspector McKinnon was not available.

'And just why is he not available, Sergeant Driscoll?'

'It is the weather, sir. He is out of the station on an investigation and his mobile isn't working. No mobiles work out here when we get one of these sudden sea storms. Even these telephones can . . . be . . . unpredictable and — '

There was a sudden loud whistling noise, then the line cut out.

Morag looked round from the office counter at Ewan McPhee who stood with a whistle halfway to his lips. Behind him Torquil stood grinning.

'Well done, Morag. And good man, Ewan,' Torquil said.

Lorna was standing with her hands in her dressing-gown pockets, a worried look on her face. 'Are you sure that was a good idea, Torquil?'

The phone rang again and Morag signalled to Ewan to be ready with his whistle.

'A necessary subterfuge,' Torquil whispered, before Morag picked up the phone.

He tapped the watch on his wrist and picked at his own dressing-gown sleeve. 'Time to get changed,' he mouthed quietly.

Five minutes later they had congregated back in the restroom.

'That was him again,' Morag said. 'I think he believed me, because he started talking quickly before he was cut off.'

'And?' Torquil asked.

'I don't know. He got cut off by the storm.'

Wallace and Douglas laughed. 'She has a wicked streak in her, true enough,' said Douglas.

'Aye, just as Ewan McPhee always says,' added Wallace.

Ewan was quick on the defensive. 'I never said any such thing, Morag. They are just a pair of *teuchters*.'

'OK, let's get back to brass tacks,' said Torquil. 'We have serious work ahead. Firstly,

Morag had better stay here and man the phones. If the superintendent calls, then the electrical interference will cut him off. If it is a genuine member of the public we deal with it as usual.'

Morag nodded. 'What are we going to do about the solstice? Are we going to cancel their meeting?'

'Impossible,' Torquil replied. 'We have no grounds. Nothing concrete except supposition. We police it as usual, but while we do so we will keep our eyes open and opportunistically interview the various people.'

The bell in the office rang to indicate that someone had entered the station. It was followed a moment later by the tread of heavy brogues on the linoleum floor and by Lachlan's dulcet tones.

'It is only me — Lachlan McKinnon. Can I come through?'

Moments later he was standing in the rest-room explaining about his meeting with the two girls.

Torquil filled him in on their conclusions, directing his attention to the whiteboard and its web of associations.

'We were just talking about whether we could cancel the meeting,' he said.

The Padre shook his head. 'You should see the numbers of folk that are finding their way up there right now. I think you would have a riot on your hands.'

'That is what we were thinking, Uncle. We were planning to interview the directors up there.'

'If we can get them away from the television crew,' Lorna said.

'If you like, I think that I could create a diversion if needs be,' the Padre suggested. 'I have had dealings with Finbar Donleavy as you know. I think I could handle him if you need to talk to the others.'

'What about us?' Wallace asked. 'Do you want us to interview any of the flower folk?'

'No, I think you will both be needed to sort out parking and make sure there are no skirmishes or anything of that sort. We have not had a big meeting like this and we have no knowledge of whether these solstice watchers will be drinkers. You two take the station Escort.

'And me, Torquil?' Ewan asked.

'You need to check out the folk at the Goat's Head Farm.'

Ewan was fiddling with the whistle that hung on the lanyard from his neck. He nodded and grinned. 'I will use the station mountain bike, if that is OK.'

'And your whistle, if you run into any bad

316

folk,' jibed Wallace, much to his brother's amusement.

'So that is set then,' Torquil said. 'Lorna and I will grab the opportunities to interview the directors one at a time and the Padre here will keep the TV bods busy if needs be.'

'And we need to talk to Eileen and Jaana,' added Lorna. 'I suggest we go in my car.'

'Fine,' replied Torquil. 'That's about all we can do. The proper investigation will start tomorrow, if we find we have enough to go official.'

Morag sighed. 'Let's just hope I can keep the superintendent off our backs until then.'

'Amen,' said the Padre.

III

A sizeable crowd had already started to gather around the Hoolish Stones. The ground was wet and the sky was virtually obscured by banks of cloud. Mist swirled eerily around the ancient standing stones.

The Daisy Institute members had assembled in the positions that had been allotted to them earlier that afternoon at Dunshiffin Castle. The three directors were standing in the middle by the chambered cairn, the white hoodied acolytes were positioned each to one of the megaliths of the inner circles, and the pink-clad inceptors were similarly placed by stones around the outer ring.

'It is impressive, Logan,' said Saki Yasuda. 'From the air this will look like a real daisy.'

Logan Burns seemed restless, a little irritable. But he nodded at her. 'Just as it would have looked in the days of Atlantis, Saki. And when this temple was built all those millennia ago, the stones would have been painted in these colours.'

Drew Kelso patted Logan on the back. 'It is all coming together for you now, Logan. Just a few hours and the sunrise on the solstice will light up the stones, just as you have predicted.'

'Yes, but where is that blasted television reporter?'

'He said he would be here for the news slot as usual,' Drew returned. 'I spoke to him just a couple of hours ago.'

Peter Severn and Henrietta Appleyard were standing a few feet away from them, each beside a great stone. 'Would you like me to go and look for Finbar?' asked Henrietta.

Logan Burns shook his head. 'There is still time. We should get ready to show the people. I will address them soon.'

'I could phone him,' Henrietta offered.

'I said there is time,' Logan Burns snapped.

'Besides, your phone won't work out here in this weather.'

'Let us hope the mists clear,' Saki said.

Logan Burns snorted irritably. It was clear to everyone around him that he seemed like a man about to fulfil his life's destiny. And he seemed scared.

He pulled up his hood and stood with his hands pressed together. 'Pass the signal. It is time to begin the chant.'

IV

Calum Steele left his Lambretta in bracken some distance from the drive leading up to the Goat's Head Farm then took to the route he had planned out, circumnavigating the cow pastures and the pig pens to get to the far side of the farm. Keeping to the undergrowth and blessing the cover of the mist he had spotted the younger Cruikshank brother positioned at the bottom of the drive by the cattle grid. Several vehicles had already gone through and made their way towards a makeshift parking area in front of the old barn.

'Looks like the old girl's tip was right enough,' he mused to himself, as he lay on his stomach peering through binoculars at the activity unfurling before him. Every now and then the door of the barn opened, light from within spilled out and he could hear a tumultuous barking and a hum of raised voices.

Then a McQueen Egg van arrived and he saw the father and son emerge, to be greeted by the older Cruikshank and disappear inside the barn.

'Time for a closer look, Calum my man,' he whispered between his teeth. Then, stealthily, when he judged that the time was right and no more cars were coming up the old track, he made his way to the rear of the building.

As he suspected, there was a window, protected by bars, yet with enough room for him to see inside. The action had already begun. He saw the cages of dogs, the crowd of men, gamblers all, encircling an enclosure inside which two men were crouched at opposite corners, holding fast to the collars of a couple of snarling, wide-eyed fighting dogs. The men were crying out, braying almost. Then at a signal from Pug Cruikshank the dogs were released. A blur of movement saw the two dogs crash into each other, jaws snapping, teeth bared and immediately blood and saliva starting to spurt.

Calum had his camera at the ready, and his tape recorder in his hand to catch the noise, yet even his seasoned sensitivities were shocked. He stood staring in horror.

Then a hand was clamped firmly over his mouth and he felt his arms pinned to his side. Something hard, like a gun barrel was jabbed into his back and he froze in terror.

V

The narrow road up to the Hoolish Stones was packed on either side with cars. The Drummond twins were doing their best to maintain some order, but the crowds were considerable and they were already having some difficulty in controlling the flow.

'No one is going to be leaving in a hurry,' Lorna said, as she edged into a free spot created by Wallace.

The Padre was the first out. 'That certainly sounds eerie,' he remarked as the monotonous chanting from The Daisy Institute members assailed their ears.

Torquil, Lorna and the Padre made their way across the moor to the edge of the great crowd that had assembled around the ancient monument, despite the inclemency of the weather. It seemed a completely disparate group: New Age people, holidaymakers and locals stimulated to find out what all the fuss was about.

Among the first people that they met as they joined the outside of the crowd were Miss Melville and Jessie McPhee, Ewan's mother.

'Are the television people here yet?' the Padre asked them.

'Not a sign of them,' replied Bella Melville. 'They are just chanting away there. I am not sure that I fancy standing here in this weather listening to them caterwauling all night until the sunrise.'

'Is my laddie Ewan not here?' Jessie McPhee, a petite lady in a duffle coat asked.

'He is on a job, investigating elsewhere,' Torquil replied. 'Now, if you ladies will excuse us, we had better have a closer look at what is happening.'

He made to move off, then snapped his fingers and turned back to Bella. 'Just one question, Miss Melville. It is about the Nobles at Hoolish Farm. Do you know if Esther Noble was happy?'

'Happy! You are joking, aren't you, Inspector McKinnon? Didn't I teach you anything? You need to keep your eyes open. No, Esther was never happy since the day she married Rab Noble. He drank and he gambled and he kept low company. It is no wonder that she was . . . tempted by other men.'

'Other men? Here on West Uist?'

Miss Melville nodded curtly. 'She left him

for a few months, you know. Went to Switzerland to sort her head out. But I think she met someone there. Anyway, it didn't last and she came back.' She shook her head again. 'No she was not a happy woman, Torquil McKinnon.'

Torquil looked at Lorna, both aware of the possible link with The Daisy Institute that they now had to follow up on. 'Thank you, ladies,' he said. 'Don't get too cold.'

They left and gradually sidled through the crowd to the edge of the stones, where the chanting hoodie-clad figures formed an impressive yet incongruous sight.

As they did so the figure of Logan Burns raised his hands and the chanting suddenly stopped. He stepped up on top of the chambered cairn.

'My friends!' he called out, his voice seeming to boom and echo around the great standing stones. 'Thank you all for coming here today, on this night to wait until the solstice sunrise. As you will all know from the televised slots on Scottish TV — although for some reason the television crew are not here tonight — the summer solstice is the longest day of the year, and on that day the sun will seem to stand still. I, my fellow directors and our acolytes and inceptors plan to stay here until the sunrise, at which point there will be a great revelation. You will all see that — '

'*Liar! You filthy liar!*' someone screamed.

Logan Burns blinked, looked slightly taken aback, then began again. 'You will see that my predictions — '

'*Liar! Bloody murderer!*' the voice screamed again. A man's voice, that quaked with rage.

Torquil and Lorna were craning their necks to spot the heckler, as were most people in the crowd.

'*You killed my girl! Now die there in your precious stones!*'

There was an explosive noise of two shots and Logan Burns spun round and seemed to be knocked backwards, to fall off the cairn, an arc of crimson trailing from his body.

The crowd immediately began to panic as people realized that a gun had been discharged.

Torquil and Lorna immediately went into action in an attempt to quieten the crowd and pinpoint the gunman, but it was in vain. They were jostled to and fro as people attempted to escape lest there should be further firing.

Then, as the crowd started to move away, Torquil saw Hamish MacRurie, advance towards the group of three inside the inner stones. All of the inceptors and acolytes had either taken cover behind their stones or had taken to their heels with the rest of the onlookers.

Logan Burns was lying on the ground, blood pumping from a wound in his chest. Saki Yasuda was kneeling beside him, attempting to cradle his head in her lap. Drew Kelso was backing away from the approaching gunman.

'Hamish MacRurie!' Torquil shouted. 'Police! Stand still!'

But the distraught father was moving as if in a trance, the gun in his outstretched trembling hand.

'Lorna, get hold of Ralph McLelland,' Torquil ordered, as he launched himself free of the crowd and charged after Hamish MacRurie. He realized that the man was not going to listen to logic. So he dived at him, ensnaring his arms and dragging him with him to the ground. The gun went flying.

The Drummond twins were quickly on the scene and ran to help.

'Help me!' Saki Yasuda screamed. 'I need a doctor here. My God! I think Logan is d . . . dead!'

VI

Calum's mind was racing and the pressure of the object in his back rooted him to the spot.

'Not a sound, Steele!' a familiar voice

hissed in his ear. 'I am going to take my hands away in a moment, OK.'

Calum made to nod and the hand slowly withdrew from his mouth.

'Good! Now let's get some proper footage of these sick bastards,' Finbar Donleavy said. 'In you get, Danny, and start shooting.'

Calum eased away to let the white-haired Danny Wade take his place with his camera.

'How did you find me?' Calum gasped.

'We followed you,' Finbar whispered back. 'We realized you were on to this lot as well.' He winced as he looked in the window at the carnage that was taking place in the ring. 'Make sure you get some pictures of the punters as well, Danny.'

'This is my story, Donleavy!' Calum said, between gritted teeth as he recovered himself.

'Don't worry, Kirstie made me promise that you'll get your credits. We will interview you properly once we get away from here, then later we'll do a stake out and confront some of these sick sods.'

'Kirstie said that? Well, get the McQueens over there,' Calum said, shooting out a hand to point at the two men through the window. But in doing so he jolted Danny Wade's hand and the camera lens struck the window.

Immediately, a man at the back of the crowd looked round and saw them. He cursed, then shouted out a warning. Before they knew it two-score or so of angry faces were turned in their direction. Worse, men were making for the door.

'Shit! Now it's hit the fan. Let's get going,' cried Finbar Donleavy.

And indeed the three of them needed no further prompting. They belted for it and were already a couple of dozen yards away when the barn door burst open and people started racing out. One of the first was Pug Cruikshank.

'Get those bastards or we're scuppered!' he cried. Then, 'Wilf, get your dogs on them!'

In the general mêlée of people running for their vehicles the three journalists ran for all they were worth. They were all too aware that in moments, as some of the fighting dogs were loosed, they could well be running for their very lives.

VII

'He is just in shock,' the Padre said, as he knelt beside Saki Yasuda and Logan Burns. 'We are getting a doctor to him as soon as possible. I am no doctor myself, but I would say that he has been lucky. The bullet has passed through the top of his chest and missed his heart. We need to keep him conscious and comfortable, and just maintain pressure on that wound.'

Saki Yasuda heaved a sigh of relief. She looked up. 'Is Drew here?'

Wallace and Douglas had come running at the sound of gunfire and were in the process of helping Torquil put handcuffs on the wild-eyed but now subdued Hamish MacRurie.

'Is that the other guy in the yellow hoodie?' Wallace asked. 'He went off with Lorna.'

'She said she was going to get Ralph McLelland and that we should help you,' said Douglas.

Torquil stood and looked round, his eyes opening wide in alarm. 'Where is the gun?'

The twins shook their heads.

'I don't like it,' Torquil said, turning and running towards the cars. People were running everywhere, cars were being started and horns beeped as everyone wanted to get away from the Hoolish Stones.

But no one could, for two cars were blocking the narrow lane, and both had their tyres slashed. Sergeant Golspie's Golf GTI was gone.

'Wallace, see if you can get through to Morag,' Torquil snapped. 'And, Douglas, try and get hold of Ralph McLelland.'

'What are you going to do, boss?'

Torquil was running for the other side of the road where he had spied Nippy, Jessie McPhee's Norton moped.

'I am going after the bastard. He's got Lorna!' Torquil exclaimed. 'And he's a murderer.'

VIII

Calum's heart was pounding and felt as if it could easily burst as he ran as he had never done before. Cars were being revved up and driven off, slewing from side to side in the mud.

'Where is your car?' Calum called to the other two.

'Miles away,' Finbar gasped.

'Fuck! The dogs are coming,' cried Danny Wade, chancing a look over his shoulder.

'Make for that Hillman Imp,' Calum said. And, as the words tumbled out, he realized that he recognized the car parked just inside the cattle grid.

The noise of panting dogs seemed ominously close and the three men tried to put on a spurt.

A stream of cars was flashing past the Hillman and, as they watched, they saw the driver's door open and an old lady got out.

'A . . . Annie! For God's sake,' screamed Calum. *'Get back in the car!'*

But the old lady just pulled the door as wide open as she could and casually reached inside and took something out. 'You get in the car, Calum Steele,' she called. 'And your friends.' And, as they approached, they saw that she had a parcel, which she tossed to the side. Then she pulled out a whistle and blew. But no noise came out.

Finbar arrived at the car first and dived in, followed shortly after by Danny Wade who tossed his camera in first. Calum brought up the rear and with what seemed the last of his strength, he dived in.

'C . . . come on, Annie!' he gasped, turning as quickly as he could to help her.

But then they saw that the old lady was doing nothing of the sort. She was standing over the two black pit bull terriers as they sniffed and snuffled over the parcel of meat. Annie had a hypersonic whistle between her lips and was blowing it. And to the amazement of the three newsmen, looking from the safety of her old Hillman Imp, the dogs began to settle and moved towards her, tails between their legs looking thoroughly cowed.

'I thought you might need a wee bit help, Calum Steele,' she said, taking the whistle

330

from between her lips. 'And see that I found a good use for your newspaper,' she added with a twinkle in her eye, pointing to the parcel of raw meat that she had thrown to distract the dogs.

IX

Lorna had been unable to do anything other than obey with the gun in her back. Then, once in the car, Kelso had produced an S&M choke chain from a pocket of his hoodie and dropped it over her head. She had gagged as he demonstrated how easily he could garrotte her.

'Just drive to that police boat of yours,' he had commanded.

Unable to do otherwise she had obeyed.

It had been difficult driving, with her as yet unsure of the roads, and trying to go quickly with repeated reminders not to do anything foolish. She had taken two wrong turns, for each of which she received a choking reprimand, yet she managed to drive to the police docking point on the harbour where the *Seaspray* police catamaran was waiting.

'Start it up and let's get off!' Kelso snapped at her. 'Set a course for the mainland. Be good to me and maybe you'll live through all this.'

Lorna acquiesced, despite her protests about being a poor sailor and getting sea-sick.

'Just go.'

'Why . . . why are you doing this?' she ventured once *Seaspray* was clear of the harbour and heading out to sea.

'I am escaping,' he said simply. 'I would have been leaving soon anyway, but that fool precipitated my egress. I had no intention of you clods getting hold of me.'

'You mean because you killed — ?'

'All of them!' he said with a laugh. 'That's right. That snivelling bitch who was going to shop me. Her cuckolded husband, that drunken idiot MacNeil.'

'And . . . and Nancy?'

'Her too. Stupid bitch. What was she doing on that vigil anyway? I was going to have a quick interlude with that little Eileen girl, but then it was the wrong one. She had to have an accident.'

Seaspray scudded over the waves and Lorna began to feel nauseated, though whether from the confession or from the buffeting of the boat, she was unsure.

'The fool Logan Burns can take the rap. It is only a matter of time before they make the link with Geneva.'

'With Jaana's sister? We . . . we know about that already,' Lorna ventured.

Kelso tugged on the chain and Lorna gagged. He laughed, and stroked her neck with the barrel of the gun. 'You are quite attractive, you know that, Sergeant? We might have a slight stop before we get to Benbecula. You might grow to like this little chain, what do you think?'

Lorna tasted vomit and retched.

Kelso looked at her distastefully. 'Still, I don't need to kiss you. Your body will do.'

Lorna felt her skin crawl as he moved the gun, letting it trace the contours of her left breast.

'You . . . you like this S&M stuff, do you?'

'I like to be in control.'

'And . . . where are you going to go?'

He laughed. A brutal laugh. 'That you will never know. Suffice it to say that I will be going to enjoy the money that I have siphoned off from this mad bastard's organization. I am going to enjoy a very long retirement, incognito.'

'You told me why you killed Nancy, but why Finlay MacNeil?'

'No reason why you shouldn't know. He saw me leave the Hoolish Farm after I killed the bitch. After all I did for her. I brought The Daisy Institute to this god-forsaken island

333

after she left Geneva. She liked it at first, being able to continue our affair, until I developed . . . other interests. Other women.'

'A crime of passion?'

'We had the passion before she telephoned that reporter, Calum Steele. She thought I had left, but I was still in her kitchen and I heard her phone. She had to die. Then her husband had to be seen to have killed her.'

Lorna chanced a sideways look at him. What she saw made her feel even more afraid. His eyes almost seemed to glow and she realized he was a complete psychopath, without remorse or guilt.

'Cut the engine!' he snapped.

'What . . . what are you going to do?'

He yanked the chain and she gagged again.

'Time for a little diversion, I think.'

He turned and looked at the tarpaulin behind them. 'We could be quite comfortable here.'

He raised the gun and looked towards it. 'It would be a pity to use this on you too soon.'

Lorna saw a slight chance. With the gun not pointing at her she made a grab for his wrist and tried to twist it. But she was a moment too slow. He yanked the chain instantly and she gasped for air and felt her body buckle. Then she saw the gun hand rise as if to strike her.

But it never fell. The tarpaulin was thrown back and Torquil McKinnon shot out, his truncheon rising and falling to deliver a numbing blow above Kelso's elbow. The gun fell from his hand and before he could lash out Torquil had given two rapid jabs, one to his midriff and the other to his throat. Then as he staggered backwards, he followed up with a haymaker that lifted Kelso off the deck and deposited him like a sack of potatoes against the side of the catamaran.

In a trice Torquil had him handcuffed and then he was beside Lorna, pulling away the choke chain and showering her with kisses.

'Torquil, thank God,' she gasped. Then, her eyes wide with alarm, 'Look out, I'm going to throw up.'

X

Ewan was not in a good mood as he rode up towards the barn at the Goat's Head Farm. He had almost been knocked off his bike twice by fleeing cars, so he had stopped and jotted down the numbers of all who had passed him. Then he had continued to the barn where he found Pug Cruikshank and Tyler Brady trying to clean up the blood-stained fighting pit.

He blew his whistle to gain their attention.

'I am arresting you two,' he said, as he entered the barn.

Tyler Brady stepped over the side and reached for the cattle-prod. 'On what charge?' he demanded.

Pug Cruikshank stepped over likewise. 'Maybe you think you would like to try taking us in, ginger. Maybe you would like another tap on the head, like the last one Tyler gave you.'

Brady suddenly made a stab at Ewan with the prod, but he was too slow. Ewan merely side-stepped, grabbed it from him and lashed out with a back-handed blow that floored him instantly.

'Well, there's a repayment, you rude devil. Call it a lesson in manners if you like.'

'Smart ass, aren't you?' said Pug Cruikshank. 'Perhaps you would like to try me instead? I was a British light-heavyweight contender.' He dropped into a fighting posture and advanced.

'Were you really?' Ewan replied. He ducked the blow aimed at his head then closed his arms around his adversary in one move, pulling him into a bearhug that would have done a grizzly bear proud. As he applied pressure Pug Crukshank's face went puce, then purple and his eyes seemed to protrude.

Ewan let him go, then before the ex-boxer could get his breath, he gave him a straight right to the jaw. As Cruikshank tumbled into the fighting ring in an unconscious heap, Ewan blew on his fist. 'Always wanted to do that,' he said. 'But I can't say that I am too impressed with this boxing of yours. You wouldn't last half a minute in a proper wrestling match.'

The caged dogs had been watching and seemed to go wild, hurling themselves against their prisons and howling.

Ewan raised his finger to his lips. 'Wheesht, doggies. You'll wake these scunners up.'

He grabbed Tyler Brady's collar and dragged him across the floor then flung an arm over the side of the fighting pit. Then he stepped inside, slipped a handcuff on the unconscious Pug Cruikshank's wrist and coupled him with his henchman.

'Oh yes, I didn't answer the question, did I? I am arresting you for resisting arrest.'

13

I

The following day, after a hectic time of interviews, meetings and reports, Torquil, Lorna and Morag sat in the sitting-room of the manse while the Padre poured drinks prior to serving dinner.

'There we are, a dry sherry for Morag and Glen Corlins for the rest of us,' he said, approaching with the small tray that he loved to use when he and Torquil entertained. 'Here is to a more peaceful time,' he said, raising his glass. 'That will help your throat, Lorna. West Uist's own malt whisky.'

Lorna self-consciously touched her bruised throat and smiled. Then she raised her drink and they clinked glasses and sipped their drinks.

Torquil glanced at the clock on the mantelpiece, then rose and switched on the television. 'It's just about time for the news.'

The Scottish TV news jingle sounded out and then Kirstie Macroon's familiar voice read out the main headlines.

'SCOTTISH FIRST MINISTER DEMANDS THE RETURN
OF THE JACOBITE HOARD.'
'SERIAL KILLER ARRESTED ON WEST UIST AND LOGAN BURNS
SHOT AT THE SUMMER SOLSTICE.'
'DOG FIGHTING SYNDICATE EXPOSED.'
'DISGRACE OF THE WEST UIST
BATTERY FARM.'

The Padre raised his eyes heavenwards as the news anchor-woman read the report about the Jacobite hoard. 'I cannot say that I like this move to separate Scotland from England. There is too much petty nationalism these days.'

And then she was reporting on the things they had been waiting to hear.

'Last night the controversial director of The Daisy Institute, which we have been featuring in our regular news bulletins over the last week, was shot during the start of the proposed night-long vigil at the Hoolish Stones. It seems that he was shot while addressing a crowd of onlookers, by the distraught father of a young woman who died in a fatal accident at Dunshiffin Castle earlier in the week.

'We have to report that evidence has come

339

to light to show that her death was not an accident, as was previously thought. Similarly, the death of noted local historian Finlay MacNeil — '

'How did Superintendent Lumsden take it all?' the Padre asked.

Torquil gave a wry smile. 'A bit like a wild boar, Uncle. He went on for about quarter of an hour about breaking me to constable, having me keel-hauled, flogged, you name it.'

Lorna gave a short laugh. 'But he had to accept that we — or rather Ewan and Calum Steele — broke that dog-fighting crowd. They will all be prosecuted.'

'And since the McQueens were in on it they have been totally discredited,' Morag added.

Kirstie Macroon went on to report about Drew Kelso's connection with The Daisy Institute and the death of Jaana Hakinen's sister in Geneva, and the fact that Esther Noble had spent time in Switzerland.

'Police are following a trail of investigation which suggests that there may be a link with the suspicious deaths last winter of Esther and Rab Noble. It had been thought that the husband might have murdered his wife and then committed suicide. The evidence now points to a double murder by Kelso.'

Morag put her sherry down on the coffee table. 'So Kelso persuaded Logan Burns to move the institute to West Uist, knowing that he would jump at the opportunity to use the Hoolish Stones to further his crackpot Atlantis theories.'

'That's right,' said Torquil. 'Kelso didn't care, because he was just siphoning money away into a numbered account in Zurich. He and Esther started up their affair again. And seemingly he was a sadist and had a passion for S&M. He must have told her everything in some of his sessions and then when he started fancying someone else, presumably Eileen Lamont, she threatened to expose him. So he killed her.'

'I feel so sorry for Nancy. She died because she was in the wrong place at the wrong time. Eileen was right, it was meant to be her. Although he might just have meant to rape her, rather than kill her.'

'We are pleased to report that Logan Burns, the Director of The Daisy Institute, is recovering in the West Uist Cottage Hospital. We talked earlier to his fellow director, Miss Saki Yasuda, who informed us that The Daisy

Institute is planning to leave West Uist as soon as Logan Burns has recovered.'

The Padre shook his head in sorrow. 'All those deaths. So unnecessary. So evil. Poor Finlay MacNeil. It was his televized outburst that made Kelso suspect that he knew about him and led to his death.'

'We turn now to the discovery of a dog-fighting syndicate, using specially, illegally bred and trained dogs on West Uist. A joint investigation by *West Uist Chronicle* Editor Calum Steele and Scottish TV's Finbar Donleavy, uncovered an illegal group. I warn you that the footage we are about to show may offend those of a sensitive nature — '

The footage was indeed alarming, but quite damning.

'That will be the end of the McQueens and the Goat's Head Farm lot,' said Morag. 'Ewan, Calum and Finbar Donleavy all come out of it well.'

'Aye, and Calum is pretty hopeful,' said Torquil. 'Apparently Finbar Donleavy has been offered a post with CNN. That would mean that his and Kirstie's relationship might be difficult, with them on opposite sides of the pond.'

'And during their investigations the police discovered that Tyler Brady had been responsible for the savage attack on Calum Steele and on PC Ewan McPhee.'

The Padre stood up. 'Well, Lorna, you have had a pretty baptism of fire on West Uist, haven't you? Are you sure that you want to stay?'

Lorna looked at Torquil and smiled as he reached out a hand to her.

'Yes, Padre, I think that I very much want to stay.'

Morag stood up. 'Let me help you serve the food up, Padre,' she said quickly. 'I — er — think we are in danger of feeling like a couple of gooseberries in here.'

The Padre grinned as Torquil and Lorna stared dreamily at each other.

He winked at Morag. 'Aye, you could be right, lassie. Bring your glass and we'll have another dram while I strain the tatties.'

We do hope that you have enjoyed reading this large print book.

Did you know that all of our titles are available for purchase?

We publish a wide range of high quality large print books including:
Romances, Mysteries, Classics
General Fiction
Non Fiction and Westerns

Special interest titles available in large print are:
The Little Oxford Dictionary
Music Book
Song Book
Hymn Book
Service Book

Also available from us courtesy of Oxford University Press:
Young Readers' Dictionary
(large print edition)
Young Readers' Thesaurus
(large print edition)

For further information or a free brochure, please contact us at:
Ulverscroft Large Print Books Ltd.,
The Green, Bradgate Road, Anstey,
Leicester, LE7 7FU, England.
Tel: (00 44) **0116 236 4325**
Fax: (00 44) **0116 234 0205**